THE SECRETS OF
ROCHESTER
PLACE

'Full of intrigue and loss, this beautifully written
gothic tale makes for a spellbinding read'
Rhiannon Ward, author of *The Quickening*

'Beautifully written with a story that draws you in'
Jane Corry, author of *We All Have Our Secrets*

'An intriguing story which skilfully entwines the
past and present'
Heidi Swain, author of *A Taste of Home*

'A beautiful story that illuminates the past and the
present and brings every moment to vivid life'
Christi Daugherty, author of *The Echo Killing*

'A rollercoaster ride of a novel . . . a love letter
to multicultural London, and shows how
ripples from the past can be felt right
up to the present day'
Sinead Crowley, author of *The Belladonna Maze*

'A warm, comforting read infused with love
of family, love of history and love of home'
Kit Whitfield, author of *In the Heart of Hidden Things*

'Intricately woven and beautifully told, I can't
recommend it more highly'
Simon Lelic, author of *The Search Party*

'A richly atmospheric story that moves between
Blitz-torn London and the present day . . . a
moving tale of love and loss'
Sophia Toibin, author of *The Silversmith's Wife*

'A mesmerizing tale about the enduring
nature of female courage'
Michelle Adams, author of *Little Wishes*

ABOUT THE AUTHOR

Iris Costello is the pseudonym of Nuala Ellwood, who was
born in 1979. She has a BA Hons degree in Sociology from
Durham University and a Master's in Creative Writing from
York St John University, where she is a visiting lecturer in
Creative Writing. The author of six highly acclaimed novels,
Nuala has a teenage son, Luke, and is based in York and South
London.

THE SECRETS OF
ROCHESTER PLACE

IRIS COSTELLO

PENGUIN BOOKS

PENGUIN BOOKS

UK | USA | Canada | Ireland | Australia
India | New Zealand | South Africa

Penguin Books is part of the Penguin Random House group of companies
whose addresses can be found at global.penguinrandomhouse.com.

First published 2022

001

Set in 13/15.25pt Garamond MT Std
Typeset by Jouve (UK), Milton Keynes
Printed and bound in Great Britain by Clays Ltd, Elcograf S.p.A.

The authorized representative in the EEA is Penguin Random House Ireland,
Morrison Chambers, 32 Nassau Street, Dublin D02 YH68

A CIP catalogue record for this book is available from the British Library

ISBN: 978–0–241–99440–5

www.greenpenguin.co.uk

Penguin Random House is committed to a
sustainable future for our business, our readers
and our planet. This book is made from Forest
Stewardship Council® certified paper.

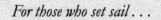

For those who set sail . . .

Twas a proud and stately castle
In the years of long ago
When the dauntless Grace O'Malley
Ruled a queen in fair Mayo.

James Hardiman, *Irish Minstrelsy*, Vol. II

Prologue

Teresa

'Time for sleep, boys and girls.'

Padre Armando's breath rises like smoke in the freezing air as he speaks.

'Now, close your eyes and listen to the Lord's Prayer. Let us ask Him to keep and protect us on this journey.'

> Gure Aita, zeruetan zarena,
> Santu izan bedi zure izena,
> Etor bedi zure erreinua
> Egin bedi zure nahia.

While the priest recites the prayer, his voice a ghostly murmur, I turn on my side and look out into the night sky, its black edges merging with the swollen sea. From this position I can hear the ship creak and groan as it moves through the waters, like a bow slowly scratching the strings of a cello. The sound reminds me of the folk songs my sister used to sing in the town square back home.

Home. The thought of it makes my heart hurt. How can it be that I am here, in the middle of the ocean, miles from everything that is familiar, all that I love?

As the prayer comes to an end and Padre Armando's voice falls silent, I think once more of my sister, but this time she is leading me through a crowd of people. We pass a newsstand and I catch the headline on the front of the morning paper: *THEY STEAL OUR CHILDREN*. I want to ask her if that is true. Is that what is going to happen to me? But I do not speak, as she has instructed me to stay silent. 'I will do the talking, little one, do you understand?' She is dressed in a dirty old overcoat and scuffed shoes, while her long, chestnut hair is unwashed and falls in messy tendrils round her face. It is odd to see my sister, who has always been so particular about her appearance, in this state. But these are different times, desperate times, and her black eyes blaze as she storms into the processing centre and thrusts me into the arms of a plump female volunteer. 'You must take her,' she pleads, her fingertips digging into my shoulder blades. There are some questions then, muffled voices that I cannot quite make out. 'Eight years old,' I hear her say. The woman looks at me suspiciously. 'Eight years old?' she repeats, taking in my tiny frame. 'You sure?'

The deck beneath me is rough and uncomfortable and I shift position, turning on my left side, away from the sea. I look at the sleeping children lying around the deck and the thin outline of Padre Armando as he sits upright in the corner by the lifeboats, his hands clasped together, his head bowed, the gold of his crucifix glinting in the moonlight.

'Come back for me,' I whisper into the freezing night air, hoping that my voice will carry across the waves, over the sea. That, wherever my sister is now, she will hear it and know that I need her. 'Take me home.'

I shake off the blanket and tiptoe across the deck. When I reach the side of the ship I stand and look out across the black water, listening for any sound, any sign that she has heard my cry. All my life, my big sister has been there for me, has swept me up in her arms when I am scared, come running when I call, soothed me with her calm voice when bad dreams wake me in the night. Yet now, as I stand here, my hands clasping the railings, the only sound I hear is the thick, black silence of night. For the first time in my life, she has not come to my aid when I call, and I realize with a sickening dread that this is it. This ship, these strangers, are all I have now.

I stagger back towards the sleeping children and collapse in a heap at the feet of Padre Armando.

'Try to rest now, child,' he says, his voice almost swallowed by the fierce wind. 'There is nothing to fear. You are safe.'

But I know, as I close my eyes and let the motion of the waves lull me to sleep, that I will never feel safe again.

I

Corinne
PRESENT DAY

'The ambulance has arrived at the house, Anthony. The paramedics will be with you any moment now.'

I breathe a deep sigh of relief as the red dot that has been flashing across the screen for the past five minutes finally settles on the address.

'Oh, thank God. Thank God,' says the man on the other end of the line, his voice trembling. 'And thanks, Corinne. For everything. I couldn't have done this without you.'

I have spent ten minutes talking this young man through CPR for his mother, who had collapsed with a suspected heart attack. He was so panic-stricken at first, I didn't think he would be able to perform the procedure. There was also the added stress of a child screaming in the background. Yet, thankfully, using all my skills as an emergency call handler, I managed to calmly coax this man into focusing on his mother until he could detect a pulse.

'You're welcome, Anthony. All part of the service.'

I hear the voices of the paramedics in the background

5

before Anthony clicks off and my shoulders loosen. The ambulance got there in time. Anthony's mother is in good hands now.

As I wait for the next call, I lean back in my seat and look around at my colleagues, who are dotted about the room. There is something about the dispatch centre – the broad, windowless room, the weighted silence broken in sporadic bursts by the voices of the operators – that makes me feel calm. No matter what might be going on in my life, when I get to my pod and put my headphones on, see the familiar red lines streaking across the map of London on the computer monitor in front of me, I enter what we refer to as 'the zone'. For the duration of the twelve-hour shift, we cannot see the outside world. We have no idea whether it is night or day, warm or cold, stormy or still out there. Our thoughts and focus are directed solely on the disembodied voices on the other end of the line.

I see Ed, leaning forward in his seat, talking urgently into his headset. Ed has only been here a few months, but he was thrown in at the deep end with a major traffic accident on his first night. That's the thing about this job: nothing can prepare you for what's going to come in. It's how you deal with it that proves whether you are going to cut it long-term. Ed, though visibly terrified, kept his nerve and handled the emergency with a calm efficiency that impressed even the old-timers like me.

I've been here ten years – my first job after university – and during that time have been privy to the worst that life can throw at a person. I have heard people gasping for breath, listened as anguished relatives tried to resuscitate their loved ones, heard screams so blood-curdling they penetrated my bones. Yet I manage to keep all those horrors contained in my pod. I never take them home.

That is because, if I let my emotions take over, I will sink. Ever since I was a child, I have been able to tap into the feelings of those around me. At school the air would buzz with the other children's thoughts, their happiness, their pain, their insecurities. It was so intense I would sometimes put my hands over my ears to try to block it all out. As I grew up, I learned how to deal with those feelings, how to keep calm and centre myself so I wouldn't become overwhelmed. Over time, this centring has become a kind of shield I place between myself and others, to the point where most people think that I am aloof or impassive. Little do they know that, if I allowed my true nature to come through, then I would be so overcome with the emotions of the people on the other end of the line I wouldn't be able to do my job. Better to have people think me cold than have that happen.

After a hysterical sous chef in Clapham suffering third-degree burns and a motorbike accident on Streatham Hill, my headset falls momentarily silent, and I feel my stomach rumble. Time for my break. I gesture to Ed then take myself off to the staffroom.

Sitting on the soft green beanbag chair, my usual spot, tucked away in the far corner of the room, I peel open my plastic takeaway box and greedily devour mouthfuls of cold – yet delicious – dosa, the hit of potato, pancake, mustard seeds and spice sending me into a temporary food coma. While I eat, I take my phone and go through my inbox, skim-reading, and make a mental note of the HR email outlining the details of an upcoming staff training day in Kent. Then I click on an online petition calling for the preservation of an ancient yew tree located in an East London churchyard, sent by my Uncle Robin at midnight. I smile as I read his accompanying message: *It would be much appreciated if you could add your name to stop the heartless bastards destroying yet another piece of London's history. Oh, and a gentle reminder that my new series starts this Thursday at 9 pm . . .*

All signed, I hastily reply. *Working night shifts this week but will watch the first episode on catch-up. Can't wait to see it xx.*

Closing my emails, I pause for a moment to scrape every last crumb from the box, the hungry feeling suddenly replaced with a shiver of adrenalin. Time to get back to it. I go to wash out the box and am just trying to locate a clean tea towel when my phone starts vibrating. My chest tightens. Calls at this time of night are never a good sign. I yank the phone out of my pocket and see the words *Unknown Number* flash onto the screen.

'Hello,' I say, placing the box on the draining board to air-dry.

There is a hissing sound on the other end of the line, like the static on an old recording. The person must be in an area with poor signal.

'Hello. Who is this?'

I can hear a woman speaking. Her voice sounds muffled, as though she is in a windowless room, or trapped underground.

'Please, you have to help me,' she cries. 'You have to find my little girl. She's trapped.'

I abruptly switch back into work mode. With the phone pressed tightly to my ear I rush back to my pod.

'It's the big old Georgian house,' she says, her words tumbling out so fast I can barely keep up. 'Rochester Place it's called, you can't miss it. It's hidden away, behind Larkin Road, down the little pathway. It has a bright red door and a magnolia tree in the garden. Telephone number: BAL 672. Please hurry. I think the house might have been hit. There's so much smoke. You have to help her. Do you promise me you will? She's just a little girl. Eleven years old. Just make sure she's okay, will you do that? My name is Mary. Did you get that? Mary.'

'Mary, can you tell me where you are?' I say, wondering if this person is someone I know, a neighbour perhaps. They are all aware that I am a first responder. 'Hello? Are you there?'

With a sick feeling I realize that the line has gone dead. And as it was an unknown number, I can't retrieve the call.

'Everything okay?' says Ed, peering over the top of my screen from his pod. 'What was that?'

'Someone called my mobile,' I say, looking down at the notes I've scribbled. *Child trapped. House has been hit. Smoke. Rochester Place. Georgian house off Larkin Road. Red door. Magnolia tree. BAL 672.* 'A woman. She said there's a child trapped in a house. I'm going to have to call it in.'

'Strange that they called your mobile and not 999,' says Ed, frowning. 'Could it be someone you know?'

'I don't think so,' I say, as I type *Larkin Road* into the system, prompting the computer to automatically dispatch the fire service. 'It came up as an unknown number and I didn't recognize the voice. She had an Irish accent, sounded quite elderly.'

Almost immediately a red dot appears on the map, hovering over the familiar broad stretch of Larkin Road. Zooming in, I see what looks to be a square patch halfway down the road, jutting off to the left. Larkin Road is just minutes from where I live, yet I had no idea it had a side street leading off it.

'Did you say the child was trapped?' says Ed, adjusting his headset. 'If so, you might want to alert the fire service first. It could be an explosion.'

'Already done it,' I say, watching as the dot on the map stops moving.

With a potential gas leak or explosion, the fire service must attend first in order to deem the area safe. I
also have an ambulance on standby, waiting for the all-
clear. I sit, my eyes fixed on the screen. This part can
take a while, and every second feels like a lifetime. But,
after just a few minutes, a male voice comes through my
headset.

'Hello, it's Ian Turner, fire and rescue. We're at the
address and there's nothing here. No house at all – just
a back alley. We've done a door-to-door of the houses
on Larkin Road that back onto the side street and there's
no one here needing assistance. Are you sure you got
the right address?'

I look down at my notes.

'The caller said it was a large Georgian house called
Rochester Place, just off Larkin Road,' I say, aware of
Ed's eyes on me and hoping I didn't mishear the woman.
'She said it had a red door and a magnolia tree in the
garden.'

'Well, if there was a house like that here we'd notice
it,' he says with a sigh. 'There's just a load of bins and
what looks like some sort of compost heap.'

'Are you sure?' I say. 'The caller was very clear and—'

'I am sure, yes,' he says, cutting in with more than a
hint of irritation in his voice. 'Now, we're leaving the
scene.'

He clicks off, and I lean back in my chair, my heart
racing.

'Hoax call,' says Ed, shrugging his shoulders. 'It happens to the best of us.'

I nod my head. He's right, of course. I have dealt with hundreds of hoax calls in my time. This was just the latest. I adjust my headset and try to refocus, try to block out what has just happened, but as I sit, waiting for the next call to come in, all I can hear is Mary's voice: *Please . . . You have to help her . . . She's just a little girl.*

2

Teresa

MAY 1937

'Good morning, my child. It seems that God has blessed us with a calm sea today.'

Padre Armando is standing above me, his face half in shadow. He clutches his crucifix in his hands and begins to mutter a prayer. Beside me, I feel warm, musty-smelling bodies twitching, and I remember, with a sick feeling, where I am.

I woke early, thoughts of home drifting through my mind. While the others slept, I watched as a black cloud crept steadily towards the crescent moon. Above it, a pinprick of light, which may have been a planet, flickered on and off, reminding me of a happy memory from three summers earlier.

It was a June morning. I was five years old and standing with my sister in the window of our small apartment. Outside, the town square was quiet and still – no market that day, not a soul about. It was warm and bright, the sun already strong despite the early hour. Katalin had her Leica camera in her hand, wanting to capture the summer morning light. I asked her how it worked, and she put it in my hands, explaining how the lens brought all the light rays together into a single point, creating a sharp image. Then, taking the camera from me and placing it carefully on the window seat, she walked over to the mantelpiece and picked up the glass ornament that had been there, in that spot, for as long as I could remember.

'Look at this, little one,' she said, returning to the window. 'This is called a prism. Our father gave it to Mother when they first met.'

I climbed into her arms, inhaling the scent of her: the citrus tang of her perfume, the medicinal herb-like odour of her shampoo, the earthy undertones of her skin.

'Watch what happens when it finds the light.'

I watched as Katalin held the glass aloft. Streaks of rainbow light fractured the glass in a dazzling display.

'Look how the light diffracts,' she said gently. 'How it splits into multiple possibilities. You know, Father used to say that the prism teaches us about life after death.'

Her eyes glistened, but I could not tell whether it was the sharp sunlight or talk of the dead that made them so.

'I like to think that this world is one of many, Teresa,' she said, sighing deeply. 'Like these strands of colour. How wonderful to think that those who have gone before, all those we have loved, may be living still, out in some other dimension alongside ours. And that, one day, those separate strands will come together again, even for just a moment.'

My sister smiled at me, her dark eyes full of hope and wonder. I reached out towards her, but her face dissolved into the darkness and I was back on the ship, surrounded by sleeping strangers.

'They're serving breakfast below stairs,' says Padre Armando, his voice rousing the other children from their sleep and sending my memory scattering across the deck. 'I recommend you visit the washrooms first.'

My legs wobble as I try to stand. Sleeping in one position on hard wood has left my body feeling heavy and sore. Above me, the sky is almost white, and a pale light envelops the deck, making strange shadows of the children as they yawn and stretch and throw off their blankets. When I get to my feet, I drape my blanket round my shoulders, my fingers brushing against the hexagonal cardboard disc they pinned to my coat at the station, the numbers 2034 stamped in the centre. My name, it seems, was left behind on the station platform at the barriers beyond which Katalin was not permitted, trailing in her wake like steam from a kettle. Gone, like the glint of light inside the glass prism she gave me as she handed me over to Padre Armando. 'Take this and remember what I told you,' she whispered. 'We will be together again very soon. No more than three months, I promise. Now, be brave, little one. Be brave.'

'I can do that,' I tell myself, as I follow Padre Armando

across the deck towards a set of wooden steps. 'I can be brave. For Katalin.'

The area below deck has been transformed into a makeshift dining room. While Padre Armando's group, and several others, had commandeered the upper deck, another set of children and their guardians had found themselves sleeping down here. I saw them on my way to the lavatory before bedtime, dozens of children crammed top-to-toe on mattresses that covered every inch of the floor. But now the mattresses have been stacked up against the wall, and rows of tables have taken their place. The air smells of burnt cooking fat, eggs and body odour. The other children hurry towards the food and I reluctantly follow. But as I get closer, the trays of grey, fatty bacon and watery tomatoes churn my stomach.

I turn to go back up the stairs to the deck but am stopped in my tracks by the tall, thin figure of Padre Armando.

'Come now, child,' he says, guiding me back towards the serving hatch. 'You must eat. We still have a long journey ahead of us.'

As a woman in pink, her hair scraped severely back, slops the food onto a plate, I think of Katalin's words at the station: *be brave*. And though my eyes are watering already at the thought of another day without her, I tell myself that I cannot fear a plate of food, no matter how disgusting it looks, not when my sister is facing untold dangers for the sake of our country.

'Good girl,' says Padre Armando, nodding at my piled plate, as I join him and the rest of the children at the table. 'Now, let us give thanks for the bounty God has placed before us this morning.'

As he says grace, I look around the table at the others. There are four girls and two boys. The girl sitting next to me, hollow-cheeked, with cropped auburn hair, looks close to my age. The others seem older. One of the boys already has the beginnings of a moustache, though he can only be fifteen at the very most. Katalin told me the authorities would only take children between the ages of five and fifteen. I have barely spoken to any of them, so terrified was I when Padre Armando pulled me from Katalin's arms at the station barriers. Crying so much I could just see a blur of colour as the priest introduced me to the rest of his charges in the cramped train compartment. I sat with my head down for the entire journey, only looking up when Padre Armando said we had arrived at the docks. When we boarded the ship, I kept my eyes lowered. If I saw the ship and the children and the volunteers, then it would be real. If I kept my eyes on my black patent-leather shoes, the shoes Katalin had bought for me on my last birthday, then I could pretend that none of this was happening, that it was all a bad dream.

Now, in the cold light of morning, I can see that the other children are as confused and wary as I am. The girl next to me hasn't looked up from her plate of bacon and eggs, and I can hear sniffling coming from one of the older girls. The sound makes me feel uncomfortable, as my own tears are never far away and I am trying my best to be brave.

'You have finished?' says Padre Armando, as I push my plate away. 'There is still some bacon there.'

He points at a congealed piece of fatty meat nestled against a soggy pile of scrambled eggs. I nod my head and am about to take my plate back to the serving hatch when the boy with the moustache leans over and grabs it from my hand. I sit for a moment and watch as he shovels the food into his mouth. I remember what Katalin told me when we arrived in Bilbao after travelling for two days – how the city had been ravaged by food shortages, its people half-starved.

'Princess. Thinks she is better than us. Probably one of them . . . a dirty Nationalist.'

I look up and see the boy who took my food sneering at me. He shakes his head and raises his middle finger. Padre Armando puts his hand on the boy's arm and whispers something in his ear. The boy nods then continues to eat. I want to leave the table, but I dare not move.

How can he think that I am a Nationalist? For someone like me, there can be nothing more damning than to be thought of as one of them. Don't they realize that I am the sister of the fearless Katalin Garro, the woman who would lay down her life to protect the Republican government – the legally elected government – from Franco and his fascists? Then I remember that here on this ship I am just another child in borrowed clothes with a cardboard disc pinned to my coat. No one here knows about my sister or her reputation. While the children eat, I close my eyes and think of the cinnamon buns Katalin used to buy for me from the bakery near my school.

I last went there just a few days before our town was wiped off the face of the earth. I had been sent on an errand by Katalin. She had told me I was to ask José, the baker, for a bag of cinnamon buns. And, though the buns would be warm and delicious, I was not to open the bag until I came home. Katalin made it clear that I should hand her the bag as soon as I got home and I would be allowed a bun as a reward. I had been doing this for a few weeks now, and though I did not really understand why I was not allowed to open the bag, I enjoyed the sense of responsibility. Katalin had entrusted me with this job and I did not want to let her down.

When I arrived that day, a queue was already forming outside the pretty white building with its bright blue shutters. As I drew near, I saw José's handsome face peeping out of the hatch, his mop of black hair, his navy-and-white striped apron smeared with flour. There were lots of people in front of me, but José, spotting me, gestured them to one side. 'Buns for the Garros,' he cried, holding up a brown paper bag.

I could hear the disapproving noises from a couple of women in the queue: what right had Katalin Garro's skinny sister to push in front, to get special attention? Though some of the men removed their caps and stood back to let me through. When I reached the front of the queue, José handed me the bag of buns as usual, but I noticed when I took them from him that his hands were shaking. 'Tell your sister,' he whispered, glancing sideways at the disgruntled women, 'that the largest bun is just for her.'

'Hey, princess.'

I look up and see the moustached boy glaring at me. Padre Armando and the rest of the children have left the table and it is just the two of us.

'Your home was completely flattened, wasn't it?' he says, picking pieces of food out of his teeth with his grubby fingernail. 'I heard there is nothing left of it.'

He stops picking and stares at me, expecting an answer.

'The priest told me where you came from,' he says, flicking a piece of gristle onto the floor. 'The spoilt little girl, looking at me, as though I was some sort of beggar, some shit on her shoe. But you're just like the rest of us. At least my city is still standing.'

He starts to laugh raucously, and I turn my face away, recalling the words of a couple standing behind us at the processing centre in Bilbao.

Nothing left? Are you serious?

As the grave. My sister is an ambulance driver. She was one of

20

the first on the scene . . . said it was like gazing into the bowels of Hell . . .

The woman spoke the name of my town then, and tutted sadly, as though she were speaking of the dead. I looked up at Katalin, who was holding my hand. She smiled, as if to reassure me, but her eyes were sad. We both knew that we would never see our home again, never walk along the cobbled streets of our town eating warm cinnamon buns, never dance to folk songs in the square, or stand at the window of our apartment and watch the morning sun rise above the terracotta rooftops. It was gone, swept away like crumbs from the bakery floor. Our lovely town was no longer home; it was just a name, a name that had horrified the world.

'Guernica.'

I turn back to the boy. His eyes are blazing.

'I can't believe you come from there,' he says, shaking his head. 'My uncle said it would have been a miracle if anyone survived. Tell me, did you see the planes approach? They say it was the Condor Legion, sent from Germany to help Franco. Is that true? Did you see them? What about dead bodies? I hear there were arms and legs flung around the market square, so many they couldn't tell which were from the butcher's stall and which were human.'

'Stop!' I cry, jumping up from the table. 'Leave me alone, do you hear me? Just leave me alone.'

I run up the wooden steps towards the deck, my heart pounding in my chest.

When I reach the top, I am almost thrown backwards by a gust of wind. I cling on to the rail and try to steady myself as I step out onto the deck. A thick fog hangs in the air, making it difficult to see where I am going. The ship tilts to one side and I sway with it, feeling the morsel of greasy bacon and eggs I ate earlier rising forcefully back up my throat. A wave crashes over the side, drenching me in seawater.

Wiping my eyes, I try to locate the place where Padre Armando put our mattresses. All around me, scenes of panic, confusion and chaos are unfolding. Children screaming, bodies tossed about the deck like rag dolls, smashing against the sides with sickening thuds. The ship tilts to one side and I sway with it, nausea rising inside of me.

I stagger towards the centre of the deck, where, I hope, there is less chance of being thrown over the side by the roiling waves. Behind me, someone screams: 'We're being attacked. He has sent his ships to sink us. The Lord save us. We're going to die.'

I was told I would be safe on the ship, that no harm could come to me once we had departed Spain. Now it looks like I will die here, in the middle of this wild, angry ocean, and I am all alone. Then, I feel someone's hand on my arm, and I am hauled to the ground.

I look up and see a girl with cropped auburn hair and

large brown eyes. I recognize her from the breakfast table. The thin girl. Her name is Ana. As another wave hits the deck, she pulls me to her chest.

'I'm scared,' I cry, pressing my face into the soft wool of her cardigan. 'I don't want to die.'

'Shh now,' she whispers in my ear. 'We're not going to die.'

3

Corinne

PRESENT DAY

Mary's desperate voice is still echoing in my head as I cross Garratt Lane and make my way to Tulsi, the twenty-four-hour café in Tooting run by my wife and sister-in-law.

When I checked my phone at the end of my shift, it showed that the call had lasted just forty-five seconds. Yet it had seemed much longer than that. Was Ed right? Had it just been a prank? It certainly seemed that way, but I've been in this job long enough to spot the hoaxes: the time-wasters who think it's funny to call 999 and fake an emergency, or the drunk revellers who ask if we can send an ambulance as it will get there quicker than a taxi. These calls are the scourge of the service. Not only do they cost money, but they put lives in peril, as real emergencies are left hanging while we attend to the jokers. I'm mortified to think that I fell for a prank and sent a full fire crew out – and with Ed watching me too.

So why do I have this certainty at my core that Mary's call was genuine? She called my mobile. How would a prankster get hold of that number? And there was no sense that this was someone playing around. I could hear the terror in Mary's voice. It was palpable. *Please* . . . *You have to help her.* The words burn into me as I walk into the café. I'm so preoccupied I barely notice the boy hurtling towards me until it's too late.

'It weren't my fault,' he cries, jabbing a bony elbow into my side which almost knocks me over. 'It was him. He pushed me.'

He points behind him to where a group of teenagers – three shaven-headed boys with surly expressions, and a smirking girl with blue streaks in her black hair – are standing next to an upturned table, a pile of broken crockery at their feet. It is then I notice my sister-in-law, Rima, standing by the counter, her arms folded across her chest, her white apron stained with yellow turmeric patches.

'I don't care whose fault it was. I won't have you disturbing my customers,' says Rima, moving back to let my wife, Nidra, through with a dustpan and brush. 'If you can't behave yourselves then you're not welcome here. Now go on. Out.'

She rushes at the boy, who looks pale and thin in his oversized blazer, his close-cut ginger hair accentuating razor-sharp cheekbones, and marches him to the door. The others follow suit, their heads bowed. Only the girl is still smiling.

'I said it weren't my fault,' repeats the boy, turning to

Rima, his voice shaking with anger. 'What right have you got to throw me out, eh? I'm waiting for an answer.'

His face is just inches from hers. I move towards them, ready to intervene if necessary, but I have forgotten how formidable my sister-in-law can be in these situations.

'Hey, tough lad,' she says, putting her hand out to ward him off, 'I don't get intimidated by skinny kids whose voices haven't broken yet. Now get out or you really will be in trouble.'

The boy staggers back while the others explode into fits of laughter.

'Ha, your balls haven't dropped,' shrieks one of them as they tumble out onto the street. 'That's what she meant.' The boy glares at Rima then shuffles out, slamming the door behind him.

'What was all that about?' I say, helping Nidra right the table and place the broken crockery into a bin bag.

'Just daft kids,' says Rima, shaking her head. 'What do you expect? Guzzling fizzy drinks at this time of day. They go mad with sugar.'

'It was a bit mean of you to say that to the skinny one,' says Nidra, tying the handle of the bin bag into a thick knot. 'Poor kid will never hear the end of it.'

'Listen, anyone who sticks their face in mine like that is going to be dealt with firmly,' says Rima, marching into the kitchen. 'Alexa, play "Smooth Operator".'

As Sade's soothing voice trickles through the café,

I take a deep breath and go to sit in my usual spot: the corner booth by the window. Placing my phone on the table, my thoughts return to the call and the woman's terrified voice.

'Everything okay?'

I look up at Nidra, who has arrived at the table with a pot of coffee and a plate of steaming dosas. A South Indian breakfast staple, these delicious pancakes stuffed with spiced potato have had people flocking to Tulsi ever since it first opened in 1996.

'I'm fine,' I say, watching as she slides into the seat opposite me. 'Just tired, that's all.'

My wife puts her head to one side and gives me that look, the one that says she can see right through me.

'Corinne?' she says, her hazel eyes widening. 'What is it?'

I take a sip of coffee and look out of the window. I am wary of telling her about the call. I know how she will react. Memories of the bleak period following her mother's death, the obsessive behaviour, the online psychics and tarot card readers, come tumbling back.

'It's not your gran, is it?' she says, placing her hand on mine.

'No,' I say, turning from the window. 'Though that reminds me, I should give her a bell . . . No, it was just a call I had at work. It's probably nothing.'

'It doesn't sound like nothing.'

I realize then that I could do with someone else's

input. Perhaps Nidra can reassure me that I'm worrying over nothing.

So I tell her about the phone call, the mysterious house, the fear in Mary's voice as she implored me to help her child.

When I have finished, Nidra looks at me in astonishment.

'Oh my God,' she says, putting her hand to her mouth. 'This is so spooky.'

That is not what I wanted to hear.

'But what I can't get my head round is how that person, Mary, got your mobile number,' says Nidra, frowning. 'And why she called it and not 999, if she was in such distress.'

'I've been trying to think if I know anyone round here called Mary with an Irish accent, but there's no one I can think of. Also, I don't just hand out my mobile number to complete strangers.'

'Yeah, but think of all the times you enter your number on online forms and shopping sites,' says Nidra, pouring herself a coffee from the pot. 'Phone numbers get around, more than you realize.'

'You're right,' I say. 'But that would only make sense if the call I'd received was some sort of sales thing. This woman, Mary, wasn't a cold-caller trying to flog life insurance, she was . . . well, she was just like the others that call in on any given evening. A real person, scared and in need of help. That's what's so weird.'

'And the guy from the fire service said there was no house there,' says Nidra. 'That's the part I find seriously scary. Maybe she was calling from beyond the grave. Maybe she was a ghost.'

I shake my head, regretting that I opened my mouth. Talk like this, however fantastical, has the potential to send my wife back to that dark place. And none of us need that. Not after everything we've been through.

'How many times do I have to tell you, Nidra? There are no such things as ghosts,' says Rima, appearing at the table. She flashes me a look, a sisterly warning. I take the hint and grab my coat from the back of my chair.

'I'd better be heading home. I need to get some sleep before tonight's shift.'

'What about your dosas?' says Rima, gesturing to my plate. 'You've barely touched them.'

With all the talk of Mary, I had completely forgotten about the food.

'I'm sorry, Rima,' I say guiltily. 'I'm afraid I haven't much of an appetite this morning.'

'I tell you what,' she says, reaching across to take my plate. 'I'll box them up and you can take them home to have later.'

She disappears into the kitchen while Nidra goes to serve a customer. Thankful for the distraction, I put on my coat and head for the door.

'Corinne,' calls Rima, as I'm making my way out, 'don't forget your food.'

She rushes towards me with a plastic box in her hand.

'Here you go,' she says. 'You'll be thankful for that later. Oh, and do thank your gran for sending that seaweed. Tell her I roasted it with some salt and olive oil, and it was delicious – like eating a big bowl of crisps.'

'She'll be delighted,' I say, picturing Gran wandering along the shoreline near her cottage, stooping to collect armfuls of thick, sodden seaweed before returning to the warmth of her sofa and an afternoon reading her favourite Dickens or Hemingway stories. 'She said there's tonnes of the stuff out there at the moment. I'm guessing she'll be spending this week stocking up. You know she swears by its nutritional value, says it keeps her young.'

'In that case, tell her to send me some more,' says Rima, laughing. 'I can get rid of the expensive face creams.'

The earthy scent of cumin and mustard seeds wafts deliciously on the crisp morning air as I head down Garratt Lane, the box of warm dosas tucked into my backpack. The temperature has dropped, and I put my hands into the fur-lined pockets of my parka as I walk, imagining how warm and welcoming my bed will be. Yet, as I reach the end of Larkin Road, something compels me to turn left and go and investigate Rochester Place for myself. I know this is a crazy idea. After all,

Ian Turner was certain there was nothing there, that the call had been a hoax. Surely there is nothing to be gained by poking around. Yet my feet are leading me onwards.

Larkin Road is an unremarkable street, with the usual South London mix of Victorian terraces and boxy new builds. I remember Gran telling me how London rebuilt itself after the war, leaving many streets looking like this one: the old world and the new jostling for space.

As I walk, I take out my phone from my pocket and look at the maps app, trying to locate the little pathway that Mary described. The map indicates it is pretty much midway down Larkin Road, on the left-hand side, just before the Victorian terraces give way to the new builds. It should be coming up any moment now.

Slipping my phone back into my pocket, I reach the last of the terraces – a rather rundown red-brick house with peeling paint on the sash windows and weeds clustered round the doorstep. And then, suddenly, it appears: a narrow, cobbled walkway, leading westwards.

There is a black patch on the wall where a street sign must once have been fixed and, without knowing why, I press my hand over it, feeling the chalky texture. A ghost sign, one of many to be found across London. The faded remains of shop hoardings, pub signs and street names, little pieces of the past breaking into the present, whispering their secrets.

'What is this?' I mutter to myself, as I follow the

uneven path. In all my years of living and working in Tooting, of spending every night staring at a map of the area, I never knew such a place existed.

An old stone wall runs the length of the pathway and is covered with bramble bushes and bracken. It is extraordinary, I think to myself – a little pocket of countryside in the heart of urban Tooting. As I walk further along the cobbles, a shaft of morning sun strikes the pathway, temporarily blinding me. White spots appear in front of my eyes. I blink and, when the spots subside, see that I have arrived in a garden, although 'garden' is rather too generous a description.

Accessed via a tall iron gate and enclosed by a honey-coloured stone wall, it might once have been idyllic: a substantial walled garden, just minutes from the bustle of Tooting Broadway. As I step further into the tall grass, taking care to avoid the broken bottles and rusted beer cans that are scattered on the edge of the uneven path, I remember Mary mentioned a magnolia tree and try to picture where it might be, but it is difficult amid such detritus. As the sun changes position, I see a flash of colour up ahead. As I draw closer, I see a seat pushed against the wall. It is one of those ornate iron benches, the kind you see dotted along the promenade at a seaside resort. It was once painted bottle green, but most of its colour has been weather-worn to rust. There is something fixed to the back of it: a small metal plaque with gold lettering. I lean forward to read what it says.

The words have been eroded by the elements, but I can just about make them out:

In loving memory of Mary Davidson and Teresa Garro . . .

My blood runs cold as I read the next line.

. . . who lost their lives here, on 15th October 1940.

'Mary,' I whisper, slumping onto the bench. 'It's not possible . . . it can't be her.'

I turn round and read the plaque again, and it is then that I notice: 15 October. Today's date.

A strange feeling, one not unlike vertigo, overcomes me suddenly. I get to my feet. I feel vulnerable, alone here in this desolate, abandoned place. Surely this is all just a coincidence? Surely the Mary who called me in the early hours of this morning is not the Mary commemorated on this plaque – a woman who died eighty years ago this very day?

4

Teresa

MAY–JUNE 1937

'Ingalaterra!'

The shout wakes me from my sleep.

It is morning. The water is still, and the attack we had feared turned out to be, as the captain assured us, just a storm after all.

As I cowered in Ana's arms the previous evening, she remained calm and told me that we needed to call out for Mari.

'Who is Mari?' I replied.

'Mari was one of the most important of all the Basque goddesses,' said Ana, raising her voice above the roar of the waves. 'She was very special because she was both a queen and a witch.'

I had never heard of the goddess Mari, but I liked the sound of her. In my head I saw a dark-haired woman flying on a broomstick with a jewelled crown on her head.

'They say that Mari lives in a cave in the mountains along with her priestesses,' Ana continued. 'Hidden deep within her cave, Mari listens out for those who might be in peril, as we are now. They say if you call Mari's name loudly, three times, then she will come to your aid. And you will know her when you see her because she will be dressed in red.'

'Ingalaterra!'

The cry goes out again, and I look up to see the moustached boy standing at the edge of the ship, looking overboard.

'Ingalaterra,' he cries, excitedly, waving his arms in the air. 'Viva Ingalaterra.'

Soon the ship is alive with cries of the same. Men, women and children chanting the name of a country that has only ever existed in our imaginations.

Viva Ingalaterra. Viva Ingalaterra.

Ana, who was such a comfort during the worst of the storm, takes my hand. Padre Armando gathers up the rest of the children and we rush to join the boy.

A sliver of green looms out of the mist, and as it slowly takes form my skin prickles, and not just from the icy sea air. I feel a strange sensation, a mixture of elation and sorrow. This is England. The place Padre Armando has told us about, where there are no bombs, no wars, no German pilots delivering death from the skies, no need for the protection of saints or the goddess Mari. A place where buses are red, and men wear bowler hats and people greet each other with 'hello' not 'kaixo'. Where the skies are grey not blue, and nobody gets killed while shopping for peppers.

35

'Isn't this marvellous?' whispers Padre Armando, appearing beside me. 'My, what stories we'll have to tell when we get home.' A spray of seawater splashes over the side of the ship, and I wipe the salt from my eyes and turn away from the priest.

I walk away from the cheering and celebrations and stand for a moment by the hatch that leads down to the bowels of the ship. Perhaps if I hide down there, where it is dark and hollow, and keep as quiet as a mouse, then I can stay on this ship when the others disembark. I can wait until it is time to go back to Spain.

'Teresa.'

I turn to see Padre Armando rushing towards me. It is too late to hide now.

'Come, Teresa,' he cries. 'We must take a roll call before we disembark.'

I make my way towards him, my feet as heavy as my heart. Then I hear a splashing sound. Padre Armando gathers me to him.

'Look,' he says, pointing at the water. 'Can you see it?'

There is something bobbing alongside the ship. I narrow my eyes, try to work out what I am looking at. Then, with an almighty whoosh, a glossy body emerges from the waves.

'A dolphin,' cries Padre Armando. 'My, Teresa, what a sight.'

We watch as the dolphin rises into the air like an acrobat, curves its back then nosedives back under the waves.

I cannot believe my eyes. Before this moment, I thought dolphins were mythical creatures, like unicorns and dragons. If only Katalin were here to see this. The photos she would take. My thoughts turn to the prism she gave me. I slide my hand into my pocket, feel its reassuring glass edges. *Remember what I told you, Teresa. Remember the light.*

'I think God blessed us just now,' says Padre Armando, taking my hand and leading me back across the deck. 'That dolphin came with a message from our Lord. He was telling us that our perilous journey is at an end. He has heard our prayers. Calm waters lie ahead.'

As the ship approaches land, I think of the smoking rooftop of the Iglesia Santa María, one of the last sights I saw as Katalin and I fled the ruins of Guernica, and I can't shake the bad feeling in the pit of my stomach, the idea that Padre Armando is wrong – that we have not sailed into calm waters but have hurled ourselves into the eye of a terrible storm.

'We sisters are gathered at this site to do God's will. We are here to minister to the poor and the elderly, to help those fleeing war and persecution, to give shelter to those in need and to nourish them with the truth of our Lord God Jesus Christ. We welcome you, our good Catholic children.'

I am not really listening to what the nun is saying, as I am preoccupied with the deep-set wrinkles on her face. Her skin is dry and cracked, and her pale eyes are so small and watery they bleed into her face like puddles. This, along with the black wimple and gown, makes her look like a ghost, a strange half-person fluttering on the steps.

I look up at the bleak red-brick building and wonder what could possibly be coming next. According to the young woman who accompanied us here – one of the Basque volunteers known as 'Señoritas' – the Congregation of St Cecilia is to be our home for the foreseeable future. I look up at Sister Bernadette. She is still speaking, though she pauses after each sentence so that the Señorita can translate what she is saying. 'We have,' she informs us, 'been in this blessed convent for one hundred and thirty years.'

'No wonder she looks so old,' whispers one of the girls. This sets off a chorus of giggles along the row.

'Girls,' says the Señorita firmly, 'where are your manners?'

Sister Bernadette, however, seems oblivious to the laughter. She has her eyes closed and is making the sign of the cross. When she has finished, she turns on her heel and heads inside. The Señorita, looking flustered, gestures for us to follow.

I am allocated a dormitory with three other girls. There is Veronica, a tall, broad-shouldered girl with brown hair, cut into a severe bob, and black-rimmed spectacles. With her imposing presence and commanding voice, she seems much older than her eleven years. Rosaria is nine and has glossy, copper-coloured hair tied back in a thick plait, and pale brown eyes that turn golden when they catch the light. She also has an unfortunate tendency to collapse into fits of giggles whenever one of the nuns speaks. Then there is Eider, a small, rather timid girl who wears a permanent expression of panic on her face and spends most of her time hiding behind Rosaria. Though she is going to be ten years old next month, she appears much younger, and with her squeaky voice and anxious twitching she has been christened 'sagu' – Basque for 'mouse' – by Veronica, a name Eider seems destined to live up to.

I got to know the girls a little in the camp at Stoneham, where we were taken after receiving our medical examinations at Southampton Docks. Though I was sceptical about the camp, with its white bell tents and loudspeakers that blasted out 'Land of Hope and Glory' each morning, it turned out to be a happy and welcoming place. It was run by volunteers who had been recruited by the Basque Children's Committee, an organization formed to evacuate us children from our war-torn homeland. The volunteers were warm and friendly and provided no end of entertainment for us all, from games of pelota to craft activities. They had even managed to create a makeshift cinema, with a projector and screen donated by a wealthy businessman, where we could sit and watch *Popeye the Sailor Man* while

39

munching big bags of popcorn. The camp had its fair share of visitors too. A famous artist called Augustus John took up residence in one of the tents and offered to draw our portraits, though I turned him down as he seemed rather scary, with his bushy beard and wild eyes.

After the turbulent sea journey, and the grim-faced nurse at the port who had removed my dress and sent it away to be burned – 'We don't want an outbreak of lice, young lady' – the camp brought much-needed fun and laughter. Though it wasn't home, I reminded myself each day of my sister's words as she bid me goodbye: *It is only for three months, remember that.* That is how I got through those first few weeks in England. Yet here I am, almost a month later, transferred to another place, with no hint as to when I shall be able to return home.

The dormitory, like the rest of the building, is sparsely decorated and smells of incense and mothballs. There are four beds with iron frames, dressed in thick white blankets. Each bed has a table beside it with three drawers, on top of which sits a white bible. I place the black-haired doll, given to me by a well-wisher at South-ampton Docks, in the bed. Her sad button eyes regard me as I tuck the thick blanket around her.

There is a bathroom across the corridor which we must share with the girls from the next room along. We are each given a face cloth, towel and bar of carbolic soap which, we are told, we are to use sparingly. 'Vanity is not looked upon kindly in the house of the Lord,'

Sister Bernadette explains as she gives us a tour of the facilities. 'You are only fully clean once you absolve your sins.'

My heart sinks as we follow the hunched old nun through the stark corridors, listening as the Señorita translates her words. I regret that I spent so much of my time at Stoneham praying for escape. Now my wish has come true, but it is a hollow victory. For Stoneham, despite my homesickness, was a place of colour and music, of movies and chocolate and smiling faces. At mealtimes, the rosy-cheeked women who ran the dining tents would greet us with 'Hello, ducky' as they served our food. Here, we are told, meals will be served and eaten in near silence.

As the nuns lead us into the dining room, where a framed picture of Jesus, with a flaming heart, looms over the tables, I feel a lump settle in my throat. It stays there while Sister Bernadette says grace; while I try to chew the bland boiled meat and overcooked carrots that have been placed in front of me; and it is there when we are dismissed from the table with an order to occupy ourselves sensibly until bedtime at 7 p.m.

It is the sadness stone – that's what Katalin used to tell me when I tried to describe how it felt. 'When we feel scared or worried or upset,' she would say as she held me in her arms, 'the sadness stone lodges in our throat and won't budge until the happy birds push it away.' 'But how do I find the happy birds, Katalin?' 'Well, that's the hard

41

part,' she'd say, her eyes glistening as she thought about her own sadness stone, the parents she'd lost who I had never known. 'You call for them and hope for them and wish for them, but they do not come, and, for a time, you think that they have forgotten you. Then, one day, you wake up and the sadness stone has gone. The birds came and got rid of it without you ever realizing it.'

I try not to think of my sister as I join the other girls in the library, which is a large room tucked away at the far end of the corridor, with a curved bay window that looks out onto the two-acre parkland. Strange to think that this place is just a few miles from London. Though the view outside is lush and green, the room is just as stark as the rest of the convent, with sickly pale blue walls, heavy hessian curtains, coir-matting flooring and rigid wooden chairs, yet it has the benefit of being lined with floor-to-ceiling bookshelves.

I sit down on the scratchy carpet in front of one of the shelves and flick through the books. Most of them appear to be religious: bibles, bible-study guides or biographies of Catholic figures. Big, heavy, leather-bound books that would take a person years to read. Then, on the bottom shelf, I see a row of slim paper-back books with coloured spines. Pink, red, blue, green and yellow. Yellow is my favourite colour, so I pull that one out to look at the cover.

It is a painting of a fair-haired woman kneeling in prayer. I can't read the title, but I do recognize one word: *Teresa*. St Teresa. I run my fingers along the raised black lettering. This might be a story about me, I think to myself as I take the book over to the chair by the bay window and sit down to look at it.

Outside, the last of the day's sunlight is turning the parkland a golden pink, and the rays pour onto my face as I open the book. Though I cannot understand the words, I enjoy looking at the pictures of St Teresa. One in particular catches my eye. It shows St Teresa, sitting at a desk with a feathered quill in her hand, looking up into a flaming sky as a host of angels descends upon her. I wonder what she was writing and if the presence of the angels meant she was going to die or that what she was writing was special.

The other girls are quietly engrossed in their own activities. Eider and Rosaria are huddled together on the floor, working on the cross-stitching project they began at Stoneham: a pair of pale pink cushion covers onto which they are stitching blue flowers. Eider is clutching her fabric tightly, as though terrified someone may snatch it away from her, while Rosaria has tied red ribbons around her plaited hair. The colour catches my eye and I get a pang of sadness as I recall the silver box of ribbons I kept on my shelf at home.

Veronica is sitting by the bookshelf at the back of the room, her legs pulled up to her chest, her head bowed over a book. I can hear the pages being turned alongside the ticking of the grandfather clock in the corridor, as I stare, entranced, at St Teresa. I am so lost in the pictures that, at first, I don't see Veronica leaping to her feet and walking over to where Eider and Rosaria are sitting. It is only when Eider screams that the spell is broken, and I drop the book in fright.

'No, it's not true,' Eider cries, pulling at her hair with her hands, while Rosaria sits stock-still, staring straight ahead.

'It is, I tell you,' insists Veronica, waving a newspaper in front of her. 'This is today's headline. I found the newspaper on the doormat. It is the truth. Look.'

She thrusts the newspaper at the sobbing Eider, who pushes it away and runs screaming out of the room – almost colliding with the Señorita, who has arrived at the door, her face as red as the erremolatxas at the food market back home.

'What is it, child?' she says, clasping Eider's shoulders. 'What is the matter?'

'I want to go home,' cries Eider, who has now been joined by a rather dazed-looking Rosaria. 'I want to see my mami and papi.'

As the Señorita ushers the girls out of the room, Veronica notices me huddled in the window and comes over, holding up the newspaper.

'Did you hear?' she says, her eyes wide and unblinking behind her thick-framed spectacles.

I shake my head.

'Look,' says Veronica, handing me the newspaper.

I cannot read what it says, as it is an English news-paper, though I see the black-and-white photograph that accompanies the headline. It shows rejoicing sol-diers, waving guns in the air, their dark uniforms with the fascist Falange emblem – the yoke and five arrows – clearly visible on their shirt pockets.

'Bilbao has fallen to Franco's forces,' says Veronica, swiping the newspaper from my hands and clutching it to her chest. 'Our parents will be dead. That nervous little sagu needed to know the truth. We are not going home, you hear me, Teresa? We are never going home.'

I stand up abruptly from the chair, the book falling from my lap onto the floor with a thud. Outside, night has fallen, plunging the parkland into darkness. It feels like the black night has seeped inside me. I cannot breathe. I must get out of here, out of this room, away from Veronica and her newspaper. I must go and find Katalin.

Running along the corridor, swerving to avoid the black-clad nuns who are filing out of the chapel, I feel as though my heart is about to burst out of my chest. When I reach the dormitory door, I rush to my bed and dart underneath it. There is only one person who can help me now. Closing my eyes, I take a deep lungful of air and shout, at the top of my voice, 'MARI, MARI, MARI.'

The name echoes around the empty room, then a heavy silence falls. I stay where I am, keeping deathly still. A couple of moments pass, before I hear footsteps coming up the corridor. The footsteps come closer and closer then stop, by the bed.

I hold my breath as the person begins to speak.

'Hello under there. Did you call?'

To my utter astonishment the person is speaking Basque, and it cannot be the Señorita because her voice is higher-pitched. Who can it be? Finally, curiosity overcomes my fear, and I open my eyes. I see a pair of feet clad in the most beautiful pair of shoes I have ever seen, cherry red with a pair of gold buttons on the side.

Eager to see who the shoes belong to, I slide out from under the bed and see a woman standing there. She has black hair that falls in glossy ringlets about her shoulders, dark eyebrows that frame her green eyes perfectly, and skin as pale as the alabaster statue of the Virgin Mary in the church back home. Her lips are painted the same shade as her shoes, and she is wearing a scarlet shirt-waisted dress and an emerald hair clip that brings out the colour of her eyes. She is the most glorious sight, like something from the movies. Looking at her, I feel overcome with warmth and happiness, and I remember Ana's words about the goddess Mari: *And you will know her when you see her because she will be dressed in red.*

5

Teresa
JUNE 1937

'Now then, how about a bedtime story?' The woman speaks softly, guiding me onto the bed and pulling up a chair beside it.

I listen carefully to her voice. Though she is speaking Basque, there is another accent buried beneath it that I do not recognize. It is not English, and it is not Spanish. It is an accent I have never heard before, and it has a rhythm to it rather like the folk music Katalin used to sing back home. That is it, I think to myself. When this woman speaks, it sounds like music.

'Right,' says the woman, tucking the covers around me as I settle into the bed. 'Shall we begin?'

Dazed, I nod my head and lie back on the pillow as the woman, with her hypnotic voice, tells a story about a brave but spirited young Irish girl who fought the might of the British navy and ruled the Irish Sea. As she continues, I try to work out who she is and where she has come from. She does not look Basque, despite her heavy dark eyebrows and a certain sparkle in her eyes,

47

but she can speak the language perfectly. It does not make sense.

'Grace O'Malley was a pirate, and a queen,' says the woman, her face deadly serious. 'She lived in a tower on a windswept clifftop off the west coast of Ireland, just a few miles away from where I grew up. She was so respected and feared that, when the British imprisoned her youngest son for treason, she was granted an audience with the Queen of England, Elizabeth I, herself. It was a great honour, though Grace, being a true Irish woman, refused to bow.'

'How could she be a queen if she was a pirate?' I say, sitting up. 'I've never heard of such a thing.'

The woman smiles then, and raises one of her dark eyebrows.

'Well, I have always thought that being a queen has nothing to do with birthright,' she says, tucking a strand of black hair behind her ear. 'And everything to do with the inner flame that shines inside a person.'

I think of the picture of Jesus in the dining room, his heart glowing red.

'Here's a little bit of advice,' she says, lowering her voice as a nun walks past the open door of the dormitory. 'There are some in this country that will try to dim your flame, but you haven't to let them, do you hear me?'

I nod my head, mesmerized by this woman and her melodious voice.

'You must always be proud of who you are and where

you come from,' she continues, her green eyes fixed on mine. 'Never forget that. Now I must be off, and you must get your rest. Goodnight, Teresa.'

How does she know my name?

'What's your name?' I say, my eyes growing heavy with fatigue, so that she is just a greenish blur in the doorway.

'My name?' she says. 'Well, I thought you already knew, seeing as though you were screaming it at the top of your voice.'

'Mari?' I say, in disbelief.

'Almost,' she replies, giggling. 'Though I like to say it the Irish way. Mary.'

'Mary.' I whisper the name under my breath as she wishes me goodnight and disappears down the corridor.

The following morning, I am still thinking of Grace O'Malley, the fearless young pirate, as I accompany the other girls to the dining room for breakfast. My thoughts wander until I am no longer shuffling along the bland corridor, the smell of stewed prunes and warm milk in the air, but am standing proud and tall in the grand court of Elizabeth I, sea salt in my nostrils, my skirts damp from the ocean spray. The red-haired queen is looking down her sharp nose at me.

The image is so real, so tangible, I am shocked when the nasal drawl of Sister Bernadette interrupts, calling for us to hurry along. Mary's story has ignited something in me, has made me hungry for more than the paltry breakfast that awaits me.

As the others turn the corner, I hang back. I see the double doors to the library up ahead. Maybe I could go and sit there, just for a few moments. I hurry down the corridor, glancing behind me to check that Sister Bernadette is not on the prowl. Once inside, I lean back against the door and close my eyes. Five minutes. That is all I need.

The library is empty, though I can see a box of books by the chairs in the window that was not there yesterday. Curious, I walk over to take a closer look.

To my amazement, the books have Basque words on the covers. I take out a bold red hardback with a striking painting of a castle on the front.

'I'd highly recommend that one.'

I turn on my heel, almost dropping the book. Crouching in front of a half-empty bookshelf is Mary.

'Oh,' I gasp. 'I didn't know anyone was in here. I was just . . . I—'

'Don't worry,' she says, getting to her feet and brushing the dust from her scarlet skirt. 'I won't tell the nuns you're skipping breakfast. In fact, you can give me a hand with these. I need to put them on this spare shelf.'

She gestures to the box of books, then fixes me with her green eyes, waiting for an answer.

'I'd love to help,' I say, placing the book I am holding

back into the box. 'Where did they come from? These books?'

'They're mine,' says Mary, sweeping a pile of them into her arms and returning to the shelf, the smell of rosewater drifting in her wake.

'But how can you . . . understand them?' I say, watching as she stacks the books carefully onto the shelf, her green hair clip sparkling in a shard of light from the window. 'How can you speak my language?'

'What? You think speaking Basque is beyond the capabilities of some silly Irish lady?' she says, with a smile. 'I'm just kidding you. The truth is, I picked up this language because it reminds me of my own.'

'English?' I say, taking a handful of books from the box.

'Irish,' she says, reaching out to take a book from my pile. 'We have our own language, you know. Though it's getting rarer to hear it now, so I'm told from my relatives back there. There was a time, Teresa, when it was illegal to speak our own language in Ireland. Imagine that? I hear the same could happen with the Basques if old Franco gets his way.'

The mention of that name gives me a start and I drop the books I am holding. Noticing, Mary comes over and picks them up, then puts her hand on my shoulder.

'I'm sorry, my wee girl,' she says, sitting down on the floor beside me. 'I shouldn't have mentioned him, not after everything you children have been through.' Her voice catches then, and she looks down at the floor. 'Anyway, I thought these books would be of better use here than in my house, for there's all you girls here to read them. Now, let's be getting them on the shelf, eh?'

She jumps to her feet and resumes the stacking, pausing every now and then to ask me questions about myself: my favourite colour (yellow), my hobbies (reading), what kind of things I like to eat (cinnamon buns and black cherries in syrup). We are so busy chatting we lose track of time, and before I know it, breakfast is over and it is time for me to go to bible study.

'Come on,' says Mary, helping me to my feet. 'I believe Sister Bernadette herself is teaching the class. It wouldn't do to be late now.'

I feel elated as we step out into the corridor. Seeing those books written in my language has lit a spark in me, made me feel that things might not be so bad here after all. As we near the main hall, a short nun with hunched shoulders and round, wire-rimmed glasses comes towards us.

'Hello,' she says, nodding her head as we draw level.

Mary goes to speak but I beat her to it.

'Hello, ducky,' I say to the nun, nodding my head just as she did.

The nun blinks her eyes rapidly, mutters something under her breath, then walks on.

I look up at Mary, waiting for her to say how impressed she is at my English, but she has her hand to her mouth.

'What?' I say, wondering what is causing her to react like this. 'What is it?'

'Oh, Teresa,' she says, letting out a little giggle. 'What were you thinking, saying that to Sister Agnes?'

'I was just saying hello,' I say, my heart sinking. 'That's what the ladies in the dining tent used to say to us at Stoneham. "Hello, ducky".'

Mary puts her hands on her hips and shakes her head.

'What are we going to do with you, eh?' she says, smiling. 'Listen, I think it's time you learned how to speak some English, and I'm going to teach you. How does that sound?'

'I'd like that,' I say, my cheeks flushing with embarrassment. 'If you're not too busy.'

'It would be a pleasure,' says Mary, clasping her long, thin hands together. 'It's why I volunteered here in the first place.'

'So, you're not a nun?' I ask, trying to stall going to bible class.

'No, I'm not a nun,' she says, smiling as she opens her handbag and takes out a slim pair of gloves, which she slips her hands into. 'I have a house and a husband.'

A house and a husband. It sounds so strange. In my head, Mary had jumped straight out of a storybook or a movie screen. She seems too magical to have anything as ordinary as a house and a husband. I want to ask her about them. What is her husband's name? Where is the house? What is it like? But before I have the chance, she turns on her cherry-red heels and walks away, leaving me standing in the empty corridor, once again wondering if she was ever here at all.

After tea, I return to the library and tuck myself into the small space beside the bookshelf, where I sat earlier with Mary. As I make myself comfortable, I notice a box of books that is yet to be unpacked. I pull it towards me and start to stack the colourful books on the shelf. I am almost finished when I notice a thick, heavy book at the bottom of the box. It is bound in brown leather and has the word *JOURNAL* embossed in gold on the front. The leather is well-worn and, on closer inspection, half the pages are missing. I run my finger along the jagged edges. Someone has ripped the pages out. Those that remain are lined and filled with rather messy, looped handwriting, with several words crossed out – as though written in a hurry. When I read the first few lines, I realize to my surprise that it's written in Basque and that it must be Mary's diary. Some weeks have an entry for each day, then there are whole months with none. I know I should put the diary back into the box and tell Mary when I next see her that she put it in there by mistake, but curiosity gets the better of me. Taking a large book from the shelf behind me, I slip the diary in between the pages. Then, stretching my legs out in front of me, I begin to read.

6

Mary
SEPTEMBER 1924
SOUTH KENSINGTON

Señor Alvariz, my employer, has encouraged me to write a diary so that I may practise the new language that he is teaching me. Basque is spoken in Bilbao, where Señor Alvariz and his family come from. It is an interesting language, not unlike my native Irish in its cadence and rhythm. According to Señor Alvariz, if I write about familiar things – my homeland, my family, my memories, my daily life – it will add depth and context to the new words I am learning.

My name is Mary O'Connor, and I am eighteen years old. I was born in a place called Achill, an island off the west coast of Ireland.

In those days, the west of Ireland was still reeling from the devastating famine and was a barren land, ravaged by poverty and hunger. My maternal grandmother, for whom I was named, perished in Black '47, the worst year of the great hunger, and her children were taken to the poorhouse. My mother got out of that terrible place when she was fifteen. By then she had met my father, a man ten years her senior, who promised to look after her. My father was a farmer, with a small herd of dairy cattle. My mother would often say to me when

I was a child that in place of love my father had given her buttermilk and beef. Better a full stomach and an empty heart than the other way round, she would retort when I asked if she even loved my father. I had not known hunger as my mother had. If I had, maybe I would have made the same choice as she.

Ours was not a large household. My mother had suffered the loss of several children in infancy. I was something of a miracle, born ten years after my brother, Fintan; a calming companion for my wayward sibling.

Fintan was a free spirit, or, as my father used to say, 'an unbreakable horse'. Like others of his generation, Fintan had witnessed the oppression and brutality enforced by the British in the years after the famine, and it had made him angry and embittered. To many he appeared frightening, with his wild green eyes, quick temper and sharp tongue, yet he and I were close. Though he was older than me, I felt protective of him. I could see the soft heart buried beneath the hard shell. He loved poetry and would often read aloud from Yeats's Crossways as we ate dinner. His favourite being 'The Stolen Child', with that beautiful and strange image of a child being pulled from a cruel world of weeping towards the magical land of the faeries.

My father, though illiterate and not one for sentiment, would fall into a reverie whenever Fintan read that poem. I would wonder where he had gone to, as he gazed into the fire; what thoughts filled his practical head. Oh, Fintan, he broke all our hearts. My parents thought that they could contain him, that if they just kept him occupied on the farm, then his anger would subside. They were wrong.

You see, in those days, the west was a hive of Republican activity, and intelligent, furious young men were quickly brought into the ranks. At first it was just rabble-rousing in the pub, hearts burning with the fire of patriotism and porter. But it was different for Fintan. Something ignited inside him. He had found his cause and he would follow it no matter what. One day, in the early spring of 1916, he came back to the farm and announced that he was leaving for Dublin, said that there was something he needed to do there. I saw my parents' faces darken, saw the fear in my mother's eyes, but I didn't understand it. I was only ten years old. What did I know of Dublin and politics?

Yet those two very things came knocking on our door, just a few weeks later. I hid in the parlour when I saw the policeman. I couldn't hear what he said, but my mother's screams will stay with me for the rest of my life. Later, I crept into the kitchen and saw my father standing rigid by the fireplace, one hand on the back of a chair, the other clutching a piece of paper. Something had altered in him, though in that moment I could not put my finger on it. It was a few days later, when I sat across from Father at breakfast, that I noticed his auburn hair and neat moustache had both turned pure white. Father, not a talkative man at the best of times, grew silent in the wake of Fintan's death. So much so that if he spoke a word, it would cause me to jump with fright, as though one of the cows out in the field had suddenly found its voice.

During those silent years following my brother's death, I grew into a young woman, though a rather insular one, prone to sitting for hours on the clifftops, staring out to sea. I lost myself in stories of adventurous women. Grace O'Malley herself had lived for a time in Achill, and I could see her tower from my perch. I used to wonder what lay out there, across the water, and whether I would ever get the chance to be an adventurer, to escape from this tiny island.

And then, one bright May morning, my opportunity arrived. Eight years had passed since Fintan's death, and my mother had grown hunched with grief, the spark extinguished from her clear blue eyes. I was a few months shy of eighteen years old and wanted to die. Why should a young girl be feeling that way, you may ask.

Well, you see, my parents had chosen a husband for me. For many seventeen-year-old girls, the idea of marriage would be an attractive prospect: the chance to run a household, have babies, become a woman. Yet I was different to other girls. I didn't want to spend the next twenty years cooking, cleaning and giving birth. I wanted to see the world – or, at the very least, see what lay beyond the Irish Sea.

What I didn't want was to be married to Pat McGinty. The man my parents had picked out for me was forty-seven years old, had a fat belly, yellow teeth and a taste for whisky. Yet Pat McGinty was also a wealthy man, a hill farmer with one hundred acres of land and a space in his bed for a young fit wife who would give him offspring and help farm the land. My mother insisted that Pat McGinty would offer me security for life. After all, as was her constant refrain, better an empty heart than an empty stomach.

I was due to visit McGinty for tea the following day. The thought made me feel sick and I was shouting this at my mother while my father sat in silence, when there was a loud knock at the kitchen door. Eager to get away from my mother, I strode across the room and opened the latch. There, standing in front of me, was a tall woman, with greying hair tied up in a loose bun. Her eyes were green and deep-set with dark shadows underneath. It was clear she had been beautiful once, though time and circumstance had left their mark on her face. As I stood there, still huffing with indignation, she regarded me curiously.

'Hello there,' she said, extending her long thin hand. 'I was looking for Mr and Mrs O'Connor. My name is Constance Markievicz and I have something for them, from their son, Fintan.'

At the sound of my brother's name, my mother came rushing to the door. 'Something from Fintan?' she cried. 'Please, won't you come in?'

Constance nodded and I followed them into the kitchen, where my father sat in his usual spot by the open range, puffing on his pipe. When he saw Constance coming towards him, he leapt to his feet, his face aghast.

'Mr O'Connor,' she said, her voice smooth as buttermilk. 'I have come about your son. My name is——'

'I know who you are,' he said, his voice ice-cold. 'And I don't want you in my house.'

'I understand, sir,' she said, backing away slightly. 'And I know you may hold myself and my comrades responsible for what happened to Fintan. However, I know that he died for a cause he truly believed in. He was a great man.'

'I don't need the likes of you to tell me what kind of man my son was,' yelled my father, his eyes blazing.

59

My hand flew to my chest in shock. I had never seen him so angry. In all these years he hadn't so much as shed a tear over Fintan's death, he'd simply shuffled around the farm in silence.

'I'm here to offer my condolences,' Constance said, remaining steadfastly calm in the wake of my father's anger. 'And also to give you this.'

She slipped her hand into the pocket of her long, green overcoat, and pulled out a book.

'It's taken many years for the possessions of those who fell that day to be collected,' she said, holding the book out to my father. 'This was found in Fintan's top pocket and was only handed over a few days ago. I'm on my way to Sligo, and thought it right that I ensure its safe return to you myself.'

I edged closer and saw the lettering on the front of the book: Crossways by W. B. Yeats. My mother let out a shriek of anguish then and, in a swift movement, my father grabbed the book from Constance's hands.

'Thank you,' he said, coldly. 'Now, if you don't mind, I would like you to leave this house.'

'Of course,' she said, with a nod. 'Goodbye, Mr O'Connor. Mrs O'Connor.'

My mother rushed to my father's side, leaving me to see Constance out.

I walked as far as the gate with her, then she turned and asked my name. When I told her, she said that I reminded her of her daughter, Maeve. 'Like the warrior queen?' I asked. 'Yes,' she replied, her eyes brightening. 'Named after her, in fact.'

Emboldened, I asked her more about herself and she told me

that she had fought alongside my brother in the Rising. 'You're a warrior too, then? Like Queen Maeve?' I asked. She went quiet then and raised her eyebrow. 'Something like that,' she said. 'In my youth, I was ready to die for Ireland, one way or another. Though now I do my fighting in Parliament. I'm what's known as a Teachta Dála. I represent the people and relay their concerns to those in power.'

She went on to tell me how, after the Rising, she had been sentenced to death. Then, on account of her sex, she had been transferred to a prison in England. While in there, she had been elected to the British House of Commons, though she had refused to take up the seat. As I stood there, listening to this talk of fighting alongside men, of votes for women, of liberty and equality, a great feeling stirred up inside me and I cried out: 'They want me to marry a fat old farmer and I don't want to.'

She paused, a frown passing over her forehead, then came closer and took my hand in hers.

'What is it that you do want, Mary?' she said.

'I . . . I want to travel,' I said, my voice shaking. 'I want to see the world outside of Ireland, have adventures.'

'Are you prepared to work hard?' she said, fixing me with those deep green eyes.

'Yes,' I said, nodding. 'I've spent years helping here on the farm.'

'I don't mean farm work,' she said, gripping my hand tighter. 'I mean work hard to broaden your mind, to learn, to read, to educate yourself. That's what every woman has a duty to do.'

'I like books and stories,' I said, suddenly finding my confidence. 'Fintan taught me to read and write.'

61

'Good,' she said. 'Then you're prepared.'

'The problem is my parents,' I said, my heart sinking at the thought of Pat McGinty. 'They have it all planned out. I'm trapped here.'

'I may be able to help you,' said Constance, looking out across the fields. 'I have a good friend who has just arrived in London, a diplomat with his family, and when I last saw him, he told me he was looking for a bright young woman to look after his daughters. Now the position may already have been filled, so don't get your hopes up, but I will enquire on your behalf today and will write to you if he is still in need of someone. How does that sound?'

It sounded like a dream come true.

'Now, Mary,' she said, lowering her voice, 'if you do take this role and come to London, you will find yourself at the heart of British politics. You'll encounter people who may not share your . . . how can I put it, your west-of-Ireland outlook. You'll need to be tough, Mary, like your brother was. You'll need to play your part and do your country proud. Do you understand?'

'Yes,' I said excitedly. 'Yes, I do.'

Though, if I am honest, at that point I did not quite grasp the enormity of what she was inferring, or just how tough I was going to have to be, and what would be asked of me. That would all come later.

'Good,' she said, removing her hand from mine. 'Then I shall recommend you. Goodbye, Mary O'Connor. It was a pleasure to meet you.'

'Goodbye,' I said, watching as she walked across the farmyard, like a warrior queen traversing the battlefield. 'And thank you.'

When I returned to the kitchen, I found my father's chair empty. Fintan's poetry book lay on the table. The cover was stained with dark brown patches. Blood. Fintan's blood. I opened the book and turned to his favourite poem and saw that he had written in the margin: 'For my sister, Mary: May you find a better world.'

Three days later, a letter arrived from Constance informing me that her friend, Señor Alvariz, was indeed still looking for a young woman to care for his daughters, and after hearing her recommendation would like to offer me a trial of one month. If all went well, the job was mine.

My father would not hear of it at first, said that Constance Markievicz was not to be trusted, that she was likely luring me to London to enlist me in some nefarious political plot. However, when I read him Señor Alariz's letter, outlining the proposed salary he was offering, both my mother and father relented. Who knows, I told my mother, as I bid her farewell a few days later, maybe this way I would be ensured of a full stomach and a full heart.

7

Corinne
PRESENT DAY

Mary's voice follows me all the way home. It is there as I arrive at the door of our neat, red-brick, new-build flat, and as I trundle up the stairs; it screams at me as I brush my teeth and wash my face in the tiny white bathroom that overlooks the backyard, and it stays with me as I fall in a twisted, exhausted heap into the freshly made bed.

Please, it cries. *She's just a little girl.*

In desperation, I take my silk eye mask and my ear plugs out of the bedside drawer. If I don't drown out Mary's voice and try to get some sleep then I will be in no fit state for my shift tonight. As I put the mask and ear plugs in place, I spritz a little lavender spray on my pillow – one more weapon in the ongoing fight against insomnia.

Curling on my side I feel my body grow heavier and heavier. But as sleep approaches I feel the atmosphere in the room alter. A light breeze tickles the skin on my bare arm and the bed begins to list.

I open my eyes and see a velvet expanse of night sky, with pinpricks of light poking through. The air is ice-cold and I wrap my blanket tighter around me. I hear waves crashing. As I slowly gain my bearings, I see that I am lying on the deck of a ship. I try to stretch my legs out, but there is a hard object blocking me. I push against it, but it won't yield. Then I hear a voice, a familiar voice, calling out a name. It's her. It's Mary. She's calling out for someone. I must help her. I try to clamber to my feet, but get caught up in the blanket. 'Mary,' I cry out into the vast black space. 'Mary, tell me where you are. I can't help you otherwise.'

I wake to find that I have yanked off my eye mask and half of the covers. I pull the duvet round me then lie on my back looking up at the white painted ceiling that, just moments before, was a starlit night sky. As I lie here, the dream hovers in the air around me. I can still smell the salty sea, hear the ringing of the ship's bell. It takes me a couple of moments to realize that what I'm actually hearing is my phone buzzing on the bedside table.

I reach out and grab it, half fearing that I'll see *Unknown Number* on the screen. Relief washes over me when I see Rima's name.

'Hey, Rima,' I say, my speech slurred with sleep. 'Everything okay?'

'Oh, Corinne, you have to come quickly,' says Rima, her voice trembling. 'It's Nidra.'

'It was the most terrifying thing I have ever seen. I swear to you, Corinne, I thought it was going to come for me.'

Nidra is sitting by the counter, sipping a beaker of water, her hands trembling.

'Shh,' I comfort her, wrapping my arm around her while, behind the counter, Rima stands rigid, concern etched across her face. 'You're safe now. Just take deep breaths and tell me what happened.'

'Rima was upstairs on the phone to the landlord,' she says, cradling the beaker in her hands. 'It was quiet, and I was in the kitchen. We've got a big lunch booking today. And they'd ordered loads of bhajees and pakoras. I wanted to make sure we had enough for them and for the rest of the service. I was going to do a big batch for the freezer too.'

The door opens and Jimmy, one of Tulsi's regulars, comes in. He waves at us then takes his usual spot in the booth by the window. Rima pours him a coffee and takes it over.

Nidra inhales deeply then continues, her voice lowered.

'I had the radio on,' she says, her eyes darting over to Jimmy, who is engrossed in the back pages of the *Evening Standard*. 'It was playing that song from *Donnie Darko*, which gives me the creeps at the best of times. Then I heard a knocking sound coming from inside the café. I thought it was a customer. So, I wiped my hands and went to look, and there was . . . there was this figure standing outside the door.'

She shudders, then takes a long sip of water. My

heart sinks as I watch her. Why did I tell her about Mary and the phone call? She is still so fragile that any talk of 'unexplained' happenings can tip her over the edge.

'Figure?' I say, trying to keep my voice bright. 'A person?'

'It wasn't a person,' she says. 'It didn't look human. It was just looming outside the door. It was dressed in an old-fashioned black coat with the hood pulled up. I could see a mane of dark hair peeping out from beneath the hood, and its face was white and hollow. I was terrified. Then it started hammering on the glass. I thought it was going to smash its way in, so I ran back into the kitchen and locked the door. I just stayed huddled under the prep table with my hands over my ears. Next thing I knew, Rima was standing over me, asking what the hell was the matter.'

'There has to be some rational explanation for this,' sighs Rima. 'You know that, Nidra.'

'Look, I know what you're thinking,' says Nidra, her voice shaking with frustration. 'That I'm imagining things again, but it was right there in front of me, and it wasn't human. God, it's times like this when I really miss Mum. She'd get it.'

'I'll remind you, little sis,' says Rima, sternly, 'that there's a difference between Mum's Hindu beliefs and practices and your obsession with paranormal activities.'

Nidra stares at her sister, pleadingly. It is horrible to see them like this. Born just eighteen months apart, they have always had an unbreakable bond. As an only child, when I first got together with Nidra I felt rather jealous of their closeness. When I was little, I would daydream about being part of a big family, of having brothers and sisters to play with and confide in. My reality was rather different. A quiet suburban semi where I lived with Gran and her books. According to her, there were advantages to being an only child. 'The thing about us onlys,' she used to say, 'is that we can make our own fun. We don't rely on other people, no matter how much we love them. And we're not scared of being alone. In fact, sometimes we even prefer it.'

'It's okay, darling,' I say, stroking Nidra's hand. 'We'll sort this out. As Rima says, there is probably a perfectly rational explanation for what happened.'

'I'm sorry for being so short-tempered, Corinne,' says Rima, glancing at me with an expression that says that, when it comes to Nidra, we have been here before. 'But my day began with a phone call from the landlord, who has informed me that he's going to be raising the rent to almost three times what we're currently paying. When I saw Nidra curled up like that, for a second I thought she'd overheard the call.'

She sighs wearily.

'We can't lose the café, Corinne,' she says, her eyes welling up. 'We can't let Mum down. This place . . . well, it's part of our DNA.'

She's right, I think, as I scan the framed photographs

that are dotted about the walls, each one bringing up a moment from the past. There's the black-and-white newspaper clipping of Saira, my mother-in-law, cutting the ribbon to formally open the café in 1996. If you study it closely, you can see Gran in the background, looking on proudly. There are pictures of the numerous community events that Saira hosted over the years: Tooting does Comic Relief 1997, when Nidra, Rima and I dressed up as the Spice Girls with Gran making a cameo appearance as 'Old Spice'. The live screening of the London Olympics opening ceremony in 2012, just after Nidra and I got together, where we ate dosas and toasted our city with ice-cold bottles of Kingfisher beer. Then mine and Nidra's wedding celebration in 2015, when Saira surprised us with a magical candlelit decking area outside the café, where a sitar player sat playing our favourite songs. Finally, in a white frame above the counter is Saira's obituary, describing her vibrant life and courageous fight to the death with cancer, just one year after the wedding. A beautiful photo of Saira taken on our wedding day, cloaked in an emerald-green dress with matching earrings, was printed alongside the piece. Saira, the Dosa Queen of Tooting.

Saira put her heart and soul into Tulsi. Along with her girls, it was her life, her everything. As I sit here, a shaft of sunlight beams into the café, illuminating Saira's face. She appears alive once more, her eyes blinking in the light. The sun fades then and casts a shadow over

Saira. As a grey gloom settles on the café, I shiver and turn my attention back to her daughters.

'That's terrible news, Rima,' I say. 'But surely he can't do that.'

'I'm afraid he can,' says Rima, rubbing the skin between her tired eyes. 'He owns the building. If he wants to increase the rent that's his prerogative. It's all perfectly legal.'

'Yes, but surely not by that much,' says Nidra, her hands still trembling as she takes a sip of water. 'We've never had a rent hike like this before. It works out as another grand per month, which is crazy. Mum would have had something to say if she were here. She would have gone straight round to that idiot's swanky offices and told him where to stuff his rent increase.'

'But Mum's not here,' snaps Rima. 'And, to be honest, the rent is the last thing on my mind right now after the fright you've just given me. I thought you'd been attacked.'

'I almost was,' shrieked Nidra, her eyes blazing. 'And I can tell by the way you're looking at me that you think I imagined that person, that I'm getting sick again. Look, I—'

'Excuse me, I hate to interrupt, but is there any chance of those scrambled eggs this side of Christmas?'

Jimmy has left his newspaper and come over to the counter. His watery blue eyes regard us as he stands there in his threadbare wool coat and flat cap. The old man is a recent addition to the Tulsi clientele, having moved to the area last year. Since then, there has barely been a morning when he hasn't been ensconced in that corner booth, huddled over his newspaper, silently eating his scrambled eggs. Despite this, I realize I know very little about him. He rarely speaks, making this sudden interruption all the more shocking.

'I'm sorry, Jimmy, that's my fault,' says Rima, leaping into action. 'One portion of scrambled eggs coming up. I'll throw in an extra round of toast too.'

'No need for that,' mumbles Jimmy, shuffling back to the table. 'Too much bread plays havoc with my insides. But if you could give me the Wi-Fi code for this place, that would be much appreciated. I don't know why you have to keep changing it all the time.'

'Corinne, love, would you do the honours?' says Rima, gesturing to the code that is written in chalk on the blackboard above the counter.

I scribble it down on a piece of paper then take it over to Jimmy, who is now squinting at his phone. He takes the paper silently, nodding his thanks.

'It wasn't in my head. You do believe me, don't you?' implores Nidra when I return to the counter, my eyes growing heavy from lack of sleep. 'I'm not getting ill again; I swear to you.'

'Listen,' I say, taking her hand. 'I think you could do with some fresh air. Can Rima spare you for half an hour?'

'We've got that big lunch booking at 1 p.m.,' says Nidra, glancing at her watch. 'Though I should be fine for half an hour. Where do you want to go?'

'There's something I want to show you,' I say, taking her coat from the hook behind the counter and handing it to her. 'Come on. It's just round the corner.'

8

Corinne

'I'm sorry, Corinne, but this place gives me goosebumps.'

Nidra shudders dramatically and places her hands into the pockets of her pale pink teddy-bear coat.

We are sitting on the bench in the garden of what was once Rochester Place, looking at the commemorative plaque, which is coming loose, the screws that once held it securely in place now rusted and worn down.

'I mean, those two people,' says Nidra. 'What happened to them? Was there an accident, or were they . . . murdered?'

'Whatever happened to them, I just find it very sad that this was the only memorial they got,' I say, gesturing to the litter-strewn patch of grass. 'Some back alley where people leave their rubbish.'

'It's so strange,' says Nidra, shaking her head. 'The name that caller gave you. The date. The fact that this place is so close to where we live. I can't imagine there being a grand Georgian house on this site. It just looks like a wasteland. Surely someone must remember a house like that being here – someone who was alive back then.'

'It was a long time ago, Nidra,' I say, with a shiver. 'Eighty years.'

'What about Jimmy?' she says, perking up suddenly.

'Who?'

'Mr Scrambled Eggs.' Nidra smiles.

'Oh, him?' I say, my voice competing with the crash of the recycling truck emptying boxes of bottles on Larkin Road. 'I hardly know the man, beyond giving him the Wi-Fi code and exchanging a few pleasantries. If I suddenly told him I'd had a phone call from a woman who died in 1940, he'd think I'd lost my mind. He was cross enough about his food being late.'

'He's actually a really interesting man, once he starts talking,' says Nidra. 'He spent years working as a patrolman at Leicester Square tube station. It was his job to walk through the tunnels, checking for any cracks or faults on the line. I'd never heard of such a job. Can you imagine spending night after night walking through dank, deserted tunnels like that, all by yourself, staring into mile after mile of darkness? Anyway, he grew up in Tooting – he left when he was a teenager then moved back last year – and he reckons this whole area around the station has a certain energy to it because of the heavy bombing it sustained during the Blitz.'

I nod my head, recalling the stories we learned at school of London during the war.

'Jimmy said he's seen all sorts of things, above and below ground. Things that just can't be explained.'

'Oh, come on, Nidra,' I say, my body tensing. 'You know what I think of all that. I'm not going to start asking Jimmy about ghosts.'

'Okay, but he did grow up here,' says Nidra. 'And he's got an encyclopedic knowledge of the area. If anyone would know about Rochester Place and the people who lived there, it's Jimmy. I've got his address. If you don't catch him at the café, you could pop in and see him on your way to work.'

'I'll think about it,' I say. 'Though I'm still convinced that the person who called me was real – that she needed help. As for the people on this plaque . . . well, it's just very sad that they seem to have been forgotten about.'

'Someone must have loved them once,' says Nidra, turning to the plaque. 'To have gone to the trouble of having this made.'

She traces the lettering with her finger.

'I hope Mum's at peace,' I say.

'Oh, Corinne, what made you think of that?' says Nidra, placing her hand on mine.

'I don't know,' I say. 'Maybe it was the way you touched the plaque just then. It reminded me of Gran when we used to visit Mum's grave. She would kneel beside it and touch my mum's name with her finger, like she was stroking her face.'

'I used to do that with Mum's cookbook,' says Nidra, squeezing my hand. 'I would trace her handwriting with my finger, try to summon her back. I'm thankful for the years I had with my mum, even though missing her feels unbearable. I can't imagine how it must have felt to lose yours when you were so young.'

'I never forgave myself for being asleep when she overdosed,' I say, recalling the smell of the flat that morning, stale vodka mixed with something else – the musty scent of death, not unlike the smell in this garden. 'For years I believed that terrible things happen when you sleep, so I stopped. I guess my insomnia was my mother's legacy to me.'

'It's not as bad as it once was, though,' says Nidra, moving closer to me, her body obscuring the names on the plaque. 'I remember when we were kids you were always yawning.'

'Really?' I say, recalling those afternoons at Tooting Library. 'Are you sure that wasn't because I had to listen to you reading me your bloody ghost stories.'

'I loved those books,' says Nidra, swiping me with her hand. 'Though I loved your gran's stories too. Remember the one about the cat?'

'Faith the church cat,' I say, smiling at the memory. 'That was a true story. Apparently, she survived the bombing of St Augustine's church in the City and was found amid the rubble, nursing her unharmed kitten.'

'That was it. And your gran had that knitted cat puppet she used to bring out for the story. She let me borrow that once. I was so happy.'

We sit in silence for a moment, both of us lost in the

mists of 1996 – a time of innocence, and knitted cat puppets.

'I never thought I'd see you again when you went to Leicester,' says Nidra, softly. 'Thank God you came back. I can't imagine what my life would have been like if you hadn't.'

I smile, recalling that night ten years ago when, newly graduated from Leicester University, I ventured back to Tooting for drinks with some friends from work. We were at a bar in Tooting Market when I saw a petite woman, with glossy black hair and mesmerizing hazel eyes, staring at me.

'You were quite tipsy if I recall,' I say. 'You kept going on about the cat story.'

'I told you it had made a mark on me,' she says, laughing. 'Poor little Faith.'

'And then I realized,' I say, kissing her lightly on the nose, 'that I'd found her again, the chatty little girl with the book as big as her head. Though I still couldn't sleep.'

'I made it my mission to cure you when we first moved in together,' says Nidra, rubbing her hands together to warm them. 'I spent hours on the internet trying to find remedies.'

'Yes, I remember,' I say, with a giggle. 'We were in that grotty bedsit in Streatham, and I used to lie there wide awake looking at the rising damp on the ceiling while listening to some guy, who was definitely stoned, telling me that I was lying on a beautiful beach with the sun on my face.'

'Oh God, yeah,' says Nidra, resting her head on my shoulder. ' "Graham's Guided Meditation". I'm sorry about that. I thought it would help.'

'It seemed to help you,' I say. 'You used to sleep soundly through the whole thing.'

'Then I'd wake up and find you sitting up in bed, watching old episodes of *Buffy* on your laptop.'

'To be honest, *Buffy* was far more entertaining than Graham and his chanting.'

'At least we tried,' says Nidra. 'Though it might have been better if one of us had finally learned to drive.'

'What do you mean?'

'Well, I remember your gran telling me that she used to put you in the car and drive round South London until you fell asleep,' says Nidra.

'Really? I have no memory of that at all. Still, I suppose it makes sense – the lull of the engine. Poor Gran. She must have been exhausted. She was grieving her daughter and she had to deal with this little kid who refused to sleep. But it wasn't just the thought that bad things happened when I closed my eyes, it was the feeling that, if I'd been awake, maybe I could have saved her.'

'Oh, baby,' says Nidra. 'You were three years old. You couldn't have saved her. By that point no one could.'

'I know that now,' I say. 'Though it's taken me years

and countless times being on the end of the line listening to the friends and relatives of someone who has overdosed. They all blame themselves. Every single one of them. But that's why I love my job, Nidra. Because I know what those people are going through, what they're feeling. It's why this thing with Mary is bothering me so much. With every other call there's a resolution, either good or bad. The person is saved or they're not. But to have no resolution, that's what makes this so hard.'

'You can't help everyone, Corinne,' says Nidra. 'You said yourself that it's not always a happy outcome. But, also, you can only deal with what's in front of you. And with this call, you did your absolute best. You sent the emergency services to the address she gave you and there was nothing there. What more could you do?'

'I know,' I say, exhaling what feels like a lifetime of pent-up tension. 'You're right. I need to shake this off.'

'And you will,' says Nidra, looking at her watch. 'I'd better be heading to the café, and you should try to get some rest.'

'I'm going to stay here for a little bit,' I say. 'Clear my head.'

'Are you sure?'

I nod.

'Okay, baby,' she says, kissing me on the cheek. 'I love you. See you at the café later, yeah?'

I watch as she walks away, her small figure almost swallowed by the long grass.

My phone beeps in my pocket. I take it out and see a Facebook notification: *We thought that you would like to look back at this post from three years ago today.* Clicking on the link, I smile as a photo of me and Gran appears, taken outside the cottage shortly after she moved in. The sea is just visible behind us, and the wind has blown Gran's white hair into her eyes, obscuring her face. Three years, I think to myself, three years of being so far from her. I close the image and try Gran's number. It rings out then goes to voicemail. I leave a message, trying not to sound too concerned, telling Gran to call me as soon as she gets it.

I'm about to get up from the bench when I feel something brush against my leg. I look down and see a cat slinking round my ankles. It is jet black with a pure white chest – a tuxedo cat. 'Hello, puss,' I whisper, bending down to stroke it. 'Where do you live, eh?'

The cat pauses to lick its paws, then looks up at me with large green eyes before scuttling across the garden, in the opposite direction to where we came from. I stand up and follow the cat towards a cluster of overgrown bushes. Most likely it lives in one of the houses on Larkin Road and will jump over the back wall any minute. Yet as we reach the garden boundary there is no brick wall, as I imagined there would be, but a short piece of wrought-iron railing with two dome-topped wooden posts either side, carved into the shape of acorns. The carvings look strangely familiar. The cat jumps up on one of the posts and regards me. The railing is chipped and rusting, but from its size and shape it must once have been a gate. I lean forward to stroke the cat and, as I do, I am suddenly back in Gran's car, looking out of the window.

I'm dressed in my favourite Spice Girls pyjamas and slippers, with my thick, grey, school duffel coat over the top, yet I am shivering with cold. The radio is playing the opening bars of 'Space Oddity' by David Bowie. It is raining hard outside. So much so that I can barely see out of the fogged-up windows. I look beside me at the empty driver's seat. Where has Gran gone? She has left the engine running and the windscreen wipers tick back and forth in time to the melody. I press my face to the passenger window and look out into the darkness. We are parked up in a back alley. There are wheelie bins overflowing with black rubbish bags lined up against the wall. Beyond the bins is an iron gate, tall and imposing, its rails rusted and chipped. The gate swings open and shut in the wind, making a low creaking noise. Then I see a dark shape coming towards me. I slam my hands down on the door lock, my skin prickling with fear. But, as the figure comes into focus, I see that it is Gran. She has the hood of her blue plastic raincoat pulled up and she is running towards the car, her neatly applied mascara smudged beneath her eyes.

'Where were you?' I cry, as she pulls the door open

and flops, sodden, into the driver's seat. 'I was scared. What is this place?'

'Don't worry,' she says, placing her damp hand on my lap. 'It's all sorted now. Everything is going to be alright.'

With that, she reverses the car out of the alleyway. I look out of the window and see the neon streetlights of South London bleeding out onto the road.

Back in the present, I blink and look up at the acorn sculptures, remembering now when I saw them before.

I noticed them as Gran came towards me that night, as she ran, teary-eyed, through a set of tall, imposing gates.

These gates.

9

Teresa

It has been two days since I last saw Mary. I look for her everywhere – when I am walking down the corridor, when I am sitting in chapel, when I'm eating my stewed prunes at breakfast – but she is nowhere to be seen. It is like she never existed, like I conjured her up in my head. Even as I read in the diary about her childhood and her journey from Ireland to London, it feels like I am reading about a fictional character, a heroine from a storybook, rather than a real person. Though there are lots of things we have in common too. She had an older sibling who fought in a war, and she loved Fintan as I love Katalin. I have so many questions I want to ask her, but I can't because then she will know that I have read her diary, and I can't admit that to her.

I have been yearning to read more of the diary but have not had the chance, as every hour of the last two days has been filled with prayer – or so it seems. The sisters have been celebrating the anniversary of the founding of the convent and have encouraged us good Catholic girls to join them in worship. We rise at 6.30 a.m. for prayers, then it's down to the dining room for breakfast before bible study with Sister Bernadette. After a lunch of soggy vegetables leached of colour, there's handwork class. I inevitably sit tying myself in knots for an hour while the other girls produce embroidered masterpieces. After that we break for a tea of bread and jam, then it is evening prayers, dinner, and a candlelit vigil through the grounds before lights out at 9 p.m.

This evening, the celebrations over, is the first time we have been allowed back into the library. My favourite place. I sit on the wooden chair in the window and look out onto the parkland, thinking of the library in Guernica and how my friends, Josephina and Valentina, and I would huddle together sharing a bag of sweets while we read our books. Those girls were true friends, people I imagined would be around forever. I get a knot in my stomach as I recall the sight of the burning city as we fled. Did Josephina and Valentina manage to escape? I pray that they did.

I get up from the chair and go across to the bookshelf that Mary and I spent the afternoon filling with Basque books. I pointed them out to Rosaria and Eider yesterday, thinking that they would be just as excited as I was – as excited as Josephina and Valentina would have been. But they just shrugged their shoulders and carried on with their silly sewing. I feel sad for Mary. She did a good deed in bringing those books here, yet I am the only one who seems to appreciate them.

As I sit, running my fingers along the spines of the books, I suddenly remember the diary. Maybe I can have one more peek at it before bedtime.

I am about to reach across to retrieve it from its hiding place at the back of the shelf when I sense movement in the room behind me. The distinctive smell of rosewater fills my nostrils. I jump to my feet and peek out over the top of the bookshelf.

'Hello, Teresa. How are you this evening?'

My heart lifts at the sight of her. She is wearing a pale pink dress that is tied in a loose bow at her neck and falls in shimmery drapes to her shins. Her hair is pinned at the side with the same emerald clip she was wearing the last time I saw her. She smiles and it is like looking up at a blue sky on a summer's day.

I greet her in Basque, and she frowns and shakes her head.

'No, no, no,' she says, wagging her fuchsia-painted fingernail at me.

Then I remember. She promised to teach me English. I try to recall what she just said.

'Kaixo, Mary . . .' I begin.

She shakes her head and comes closer, pointing to her mouth.

'He-ll-o, Ma-ry,' she says, slowly, so I can see the

shape the words are making in her mouth. 'How are you this eee-ve-ning?'

I repeat. The words feel strange, like I am speaking underwater.

'Now, I want you to repeat that ten times more,' says Mary, speaking in Basque this time.

I do as she says, feeling proud of myself that I have spoken my first real English words.

'Well done,' she says, folding her arms across her chest. 'Right, come with me.'

'Where are we going?' I ask, as I follow her out of the library and into the deserted corridor.

'We are going on a word hunt,' she says, looking at me over her shoulder. 'When I point something out, I shall say it in English and you will repeat it five times, alright?'

I nod my head and skip excitedly after her. After days of dull lessons and prayers, it is fun to have a game to play.

'Door,' says Mary, pointing her manicured finger ahead of her.

'Door,' I say, making an oval of my mouth. 'Door.'

'And again!'

'Door.'

I repeat it twice more, then hurry after Mary, who is heading across the dining room. By the end of the game, we have walked the length of the convent and I have a pile of words, all stacked up in my head, which

Mary asks me to recite as she leads me back to the library: door, table, floor, picture, cup, book, girls, dress, shoes, window, lamp, chair, shelf, bed, drawers, clothes, basin, tap, rosary beads, bucket, hairbrush, flannel, pencil, paper . . .

My head feels like it's about to burst by the time we return to the library, and I flop down onto my chair.

'Now, tomorrow,' says Mary, watching me from the doorway. 'We shall learn how to put those words into sentences. I'll be here at the same time. Eight p.m. sharp.'

I hear her heels clicking along the corridor, then the room falls quiet. I sit for a moment, the new English words tumbling round my head like leaves in the wind. I try to catch some of them, to remember how Mary pronounced them. Three words have lodged themselves in my brain: door, dress, lamp. I repeat the words over and over, like a strange nursery rhyme, tapping my hand on my knee in time to the rhythm: 'Door, dress, lamp. Clap clap. Door, dress, lamp. Clap clap. Door, dress—'

'Bedtime, girls.'

Sister Claire's sharp voice, calling down the corridor, cuts into my chant. I get up from the chair and reluctantly make my way back to the dormitory. When I get there, Veronica is already in bed. She is sitting propped up against the pillows, her eyes on me. Eider and Rosaria's beds are empty, which is odd, as they are usually asleep well before lights out.

'Where are the girls?' I say, sitting down on the edge of my bed to remove my shoes.

'You haven't heard?' says Veronica, folding her arms across her chest. 'They have gone home.'

'Home?' I say, letting my shoes drop to the floor with a clatter. 'What do you mean?'

'Exactly that,' says Veronica, with a look of sadness mixed with defiance. 'They have been sent home to Spain. Their parents were contacted and were found to be in a safe place. They wanted to have their children back.'

I look at the empty beds, my stomach twisting.

'But they said it would be three months,' I say, recalling Katalin's pained face as she kissed me goodbye. 'They said it was not safe to return.'

'They said a lot of things,' says Veronica, with a cynicism beyond her years. 'On the coach here, I overheard the Señorita saying that the charity is running out of money. Those of us whose folks are . . . not around – well, we'll be sent to orphanages. Great, eh?'

I cannot believe what I am hearing. I feel like someone has taken a knife and plunged it into my chest.

'That can't be true,' I say, my voice trembling. 'Only people without families go to orphanages. I have a sister. She said she would send for me in three months.'

'Your sister?' says Veronica, shaking her head. 'Didn't you say she was fighting out there, no? And from what I have heard, things are not going well. The chances of your sister still being alive are rather slim. What about your parents?'

'They . . . they died when I was a baby.'

Our parents were killed in a train crash when I was eighteen months old – a derailment on a narrow track just outside Bilbao, a disaster that made the headlines as well as making a mother figure of Katalin at the tender age of sixteen. I have little memory of my parents beyond a faint image of an auburn-haired woman with amber eyes, leaning over the bars of my cot, and a broad-shouldered man in a wide-brimmed hat whose shape I would see in the courtyard, the scent of cigarette smoke drifting up to my bedroom window. There was little talk of our parents at home, though I sometimes found my sister sitting at the window, the prism gripped tightly in her hands, looking out across the town square as though searching for something, someone.

'So you're an orphan,' says Veronica emphatically. 'And where do they send orphans?'

I shake my head. It cannot be true.

'Anyway, we'll find out in the next few days,' says Veronica, pulling the covers around herself. 'I hear that Sister Bernadette is going to talk to the remaining girls individually. I suppose that is when she will break the news about your sister.'

Just then Sister Claire pokes her head round the door and switches off the light. I get into bed and pull my knees to my chest, Veronica's words still pounding against my skull.

I close my eyes and find myself back in Guernica. It is St James's Day, a special feast day in the Basque calendar. After a day of festivities and dancing, by nightfall the people of the town are in the mood for something slow and reflective, something to bring tears to their eyes, to drown the fires in their bellies. Katalin knows just the song, and as she sings the first note of 'Lua, Lua', the crowd cheer. It is *their* song, the song of their land, sung in their language. A song about a young boy whose mother watches over him from heaven, telling him to 'sleep, sleep' while angels guard his bed. For the people gathered in the square, for Katalin on the stage and for me, the little girl curled up in her bed by the open window of our apartment, the song is a reminder that nothing – not love, not home, not family, not language, not nations – can last forever.

The music stops, and the only sound I can hear is the faint ticking of the clock above the bed. It all makes sense now, why I was taken from the camp and sent here. The Basque Children's Committee must have known I would need a more permanent home. They must have known that my sister, my darling Katalin, the only family I have left, would not be coming back for me, not in three months, not ever, because she is dead.

10

Mary
MARCH 1926
WESTMINSTER

They say all good things must come to an end, and so it was, after just a year, I found myself bidding farewell to the Alvariz family. It happened in late October. I was sitting at the table in the nursery with the girls, carving jack-o'-lanterns out of turnips in preparation for Samhain, when Señor Alvariz came and told me the news.

He had been called back to Bilbao to take on a more senior role in the Spanish government. He would be returning, with his wife and the girls, at the end of the year. He explained the role and what it was, but I am afraid I did not take in the details, as all I could think was myself and how my time in London was coming to an end. As I sat there at the table, the paring knife in one hand, a half-rotten turnip in the other, my eyes filled with tears. Noticing my distress, Señor Alvariz told me that my role as the girls' nanny was still open and that I was more than welcome to join them in Bilbao. It was a wonderful offer, and most people in my position would have jumped at the chance to move to Spain; yet, as kind and warm as they were, it was not only the Alvariz family that I would miss, it was London. The city had cast a spell on me, and I felt sick at the thought of leaving.

A couple of days later, I found my solution, hidden amid the Classified section of The Lady.

'WANTED', it read. 'Nurse to take charge of two children in prominent London household. Must be respectable, hardworking and have a twelve-month character reference from her last situation. NO IRISH NEED APPLY . . .'

The advertisement went on for another three lines, but I couldn't continue reading. My hands were trembling so much I almost dropped the paper. No Irish need apply? As I had never actively searched for work in London, I had never come across this before. My cheeks reddened and I felt shamed. I wrote to Constance to tell her about it, my letter full of rage and indignation. But her response was calm and unruffled. She reminded me that, for an Irish woman, such prejudice and hostility was to be expected in England, and that I would need to be tough if I wanted to achieve my goals. I would need to be 'as wily as a fox'. 'Sometimes, Mary, we must adopt certain tactics to outwit these people. If this man only wants English staff in his house, then the young woman who arrives on his doorstep will be exactly that. Do what you need to do and keep your eyes and ears open.' Emboldened by her words, I told myself that if this role could ensure my staying in London and earning a good wage, where was the harm in a little subterfuge?

Still, the idea of hiding my Irishness made me feel guilty. I thought of Grace O'Malley. Hadn't she sailed across to England and confronted Queen Elizabeth? And here I was, thinking about concealing my identity and duping a powerful family. I felt as wicked as Peter when he denied Jesus three times the night before his death. But the lure of London, and Constance's reminder that I needed to play my part by whatever means, proved greater than my guilt, and I applied for the job. To my surprise and terror, I got it.

So, after one last Christmas with the Alvariz family, where they presented me with a box of delightful Basque storybooks, I found myself, on a cold January morning, standing on the doorstep of Pevensey House. After a brief meeting with the children, six-year-old twins Daphne and Albert – the former, bright-eyed and curious, the latter, surly and watchful – I was summoned to the study of Oliver Davidson, or Air Marshal Davidson, to use his full military title, a high-ranking officer of the RAF.

There I found a tall, thin man, with a receding chin and cold, grey eyes that rather resembled those of a seagull. He did not greet me as I entered the dark, wood-panelled room, but stayed seated behind his large, green-leather-covered desk. My heart felt like it was going to jump out of my chest when he asked me to tell him about my background. Though I had concocted a story when I applied for the role, I was still terrified of slipping up. With Davidson's eyes on me, and focusing hard to maintain my English accent, I told him that I had been born and grown up in Surbiton, a place that had been described as a 'respectable suburb' in The Lady, and that I had been employed by the Alvariz family on the recommendation of a family friend, a woman of good social standing. I smiled to myself at the thought of Constance, the Irish rebel, with her green uniform and concealed gun, being referred to in the presence of this pillar of the British establishment. But Davidson seemed convinced, despite staying silent while

I rambled on about the duties I had performed for the Alvariz children: trips to Kensington Gardens, the library and the theatre. When I had finished, he took a piece of paper from the desk drawer.

'You come with a glowing reference, Miss Connor,' he said, staring at me intently. 'Now, as you may know I am a military man, and I don't set much store by trips to the theatre and story-books. What I require you to provide for my children is consistency, discipline and order. Do you understand?'

I nodded my head, remembering Señor Alvariz's face when I had shown him Davidson's advertisement, his eyes alighting on those words: 'NO IRISH NEED APPLY.' He had frowned at the page then looked up at me. 'Mary?' he said, his expression a mixture of kindness and sorrow. 'Are you sure you want to apply for a role in a place like this?' I told him that I wanted to stay in London, that my parents needed the money I sent them, that I could do what needed to be done. That I would even drop the 'O' from my name to make it sound less Irish. He nodded his head sadly, then told me that he would write me a reference. 'But please, Mary,' he said, as I left the room, 'be careful.'

Those words returned to me as I sat looking into the icy eyes of Air Marshal Davidson, and as he continued to speak, a chill went right through my body. Could I really get away with this?

'If I find that their heads are being filled with anything except what their tutor is instructing them in – and, in Daphne's case, needlework – I shall have no choice but to reconsider your pos-ition, is that clear?'

'Yes, sir,' I replied, squeezing my hands together to stop them from shaking.

'That will be all, Miss Connor,' he said, dismissing me with a wave of his hand.

The two months that have passed since then have been as cold as the atmosphere in Davidson's study. The house is run with military precision. The staff scurry about with their eyes fixed on the floor, there is no laughter, no pleasant chatter, no music, no dancing. The only books in the house are the ones I spotted in the study: heavy tomes of military history. Mrs Davidson, who is twenty years younger than her husband, spends much of her time visiting friends, leaving the children in my care. Albert appears to have inherited his father's imperiousness and refuses to do as he is told. If I ask him to make his bed, he will remind me that I am a servant, and he is the son of a double ace, a feat he himself will achieve one day because 'Davidson men always come first'. At six years old, his single-minded self-belief is both impressive and alarming. Daphne, on the other hand, is gentle and rather shy. With her pale skin, golden ringlets, and blue eyes that appear too large for her tiny face, she reminds me of the porcelain dolls I see in the window of Hamleys. She is such a gentle soul, fond of stories and writing, yet, unlike for the Alvariz girls, neither of those pursuits is deemed to be suitable for her. The poor mite is also rather anxious. She follows me around the house, sucking her thumb, until she sees her father, when she'll yank the thumb out of her mouth and stand to attention.

Even when he's not physically present, I feel Davidson's eyes on me as I pass through the house, watching me, waiting for me to

95

make a mistake. The need to keep up the pretence of being a respectable Englishwoman is exhausting. Every so often my accent slips, though thankfully that has only happened in the presence of the children and not in front of Davidson, who would have me out of the house in a heartbeat if he discovered where I am really from. The atmosphere in the house has been so intense that it was a blessed relief when Peggy, the housemaid, came to find me in the nursery and told me I had a visitor.

I found Constance standing by a red pillar box on the opposite side of the street, having declined Peggy's invitation to wait for me in the drawing room. She knew that her presence would blow my cover and cause no end of difficulty with the Davidsons. After all, in the wake of the Rising and its weighty press coverage, Constance Markievicz is a controversial and instantly recognizable figure in most English establishment households. Yet, that morning, she looked less the formidable warrior rebel and more the kind human being who had spoken so warmly about my brother to my grieving parents.

When she spotted me, she gestured for me to walk with her to the end of the street. 'There are eyes everywhere, Mary,' she said, her voice barely a whisper. 'Well, they're obviously feeding you well,' she said, taking in my appearance. 'You've acquired a rosy bloom.' I wanted to tell her that it was London and not Cook's meals that had brought colour to my cheeks, but before I could get the words out, Constance reached into her handbag and brought out a sheaf of papers. Her eyes darting down the street, she thrust them into my hands. 'Something for you to read at bedtime,' she said. 'I knew that I would have to get them to you, though I didn't want to cause any problems with your current position. Really, I should have arranged to meet in a café, but things are so busy at the moment I scarcely have time to breathe.'

It was then I noticed the wheezing in her chest, the dark circles round her eyes that had become even more pronounced in the eighteen months since I had last seen her. 'Are you alright, Constance?' I asked her as I watched her start to cough. 'I'm grand,' she said, briskly, as she regained her composure. 'Just overworked. I won't keep you any longer, as your absence will arouse suspicion. Get back to the house now and keep up the good work. And, as always with these people, tread carefully, Mary.'

She winked, then sped off down the street without a second glance. As I stood, watching her depart, a pang of homesickness lodged itself in my stomach. Constance was a physical reminder of Ireland, of Achill, Fintan, Mother and Father. Was it worth it? The thought flashed momentarily in my mind. All this deception? Wouldn't it just be easier to hold my hands up and surrender, return to my people, away from Davidson and his watchful gaze?

I was so absorbed in these thoughts as I made my way back to the house, I did not notice Mrs Davidson standing on the doorstep. Was it my paranoia, or was she looking at me strangely? Panic surged through my body. Did she suspect something? 'Mary,' she said, in that clipped, dismissive way of hers, 'collect your coat.' My heart lurched. She was firing me. She had seen me with Constance and put two and two together. Oh, God, what would I do? 'And a sturdy bag,' she continued. 'I have a parcel that needs collecting from Fortnum's.'

I was safe. She was just sending me on an errand. With a sigh of relief, I went inside and hid the papers Constance had given me under my mattress. Then, retrieving my coat and bag, I made my way to Piccadilly. Little did I know that the simple excursion would make me rethink everything. After collecting the package, I walked back to Pevensey House via St James's Park, stopping by the lake to admire a heron. He was standing on one leg, peering into the water, preparing to catch a fish. The grey skies that had threatened rain earlier in the day darkened even further, and a gust of wind whipped round me, sending my hat flying. I tried to catch it, but it went fluttering across the lake and landed right in the middle. My heart sank as I watched it bobbing forlornly on the water. I had saved up for months to buy that hat – a fashionable taupe cloche with a brown velvet ribbon and soft partridge feathers – and I had lost it. Not only that, but I would have to return to the house bare-headed, which would not be received well by Air Marshal Davidson. Tears were pricking my eyes when I heard someone shout, 'Don't worry. I've got it!' I turned to see a young man waving to me. He was removing his socks and shoes and rolling up the trousers of his green wool suit and, before I could stop him, he had waded into the lake.

He picked up a thin branch that the wind had loosened and poked it towards the hat. Behind me a group of onlookers had gathered, and I heard a gentleman mutter something about the 'silly young fool' catching his death of cold. Despite his good intentions, the young man did not look too steady on his feet, and the constant prodding with the branch was serving only to push the hat further into the lake. When it looked like he was going to lose his footing, my instincts got the better of me and, to the collective

98

horror of the ladies and gentlemen gathered around me, I set down the parcel, whipped off my shoes and stockings and went wading in after him.

He looked utterly bemused when he turned round and saw me splashing through the water. As I drew level with him, knee-deep in green, algae-infested water, my stomach fluttered. He was the most handsome man I had ever seen, dark-haired with an olive complexion, a strong nose and pale blue eyes framed by long lashes. But it was his smile that threw me. When I had grabbed the stick from him, muttering 'eejit' under my breath, and managed to retrieve the hat, now sodden and covered in algae, he turned to me and began to laugh. Now, if anyone else had laughed at me in those circumstances, it would have driven me mad, but his smile was so warm, so vital, like the sun shining on your face after a long winter, that I found myself joining in. We laughed like two old friends as we waded back to shore. So lost were we in each other's smiles, we barely noticed the chorus of disapproval that greeted us from the elderly onlookers.

Yet, before I could thank him properly, he had run on ahead and retrieved his socks and shoes. As he hurried away, I was left to face the wrath of an old dowager, who shook her parasol at me as I pulled on my stockings and shoes, and told me that I was shameful.

I thought about that young man all the way home, wondering where he had run off to, and why it was I had felt so giddy when he smiled at me. Yet I told myself that it was just a brief encounter, a frivolous moment of madness, perhaps one I could draw upon when I was lying alone in the wee hours of the morning.

So imagine my surprise when I came down to dinner yester-day evening to find that very man sitting at the table. 'Mary,' said Mrs Davidson, 'I'd like you to meet Ronald, Air Marshal Davidson's eldest son.'

He looked up at me and smiled, the same smile I last saw when we were both knee-deep in lake water, though thankfully he made no mention of our escapade as he got to his feet, his blue eyes glinting in the candlelight.

'Hello, Mary,' he said, shaking my hand. 'Delighted to meet you.'

He gave a little wink, which made me feel warm inside. It made me feel, for the first time since I had arrived at Pevensey House, that I was welcome. Then he gestured to the seat beside him and, for the next two hours, I sat spellbound as he regaled us all with his stories. Over dinner, he told us about his studies at Oxford and about his tutor, a young don called Clive Lewis, who, Ronald said, was writing a novel and who had inspired him to do the same. I recalled what his father had instructed me in the study, and wondered at how someone so lacking in imagination had produced Ronald. His father's displeasure was palpable, and he reminded his son that he wasn't to get so excited about literature, that he was only at Oxford to receive an education and he would then be following him into the RAF. When he said this, the temperature of the room plummeted. Ronald excused himself from the table and left the room. I noticed, when he left, that his father gave a satisfied smile.

Later, as I was going to bed, I saw that the front door was ajar. As I drew closer, I saw Ronald sitting on the front step smoking a cigarette. When he saw me, he asked if I would join him and offered me a smoke. As we sat there in the chill air, he enquired after my hat. I told him that I had it drying out by the fire in the nursery and was hopeful it would hold its shape. He smiled and said he had never been rescued from a lake by a woman before. I began imitating him attempting to rescue my hat with the stick and we laughed so much my sides began to hurt.

Once our giggles had subsided, he told me more about Oxford and the story that he is writing. It doesn't have a name yet, but it is about a group of islanders who must fight to defend their land and their culture from invasion. His passion for the story was so exhilarating I almost forgot myself and was about to blurt out the story of my brother fighting for Ireland and Grace O'Malley standing up to the Queen of England. Then I remembered where I was and who I was supposed to be. Instead, I told him that the story sounded fascinating and that he should carry on writing it, no matter what his father said. When I had finished speaking, he looked at me, and his face was so stern I thought I had spoken out of turn. I went to speak, to apologize, but before I could get the words out, he leaned forward and kissed me, very lightly, on the cheek. 'Goodnight, Mary,' he said, getting up from the step. 'It has been a pleasure talking to you.' With that, he went inside, leaving me sitting there, dazed, the touch of his lips still warm on my cheek.

11

Teresa
JUNE 1937

Three days later, as Veronica predicted, I am summoned to Sister Bernadette's office.

My hand trembles as I lift it to knock on the thick wooden door. Sister Bernadette calls for me to 'enter' but I stay where I am, hoping to prolong the moment when I will hear what is sure to be dreadful news. After a few seconds, I hear footsteps drawing closer. Then the door swings open and, to my surprise, I see Mary standing there.

'Teresa,' she exclaims, her eyes shining. 'How lovely to see you. Come on in?'

Maybe it is Mary's kind voice, or the sight of Sister Bernadette sitting grim-faced behind her desk like some brooding crow, but as I enter the room I dissolve into tears.

'Please don't say it,' I cry, slumping onto the floor, my head in my hands. 'It is not true. She is not dead. My sister is not dead. You can't send me to an orphanage. You can't.'

'Mrs Davidson, what is the child saying?'

I don't understand Sister Bernadette's words, but her stern voice cuts through my sobs. Mary replies in English, then gently scoops me off the floor and leads me over to the pair of stiff chairs in front of the desk.

'Shh, now,' she says, as we take our seats. 'You're right. Your sister is not dead, and you're not going to an orphanage.'

I look up at her through a blur of tears. Mary has always been so kind to me. Surely she wouldn't lie.

'So why am I here, then?' I say, wiping my eyes with the back of my sleeve.

Mary turns to Sister Bernadette, and they start to talk in English. Finally, after what seems like forever, they stop, and Mary takes my hand.

'Now Teresa,' she says calmly, 'as you will have already noticed, a few of the girls have been sent home to Spain.'

I nod my head, waiting for her to deliver my fate.

'That is because the Basque Children's Committee had managed to locate their parents and found that they were in safe places, which meant their children could return,' she says, glancing at Sister Bernadette then back at me. 'You see, because the government are not funding the care of the children, the voluntary organizations have found themselves struggling, though they have tried their best all these months.'

'What is going to happen to me?' I say, feeling like I might burst with fear and impatience. 'Am I being sent to an orphanage? That is what Veronica said. Tell me it isn't true, Mary, please. I am not an orphan. I have a sister. She said I was only going to be here for three months and then I would be sent back to her. Back to my home.'

Sister Bernadette, startled by my outburst, turns to Mary with a grave expression and says something to her. I catch the word 'tragedy', something the volunteers at Stoneham used to say, sadly, when they saw us children, and my heart somersaults in my chest. It *is* bad news. I know it. I grip Mary's hand and look up at her, pleadingly. She nods, then says something to Sister Bernadette.

'Teresa,' she says softly, turning back to me, 'why don't we go for a little walk in the grounds, and I will explain everything.'

Only once we are outside, walking across the parkland with the convent far behind us, does she finally speak. I am expecting her to break the news that I am being sent to an orphanage, but instead she tells me the story of a battle that took place in Dublin, in 1916, known as the Easter Rising. I recognize the name from her diary, though I had thought it had something to do with Easter and Jesus rising from the dead. But Mary says it was a day when men and women came together to stand up for what they believed in, even though many of their own countrymen hated them for it. They even spat on the protesters as they made their way through the city. 'Whatever you think of their beliefs,'

Mary tells me, as she strides across the grass, 'those rebels were brave because they were rising up and fighting for what they thought was right. My brother was one of them. He believed in his cause, and he paid for it with his life.'

I am about to tell her that I know all about her brother, that his name was Fintan and his father described him as an unbreakable horse, but I quickly stop myself.

'Your sister is brave too,' she says, her eyes fixed on the horizon as she speaks. 'The Basque Children's Committee is aware of the work she is doing over there, the danger she is facing. It is good that she is standing up for what she believes in, though that means she might not be able to get home for a while. That, for now, she cannot be your guardian. It is not safe for you to return just yet. Do you understand, Teresa?'

I think of the moment we said goodbye. I pleaded with Katalin not to let me go. I told her that I could help her, that I would run as many errands to the bakery as she needed. I cried and screamed that I could not be parted from her, that I needed her. At that point, Padre Armando intervened and prised my hand from Katalin's. As he led me away, I turned to see Katalin. She was holding up three fingers. Three months. That is what she had promised me, as we made our way to the station: that I would only be gone for three months. The only reason she would break that promise is if something terrible had happened.

'Mary, did you mean what you said back in Sister Bernadette's study, that my sister is still alive?'

She stops walking, then turns to me with a sorrowful expression that makes my heart lurch.

'We think she is still alive, yes,' she says. 'Though the Basque Children's Committee has reason to believe that she has been captured and placed in a prisoner-of-war camp. Several witnesses in the hills outside Guernica say they saw her ambushed and taken away.'

I try to speak but I cannot find any words. Katalin is a prisoner? She is not in Guernica? All these weeks, when I have thought of her, I see her sitting in the town square or having coffee on the balcony of the apartment. How foolish I have been – trying to wish away the bombing, to imagine that everything in Guernica has been magically restored.

A tear falls down my face as I stand looking out at the freshly cut grass. Mary places her hand on my shoulder. I look up at her and feel safe. Mary has told me the truth, and I will never forget that.

'Teresa,' she says, crouching down in front of me and wiping my eyes with the corner of her handkerchief, 'I wanted to ask you something.'

'You want me to go to an orphanage,' I say, my heart pounding. 'That is what Sister Bernadette was talking about, wasn't it? She has got you to come and tell me. If my sister is a prisoner, then Veronica is right, I am an orphan and—'

'Shh, now,' says Mary firmly. 'No one is going to an orphanage. What I wanted to ask you is whether you might like to come and stay with me and Ronald at our house, just for a little while, until your sister is released.'

I look at her in wonder, not quite sure if I have heard her correctly.

'Stay with you?' I say, the pounding in my chest subsiding. 'You mean, live with you?'

Mary smiles and nods her head.

'Only if you want to, dote,' she says. 'It's a rickety old place and the chickens never stop clucking but there's plenty of room and—'

'Mary,' I say, interrupting her. 'What does "dote" mean?'

'It's an Irish word,' she says, smiling. 'My mother used to call me it. I'm not sure of its proper meaning but I have always taken it as a word to be used for someone lovely, someone you treasure.'

'You think I'm lovely?'

'I do, yes,' says Mary, her eyes twinkling.

'Well, I think you're an angel,' I say. 'You appeared like one when I called for you that day.'

'I'm honoured,' says Mary.

'My aingeru,' I say.

'Aingeru,' she says. 'I like that. It sounds a lot nicer than boring old Mary. Now, my dote, what do you say, would you like to come and live at Rochester Place for a wee while?'

Rochester Place. I let the name roll around my head for a moment. It sounds like a spider's web or a piece of lace, large and mysterious and full of curious hidey-holes. It sounds exactly like somewhere Mary would live and somewhere I would love to stay.

'Yes,' I say, throwing my hands around her waist and inhaling her sweet rosewater scent. 'I would like to come to live with you. I would like that very much.'

12

Corinne

PRESENT DAY

'Well, this is a surprise,' says Uncle Robin, beaming as he opens the door. 'I thought you were working nights this week.'

'I was. I am,' I say, as I step inside the house. 'I just . . . well, something happened at work, and I wanted to ask your advice.'

I realized, as I left the garden, that my uncle is the only person who might be able to shed light on what I experienced when I saw those gates. So, though I should really have gone straight home to catch up on my sleep, I found myself heading to the tube, bound for East London and answers.

'Sounds intriguing,' says Robin, leading me through to the reception room. 'I'll put the kettle on.'

Visiting Uncle Robin's house, hidden down a narrow courtyard in Spitalfields, is like stepping inside a museum. Built in 1729, it once housed generations of Huguenot silk-weavers, and the presence of those Georgian artisans is still palpable all around, as though the house has trapped the looms and held them to its heart forever. If the past can be said to live on in some parallel universe, then Uncle Robin's house is the closest I have come to proving that theory. The panelled walls are painted a deep mulberry. There is a grand fireplace where the remnants of a log fire are gently smouldering, making the air taste of smoke and fog. Robin's favourite armchair – an eighteenth-century French wingback that he found in a house clearance while on holiday in Sancerre – sits in the corner of the room, dust motes hovering over it like fireflies round a flame. There is a thick TV script lying on the arm of the chair, covered in red scribbles.

Uncle Robin catches me looking at it. 'My latest *House Detective* episode. They had me investigating a fascinating little street of cottages in Whitechapel for this new series. My, what a story I uncovered there. I can't wait to hear what you think of it. Now let's have some tea, eh?'

He gestures to the little hidden stairway that leads off the reception room.

'I know I say this every time you come, but mind your footing,' he says, as we walk up the rickety wooden steps. 'What can I say? They didn't give much consideration to health and safety in the 1700s.'

I smile as I follow his crooked form up the equally crooked steps. If a house can be said to resemble its owner, then this higgledy-piggledy Georgian townhouse is a perfect reflection of Uncle Robin. At the top of the stairs, we step onto a square landing. The walls and floorboards have been painted dark blue and there is an ornate stained-glass window that pours coloured light onto the oak sideboard. A black candle in a pewter candlestick sits in the centre of the sideboard. Robin once told me that this was where the weavers would gather to say their prayers after a busy day at the looms in the workshop below. It still feels like a space for quietude and reflection, all these centuries later.

'Earl Grey alright for you?' asks Uncle Robin, walking ahead of me to the kitchen, which is accessed through an arched doorway just off the landing. 'Or would you prefer something herbal? I think I might have some peppermint knocking around somewhere.'

'Earl Grey is fine,' I say, following him into the kitchen.

The dining table is strewn with old documents, maps, deeds, street directories – the tools of Robin's trade as a house historian. They jostle for space amid the clutter of half-empty teacups, a box of cat biscuits and, bizarrely, what looks like a stuffed peacock.

'That's Percy,' says Uncle Robin, glancing over his shoulder as he spoons tea leaves into a chunky red teapot. 'I got him from a house clearance in Kew the other week. I was over there visiting the National Archives and, as I headed back to the station, I spotted him sitting on the pavement outside one of those lovely Victorian townhouses by the green. He looked so forlorn, I felt compelled to go and take a closer look. Anyway, next thing, a chap came out of the house, saw me admiring him and told me I could have him, that he was bound for the rubbish tip otherwise. I must say I got a few off glances on the way home. Still, that's nothing new, eh? I'm not sure where I'm going to put him yet but he's a pleasant addition to the house, and Nicholas Culpeper seems to like him, which is always a good sign. It's awfully tiresome when he takes against something.'

'It's ... he's marvellous,' I say, shaking my head incredulously, both at the peacock and the thought of Nicholas Culpeper, Uncle Robin's elderly ginger cat, having the final say when it comes to matters of house-hold decor. Still, knowing Uncle Robin, that stuffed peacock is likely going to remain on the dining table for many years to come, gathering dust along with all his other bric-a-brac finds. As a self-confessed neat freak, Uncle Robin's house ought to bring me out in hives, but, strangely enough, I find it rather comforting.

I remember when I first brought Nidra here. It was like all her birthdays had come at once, and she spent the entire evening quizzing Uncle Robin about haunted houses. Like everyone who meets him, she was inspired by his passion for old properties – restoring them, researching their stories, bringing them back to life – even if he does rather resemble an old ghost himself, shuffling through his museum of knick-knacks.

Today he is dressed in a brown cable-knit cardigan that is at least two sizes too big, brown slacks, an olive-green shirt and a thick woollen tie. His face is flecked with grey whiskers, and his mop of salt-and-pepper hair is as unruly as ever. His hazel eyes peer out over the top of his wire-rimmed spectacles and I smile. As my only living relative besides Gran, there is something reassuringly comforting about Robin and his unapologetic quirkiness.

'Right, how about we have our tea in the snug?' he says, loading a wooden tray with the teapot, two mismatched polka-dot mugs, a silver sugar bowl and a pewter milk jug. 'It's warmer in there. Oh good, we've got biscuits.'

I watch as he lifts a jar from the recessed shelving unit by the door, where once the weavers would have stored their boxes of ribbon and thread, and takes out a handful of rather stale-looking shortbread.

'After you, my dear,' he says, gesturing to the narrow doorway that leads to the snug.

The snug, with its battered old soft cream sofas, sage-green walls and wood-burning fire is just as cosy as ever, and Nicholas Culpeper is happily ensconced in his usual spot in the armchair by the fire.

'Hello, stranger,' I say, giving him a little tickle under the chin. 'Gorgeous as ever, I see.'

'Lazy as ever,' says Uncle Robin, with a smile, as he places the tray on the low coffee table and begins to pour the tea. 'Oh, to be a cat, eh?'

I wedge myself onto the armchair next to Nicholas

Culpeper, feeling the warmth of his fur beside me and the comforting vibration of his sleepy purring. I am just leaning across to help myself to a biscuit when my phone rings. My heart lifts when I see Gran's name displayed on the screen.

'Oh, Gran, thank goodness,' I say, easing back into the chair. 'Where have you been?'

'Corinne, it's Annie,' says a voice on the other end.

At those words, my chest tightens. Annie is Gran's neighbour.

'Annie, is everything okay?' I say, breathlessly. 'Is it Gran?'

'She's fine, love,' says Annie. 'I just heard a phone ringing when I was sitting here watching the television, and I found your gran's phone tucked down the side of the sofa. She must have left it when she was here at the weekend.'

'Ah, so that's why she hasn't been getting my messages,' I say. 'I wish she'd be more careful with her phones. She's lost four of them since moving there.'

'Well, I'll make sure I pop it back to her,' says Annie. 'She probably doesn't realize she left it here. Mind you, she might be preoccupied. I think she's had company these last few days.'

'Company?'

'Yes. I saw her coming back from the shops on Monday, laden with groceries, like she was expecting someone for dinner. Then yesterday when I walked past with the dog, I heard voices in there, a man and a woman chatting away. Sounded like they were having a right good natter.'

'Oh,' I say, trying to think who could be visiting Gran and why she hasn't mentioned it to me. 'Anyway, Annie, thanks for letting me know about the phone. That's put my mind at rest.'

'Not a problem, love,' says Annie. 'I'll drop the phone off this afternoon on my way to work. You take care, and hopefully we'll see you on the island again soon. Bye now.'

'Bye, Annie.'

'Everything okay?' says Robin, peering at me over his lopsided spectacles.

'Er, yes,' I say, tucking my phone into my pocket. 'Gran left her phone at Annie's. That's why she wasn't getting my messages. Also, it seems she's been busy these last few days. According to Annie, Gran's got visitors at the house.'

'Really?' says Robin, dunking a biscuit into his tea. 'I wonder who.'

'A man and a woman, according to Annie,' I say, an odd sense of unease creeping up my spine.

'I thought there must be something up when she didn't reply to my email about the yew tree petition,' says Robin. 'She's usually so prompt, particularly when it comes to matters of conservation. A man and a woman? How intriguing. Your gran hardly ever has visitors. You know how much she enjoys her own company. She was always rather a lone wolf, but since moving out there she's become even more so. When I went to stay with her last year, she practically chased me out of the kitchen when I offered to put the shopping away.'

I nod. Gran is fiercely independent. Always has been.

'I think it's because of what happened with Grandad Len,' I say. 'When he left, it changed her. She tried to hide it, but I knew even then, though I was only little. I remember hearing her crying at night when she thought I was asleep. But as time went by, she developed this tough exterior. I think she wanted people to know that she could survive on her own, that she could cope without him. It's part of the reason why she moved to the island and started living like Robinson bloody Crusoe when most people her age are slowing down and taking to their armchairs for a spot of knitting. I suppose if she has made some friends then it's a good thing.'

'Joyce is the strongest woman I know,' says Robin, smiling. 'Life has thrown so much at her, and she refuses to be broken by it.'

He gestures to the mantelpiece and a framed photograph.

'That was the last time I saw your mum,' he says, sadly.

I nod my head. That photo, taken by Uncle Robin, is imprinted on my mind. My mother staring questioningly at the camera, pale and hollow-eyed, wearing a Nirvana

T-shirt – the band whose songs she would drunkenly play over and over – and cut-off denim shorts that hang from her thin frame. My gran stands beside her, demurely dressed in a claret-coloured blouse and navy pleated skirt, her dark hair immaculately curled and set. She is smiling but her eyes are sad and wary as she holds me, her tiny granddaughter, protectively in her arms. Keeping both of us at a safe distance from my mother. As Robin takes a sip of tea, the past encroaches on the room and I am three years old again, standing over my mother's body with the phone in my hand while 'Smells Like Teen Spirit' blasts on a sickening loop. The calm voice of the emergency responder on the other end of the line asks me if my mummy is breathing.

'I think it was "Storytime with Joyce" that saved her,' says Robin, leaning across to refill my cup. 'She loved that job. And the children.'

I smile as I recall accompanying Gran to the storytime sessions she gave at Tooting Library. It was there, one rainy afternoon, that I spotted a tiny girl around my age, sitting on a beanbag with a giant book of ghost stories spread out on her lap. I sat down next to her, and she looked up and said: 'I'm Nidra. Do you believe in ghosts?'

'Anyway,' says Uncle Robin, placing his empty cup on the table and leaning back into the folds of the sofa. 'We've digressed. You said there was something you wanted to ask me?'

'Yes,' I say, thankful for the change of subject. 'It was something that happened at work last night. You see, I had the most peculiar phone call.'

I begin to tell Uncle Robin the story of Mary. I tell him about the firefighters' discovery that the house does not exist, and about the overgrown garden and the plaque commemorating the death of a woman called Mary, who lost her life on this day in 1940.

'My goodness,' he says, when I finish talking. 'What a strange thing to happen. I mean, the fire chap has a point, it could have just been a prank, though I can see by looking at you that you're not convinced.'

'She was genuine, Uncle Robin,' I say, taking a sip of tea. 'I know she was. I've taken hundreds of hoax calls in my time and this wasn't one of them. Plus this call was made to my mobile.'

'Well, that bit is most confusing, and has me stumped,' he says, removing his spectacles and giving them a rub with the sleeve of his cardigan. 'Also, the house she described sounds rather out of character for that part of London. I know that area near the station pretty well and, as far as I'm aware, the bulk of the older properties are Victorian, not Georgian. And you say there's just a garden there now, in . . . what was the name of the street?'

'Rochester Place is the name of the house,' I say. 'There is no street name. It's more a hidden corner.'

'London is full of hidden places,' says Robin wistfully.

'I've been lucky enough to discover quite a lot of them though, over the years. There was the derelict Gothic chapel I found as a boy, hidden in the woods at Abney Park Cemetery; then the secret gardens tucked away behind the houses on Princelet Street, here in Spitalfields – such peaceful little pockets, and just spitting distance from the bustle of Brick Lane. The most memorable though were the ancient terraces I investigated for one of my very first television jobs. A row of houses on the west side of Newington Green that are said to be the oldest remaining terrace in London. They were built in 1658 and are still standing. Imagine that? An unremarkable set of buildings that withstood the Great Fire of London and the Blitz. I tell you, this city never fails to astound me. And this house of yours, Rochester Place . . . well, it sounds most intriguing.'

'It is,' I say. 'I took some photos of the garden. It's a complete mess now, but it was clear that it must have once been enchanting.'

I slip my hand into my pocket to retrieve my phone, and as I do I pull a piece of paper out along with it. Opening it up, I see that it is the notes I scribbled down when Mary called.

'Gosh, I forgot about this,' I say, handing the scrap of paper to Uncle Robin. 'Mary said this was her telephone number. What do you make of it?'

'BAL 672,' says Uncle Robin, peering at the piece of paper through his bifocals. 'Hmm. I think I know what this is, but I'd have to check. Bear me with a moment, my dear, while I get my laptop from the kitchen.'

He puts the note down on the coffee table then pads out of the room, almost stumbling on the uneven floorboards. Beside me, Nicholas Culpeper snores contentedly, while outside the bells of Hawksmoor's Christ Church ring out the hour. Four o'clock already. Time seems to have quickened this afternoon. I feel an odd sense of disorientation as I sip my tea.

'Right, let's see what this is,' says Uncle Robin, returning with the laptop. 'Read that out to me again will you, dear?'

I lean across and take the piece of paper from the coffee table.

'BAL 672.'

I watch as Uncle Robin types it in, his face so close to the screen his nose is almost touching it.

'Ah, as I suspected,' he says, looking up. 'Come and see.'

I join him on the sofa, and he turns the screen towards me, pointing at the web page he has brought up. I read the title: *Lost Numbers of London*. Below it is a list of London place names. Alongside each name is a code. The code Mary gave, BAL 672, has been highlighted in yellow. Next to it is written *Telephone Exchange Number for Balham and Tooting*.

'As I thought, this is an old telephone exchange code,' says Uncle Robin. 'But look what it says here.'

He points at the screen and, as I read, a cold sensation ripples through my body.

This was the number for the telephone exchange covering Balham and Tooting during the 1930s and early 1940s. The number became obsolete in 1945, shortly before the end of the war . . .

I look up at Uncle Robin in disbelief.

'Balham and Tooting in the 1930s and '40s,' I say, my voice trembling. 'So, this means that . . .'

'The number your caller gave you would have been the exchange code for Rochester Place,' says Uncle Robin, his voice full of gravitas as though delivering the summary at the end of one of his *House Detective* episodes. 'The house that your caller said she lived in. The house where someone called Mary died in 1940.'

13

Teresa
JULY 1937

A week later, my bags packed and final farewells made, I find myself on the train with Mary, bound for London and a new adventure. When we arrive at Tooting Broadway station, I am overcome by the noise. A man selling newspapers on the platform cries out as I pass, making me jump. I cling to Mary's arm and glance at the headlines on those papers. In the last week, Mary has taught me how to construct sentences in English. Though that has been beneficial in that I am able to converse a little better, it also means that I can now recognize words like 'death' and 'defeat' and 'Spanish Civil War' – the words splashed across the front of the newspapers. I turn my head away. I know that I shall find out what is happening at home soon, but today I want to banish it from my thoughts. Just for one day to pretend there is no war, no death.

Crowds of people cram against us as we reach the ticket hall. My heart starts to pound as I recall the same press of bodies in the market square once the bombing stopped – people rushing to safety, knocking each other as they ran, no care for anything other than saving themselves.

Mary seems to sense my anxiety and, as we make our way towards the doors, she squeezes my hand and pulls me closer.

'Here we are in Tooting, Teresa,' she says, as we exit the station and step out into a bustling street. 'What do you think?'

'This . . . this is London?' I ask, looking up at Mary. 'Where the King of England lives?'

'It's a district of London,' says Mary, guiding us away from the congested station entrance. 'There are lots of little areas like this that make up the city. It is rather like the head of a sunflower, with all the petals striking out from it – like the rays of the sun, I suppose. The King lives a little closer to the centre.'

We stand for a moment, then I feel a juddering beneath my feet as a train enters the station below. A shout cuts through the air and I turn to see a flower stall to the left of the entrance. The stall holder, a man in a brown flat cap, is holding up a bunch of roses. The sight of the flower stall and the rumble under my feet make my stomach lurch. I want to get away from here.

'Can we go to your house now?' I plead, turning to Mary.

'Of course we can, dote,' says Mary, taking my hand in hers. 'You'll find it is much more peaceful at Rochester Place.'

We turn from the station and make our way along the high street. A strange-looking bus that doesn't appear to have wheels hurtles past us, its bell ringing. That, Mary informs me, is a trolleybus. It doesn't have wheels because it moves along rails that are built into the road, rather like a train. I watch the bus as it weaves around the curves of the road and wonder to myself if everything in London is as topsy-turvy as it seems.

'Ronald is looking forward to meeting you,' says Mary, as we turn right off the high street and head down a quiet, tree-lined road. 'I have told him how much you love books and stories and that made him smile. You see, Ronald loves stories just as much as we do. That is his job.'

'He writes stories?' I say, looking up at the red-brick houses we are passing. Outside one of them a small boy sits on the step, playing with a toy car. When he sees me looking he sticks his tongue out. I turn the other way and pretend I haven't noticed.

'He does write stories, and very clever ones at that,' says Mary. 'But that is not his paying job, not yet anyway. No, his job is publishing books.'

'What does that mean?' I ask, my eye suddenly drawn to a pretty café with a red-and-white awning which has appeared up ahead.

'It means he puts together the books that we see in bookshops and libraries,' explains Mary. 'He is sent lots of stories and he gets to choose which ones end up as books.'

I nod my head, trying to imagine such a job. I see Ronald sitting in a room full of stories, the words spinning around his head, and him reaching out to catch the best ones in a giant, hardback book. *Bang.* He slams the book shut and the stories are captured there forever.

As the wind changes direction, a familiar smell wafts on the air. A scent I haven't encountered since I left Spain.

'I smell garlic,' I say to Mary, pausing to inhale the delicious aroma.

'That will be Mario's café,' says Mary, pointing out the café I spotted earlier. 'Mario makes the best spaghetti sauce I have ever tasted.'

The smell gets stronger as we draw near, and my stomach rumbles. The red-and-white awning flutters in the breeze and, as we pass, I catch the sound of merry voices and laughter coming from inside. Through the window I see a man with curly dark hair standing by a table. He is wearing a blue shirt and has a white apron tied around his waist. He looks up as we pass and waves his hand.

'There he is,' says Mary, waving back. 'Mario. He's one of life's good chaps.'

I look up at his name, printed in squiggly red lettering above the awning. We walk on, the smell of garlic drifting behind us. If I close my eyes, I could be back home.

'Almost there,' says Mary, as we turn left. I see a sign

on the corner that says *Larkin Road*. We pass more red-brick houses, these ones slightly more rundown. 'I don't know about you, but I'm gasping for a cup of tea.'

She takes my hand and grips it firmly as we approach the last house on this stretch. It has weeds growing by the doorstep and paint peeling from a door that must once have been white but is now a dirty grey. As we pass, I can feel someone's eyes on me. I turn to see a man standing in the window, his hand holding back a yellowing net curtain. The man has a bald head and small beady eyes. He is staring so hard at us that I assume he must know Mary. I smile at him, but he scowls and shakes his head.

'Don't mind him,' says Mary, looking up just as the man drops the curtain and steps away from the window. 'Fred Harding's what we call a bigot.'

'What does that mean?' I ask.

'Well, he seems to think that this city is purely for the likes of him,' says Mary, raising her eyebrow. 'What does he describe himself as again? Oh, yes, "the Native English". As if such a thing exists. He's just an angry old man who thinks that civilization is ending because an Italian café has opened up round the corner from him.'

I can hear the raw fury in Mary's voice as she talks about Fred Harding.

'Anyway, forget about that silly man,' she says, her voice softening. 'This way to the secret square.'

We take a left turn off the road, leaving Fred Harding's hostile face behind us, and enter a narrow, cobbled pathway. A honey-coloured brick wall lines the lane and there are bramble bushes threaded around it. As we walk, I feel something touch my leg. Looking down I see a cat. It is black with a little white patch on its front, which makes it look like it is wearing a suit. I crouch down to stroke it. Up ahead, Mary stops and heads back towards me.

'I see you've met Jeeves,' she says, bending down to join in the stroking. 'Where have you been, old boy, eh? Off scrounging for food from the neighbours as usual?'

'Is he your cat?' I say, tickling him under the chin.

'Yes,' says Mary, getting to her feet. 'We got him as a kitten when we were first married. He was going to be a companion to . . . Well, things didn't turn out as expected, but we have a lovely feline friend in Jeeves.'

A shadow passes across her face as she speaks, and her smile fades. I wonder what she could have been about to say. Who was Jeeves going to be a companion to? I don't have the chance to ask because suddenly Mary is striding off down the pathway. I get to my feet and hurry after her, Jeeves weaving in and out of my legs as I go.

'Here we are,' she says, stopping in front of a rather grand iron gate. 'Home at last.'

She turns round and smiles. A real one this time.

'Welcome to Rochester Place, Teresa,' she says, holding out her hand.

I slowly make my way towards her, my eyes fixed on the house. It is the most beautiful house I have ever seen. It rises in front of me, like a storybook castle, its chimneys pointing up to the sky like turrets. It is made of golden-coloured bricks and has tall windows with arches above them. The door is cherry red, the same shade as Mary's shoes, and has a brass knocker in the shape of a bumble bee. Above the door is a black lantern, its glass twinkling in the afternoon light. In front of the house, beyond the iron railing and gateway, is an immaculate garden. As we enter the gate and walk down the path through the garden, I see a large silver globe on a raised stand, which Mary tells me is a sundial. There is another object, a tall white pole with what looks like a miniature white house on top. 'That's our bird table,' says Mary, as we pass. 'We leave breadcrumbs and seeds on there for the robins in the colder months.' To the left of the path is a magnificent tree with pink-and-cream flowers shaped like candle flames. 'That's a magnolia tree,' says Mary, brushing her hands along the branches. 'Ronald's favourite.'

When we reach the door, I turn to look out at the garden through which we have just walked. There is a bench at the far end of it, and rows of fruit bushes clustered in the corner. Standing here, it is hard to imagine that we are in the city. It is so peaceful and still, so lush and green.

'Ready to go in?' says Mary, as she adjusts my hair.

I nod my head, though my heart is pounding in my chest as I watch her put the key in the lock and open the door.

14

Teresa

Mary steps across the threshold, while I stand, rather awkwardly, by the door and watch as she removes her hat and hangs it on a tall wooden stand.

'Right,' she says, turning to me with a smile. 'Let's go and find Ronald, shall we?'

I follow her across the entrance hall, a vast space that is almost the size of our apartment in Guernica. The floor is covered in black and white tiles, like a chess-board, and Mary's red shoes make a clickety-clack sound as she strides across them. Rays of sunlight pour in from a window on the far side of the hall, casting rainbow strands on the pale walls as they catch the glass droplets of the chandelier that hangs from the ceiling. The sight reminds me of Katalin's prism. *There are other worlds, Teresa* ... How right she was. I feel like I have spent the last few weeks stepping from one new world into the next, never staying long enough to catch my breath. From the freezing deck of the ship to the bell tents and chocolate at Stoneham, to the prayers and prunes at the convent, and now here. However, unlike those other places, there is something about this house that intrigues me, some strange magic lurking inside that is drawing me in.

Mary stops at the end of the hallway and beckons to me. I follow her through an arched doorway into a large, bright room with high ceilings, tall windows, and a stone fireplace that fills the whole of one wall. There is a man standing by the fireplace, with a pipe in his hand. The air smells of woodsmoke and cinnamon.

'Teresa, I would like you meet my husband, Ronald,' says Mary, taking my hand and leading me over to the fireplace.

'How do you do, Teresa?' says Ronald, placing his pipe in the corner of his mouth and extending his hand.

'How do you do, Ronald,' I say, remembering the greeting Mary taught me.

I shake his hand. His skin is soft and warm. I stand and stare at him for a moment. He is different to the other men I have met in England so far. Like Mary, he has a certain expression on his face that is more common in children than in adults, a light that glows from within. He is wearing baggy, biscuit-coloured trousers, a pale blue shirt with the sleeves rolled up and a navy-blue pullover. His red tie matches Mary's shoes, and I can see a flash of green sock peeking out from above his brogues. His eyes are pale blue and framed with thick, dark lashes, and his mouth curls in such a way that it looks like he has just heard the most splendid joke. My cheeks redden as I recall how Mary described him in her diary – as the most handsome man she had ever seen. I don't want to look Ronald in the eye in case he can somehow tell that I have read Mary's private thoughts.

'I bet you're hungry after your train journey,' he says, lightly tapping his pipe with his forefinger. 'How about we have a spot of tea, eh?'

He gestures to Mary, who is standing by a large oblong-shaped table by the window. It is draped in a pretty blue-and-white, floral-patterned tablecloth and is laden with food.

'Mary spent the whole morning baking,' says Ronald, as we walk over to the table.

I only catch a little of what he is saying as my English is still not that good, but I smile and nod my head politely. I notice that his accent is different to Mary's. Though both are soft and musical, Ronald's is more clipped, a snare drum to Mary's harp.

'Take a seat, Teresa,' says Mary, gesturing to the high-backed wooden chair next to her.

I sit down and gasp at the sight in front of me. Mary has prepared all my favourite things. There are cinnamon buns, honey cakes, morello cherries in syrup, cheese and grapes, a jug of creamy milk, and even a little dish of salted almonds. My stomach rumbles as Ronald passes me the plate of cinnamon buns.

'I hear these come highly recommended,' he says, taking one for himself after I have chosen mine.

Mary translates for me – then, turning to Ronald, I try to remember some of the words Mary has spent the last couple of weeks teaching me.

'They . . . my . . . favourite,' I say, pronouncing each word carefully. 'In Guernica . . . we eat them . . . er . . . before school . . . from the . . . ogindegia . . .'

'The bakery,' interjects Mary gently, nodding her head encouragingly.

'Yes,' I say, committing the word to memory. 'From the bakery. For . . . breakfast . . . we, er . . .'

I pause, remembering my errands to José's bakery, the intense stare he gave me as he pressed the bag of buns into my hands. One afternoon, after handing Katalin the bag, I lingered by the door, my curiosity piqued. To my astonishment, I watched as my sister took an oversized bun, ripped it open and removed a folded piece of paper. I watched as she read it, the colour draining from her cheeks, then I slipped into the shadows. Some things were not for my eyes. I realized then that my trips to the bakery were part of something bigger, something to do with the people who gathered with my sister in the kitchen each evening in a cloud of cigarette smoke, José amongst them, and who spoke in loud, animated voices about Franco and the need to fight back.

If only Ronald and Mary knew that I was an active participant in the Loyalist cause. What would they say? Mary, with her rebellious brother and love of pirate queens, would be proud of me, I know. As for Ronald? I will have to wait and see.

'You know what I say,' says Ronald, his resonant voice interrupting my thoughts. 'I say these buns are so delicious we should have them at every mealtime. Hooray for cinnamon buns!'

He takes a big bite of the bun then grins at both of us in turn. I have only a vague idea of what he has just said, but he pulled such a funny face as he said it that I start to laugh and, before we know it, we have all caught the giggles.

'Oh, Ronald,' says Mary, regaining her composure, 'do behave. You'll give poor Teresa the hiccups.'

At that, Ronald takes a sip of tea from the porcelain teacup then proceeds to make silly hiccuping noises while rolling his eyes.

'Right, enough of this nonsense,' says Mary, shaking her head good-naturedly as she rises from the table and turns to me. 'How about we give you a little tour of the house. Would you like that?'

I nod my head, then, after popping the last bite of the cinnamon bun in my mouth, push my chair back and follow Mary and Ronald back into the chessboard hallway.

'Now the thing to remember about this house, Teresa,' says Ronald, placing his hands on his hips. 'Is that it's rather like a map of the world. It has its mysterious areas, its freezing parts, its hidden corners and dark underbelly. Those areas that are best left alone. The basement, particularly. I'd rather you didn't go down there. But the important thing to remember, should you ever get lost, is that this spot by Mousey is the mid-point. Rather like the equator, with some bits below and some above. Middle of the earth, one could say. Now, if you take Mousey as your guide, you'll always find your way back.'

Mary translates and, taking my hand, shows me the mouse Ronald is referring to. It has been carved into the panel at the side of the grand wooden staircase. I have never seen anything so exquisite. I run my fingers along the mouse's curves, feeling his pointy ears, his sharp nose, his spiky whiskers.

'He's a friendly old chap,' says Ronald, crouching next to me. 'And he's looking well for a mouse that was around at the time of George III.' Sensing my confusion, he adds: 'Very old, Teresa. Mousey is very old.'

This I understand.

'Right, race you to the top,' cries Mary, slipping off her shoes and running up the stairs. 'Come on, slowcoaches.'

Ronald gives me a head start then pretends to collapse from exhaustion halfway up. I start to giggle and have to clutch the banister to steady myself.

'Well, I declare myself the winner,' says Mary, standing at the top of the stairs. 'I don't know. You two would make hopeless mountaineers.'

When Ronald and I gather our wits and get to the landing, I am met with the most wonderful sight: an enormous library running the length of the first floor, with more books than I have ever seen in my life. Shelves line the walls, and there is a wooden ladder propped up in the centre, with wheels attached to the base.

'Would you like to climb it?' asks Mary, noticing me staring at the tall ladder. 'It's a lot of fun.'

I nod my head and she leads me over to it. While Ronald steadies the ladder, Mary guides me up. It is scary at first, but when I get to the top it feels like I am sitting on a mountain made of books.

'Toot, toot,' cries Ronald, sweeping the ladder gently across the floor. 'Next stop, encyclopedias and medical anthologies.'

I gasp as the ladder glides across the shelves, the titles of the books blurring in front of my eyes.

'I'm flying,' I exclaim, excitedly, as Ronald whooshes me back in the other direction.

'Up, up and away.' Ronald's voice echoes round the room.

'Like a bird,' says Mary, beaming at me from below. 'Now let's stop there for a moment. We don't want you to get dizzy.'

Ronald brings the ladder back to the centre, then holds it steady as I carefully make my way down.

'That was fun,' I say, surprising myself as the English words spring from my mouth.

Mary takes my hand, and we walk across to the tall window at the far end of the library.

'Now, if you stand on that, you can see the garden,' she says, gesturing to a broad ledge under the window.

But my eye is drawn to the large table to the left of the window. Unlike the dining table, this one is bare wood and is covered with squares of paper with scribbled writing, drawings and what look like maps on them.

'What are they?' I ask Mary.

She pauses then nods at Ronald, and they both join me at the table.

'This, Teresa,' she says, running her hands across the papers, 'is *The Other Lands*. It's a story that Ronald is writing.'

I look at the scribbled handwriting on the papers, then at Mary and Ronald standing there with the walls of bookshelves behind them. How can an ordinary person write stories? Surely you can't just jot them down, like one would write a shopping list or a letter.

'How is that possible?' I say, to Mary, in Basque. 'I thought stories were just out there, like the sky or trees or flowers, and people found them and told them to their friends and family, and they were carried along on the wind like little seeds.'

Mary smiles, then translates what I have said for Ronald. His eyes light up and he comes over and pats me on the head.

'You're absolutely right, Teresa,' he says. 'Stories are just like seeds. You scatter them on fertile ground, then nourish and tend them lovingly. It takes a lot of dedication and patience to bring them to fruition, and sometimes a few of them get eaten by birds or frozen by ice and frost. The trick is to keep going, to keep believing that just one of those seeds will blossom into a dazzling flower. That's the magic of writing stories. But like all magic, you have to believe, otherwise it won't happen.'

As Mary translates for me, Ronald smiles gently. I look up at him as she finishes, feeling an overwhelming urge to tell him my story: about the prism and the bakery, the marketplace and the storm. But I hold myself back. There will be time to tell him those things. What I do know is that if Ronald Davidson believes in magic, then he is a man to be trusted.

'Right, who's for a glass of lemonade?' says Mary, clapping her hands and snapping me out of my trance. 'After all this mountain climbing and flying on ladders, I bet you're parched, Teresa. Come on, we can have it in the garden, and I can show you my flowers.'

She takes my hand and we skip back down the stairs and across the chessboard hallway, but this time, instead of walking through the archway on the left, we turn right and step into a round, glass room.

'This is the orangery,' says Mary. 'It leads out into the garden.'

Long trestle tables covered in exotic potted plants line the room. It is very hot and sticky in here, and my mouth feels dry.

'This way,' says Mary, opening a set of glass doors. 'Oh, look, Jeeves has beaten us to it.'

I follow her and step into an explosion of colour and scents. The garden is surrounded by a high brick wall, on top of which sits Jeeves the cat, cleaning his paws. A long honey-coloured path snakes its way through the neatly cut grass and is lined by tall blue flowers. There is a table by the wall swathed in a pale-pink-and-white striped cloth and surrounded by white wicker chairs with soft pink cushions. Halfway down the path, I pause to inhale the floral scents that hang in the air. The smell reminds me of Katalin's perfume, the one in the big green bottle with the butterfly stopper that she would spritz onto her wrists each morning. At the thought of my sister, a lump appears in my throat. The sadness stone. I quickly gulp it back as Ronald emerges from the orangery.

'Drinks are served.'

He bustles towards us, carrying a tray laden with glass tumblers and a green glass jug.

'Do sit, Teresa,' says Mary, beckoning me to the table where she is already seated. 'Would you like me to tell you about the plants and flowers?'

I nod my head. Ronald joins us and pours each of us a tumbler of fresh lemonade. It is cold and sweet and sharp. I take a big gulp of it as Mary tells me about the raspberry bush that she planted last year.

'I'm hoping come harvest time it will bear enough fruit to bottle up a good hoard of jam,' she says, pausing to sip her lemonade. 'There is nothing quite like a slice of warm bread with a slathering of homemade jam on it.'

I am about to add that I prefer apricot jam to raspberry, when a boy's face appears above the wall.

'Good afternoon, Mr and Mrs Davidson.'

'Good afternoon, Luca,' says Mary, waving her hand. 'This is Teresa. She has travelled to England all the way from the north of Spain.'

The boy, who has curly black hair, heavy dark eyebrows and a round, tanned face with pink cheeks, waves his hand at me.

'Hello there, Teresa,' he says, smiling broadly. 'Welcome to Blighty. I hope you enjoy your stay.'

I smile politely and wave my hand, having only grasped a couple of his and Mary's words.

'Luca is the son of Mario, the man who owns the café we passed,' says Mary, leaning down to stroke Jeeves, who is slinking around our legs. 'Behind that wall is the back of the café. When the wind is blowing in the right direction you can smell all that delicious food being cooked. Makes my tummy rumble!'

'I have an idea,' says Ronald, getting up from his chair. 'Won't be a moment.'

He hurries into the house, reappearing a few moments later with a camera in his hand. It is a Leica, just like Katalin's.

'Now, Luca, would you do the honours?' says Ronald, holding the camera towards the boy. 'I'd like to take a photograph of the three of us, to mark Teresa's first day.'

'Gladly,' says Luca, jumping down from the wall.

'What a lovely idea,' says Mary, getting to her feet and gesturing for me to do the same. 'Though I look an awful mess.'

She puts her hand in her pocket and takes out a silver compact and a tube of lipstick, then touches up her lips with the familiar red matt stain.

'Nonsense,' says Luca, rolling his eyes. 'You always look so glamorous. Papa says you're a dead ringer for Ava Gardner.'

He glances at me and smiles.

'Movie star,' he says, slowly, sensing I don't under-stand. 'Very beautiful. Mary is very beautiful.'

This I do understand. I look down at my brown cord dress and matching cardigan, recalling the delicately embroidered dress I was wearing that day – the day my life changed forever – and the knot in my stomach tightens. Mary seems to sense my discomfort and takes my hand in hers.

'Now,' says Luca. 'How about you stand in the centre, Teresa, and Mr and Mrs Davidson, you two go either side of her.'

Ronald comes to stand next to me. Mary smooths down her tweed skirt and adjusts the emerald hair clip that holds her dark curls perfectly in place, while I tuck my unruly hair behind my ear. Then they place their hands on my shoulders and we look up at Luca.

'Say cheese,' he cries.

We do as he says, and, with a flash, the image is captured.

15

Teresa
JULY 1937

'How about you children go and play while we clear away the dishes,' says Ronald, taking the camera from Luca and placing it carefully back into its black leather bag. 'Might be wise to go indoors for now. Those clouds look rather heavy. If I'm not mistaken, I'd say there's a rainstorm on its way.'

I look to Mary to translate what Ronald has said, but before she can, Luca has grabbed my hand and whisked me inside the house.

'This way,' he shouts as we run through the orangery, shapes and colours blurring before my eyes, then out into the entrance hall.

'Do you believe in ghosts?' says Luca, stopping at the top of a flight of wooden stairs that lead to the basement, the area Ronald described earlier as the 'underbelly' of the house – a place I was not to go.

'I . . . I do not understand,' I say, shrugging my shoulders.

'Whoo,' cries Luca, flapping his arms up and down. 'Bogeyman. Il fantasma. Comes to get you in the night.'

'Oh, er . . . mamu,' I say, recalling the story in one of Mary's books at the convent, where a child dressed up in a white sheet and pretended to be a ghost. 'You are . . . ?' I rack my brain for the English word, the word he just used. 'You are . . . a ghost?'

'I'm not a ghost,' he says, shaking his head. 'The ghosts are down there.'

He points down the wooden staircase and an icy chill goes though me.

'No,' I say, backing away from the steps. 'Ronald . . . he . . . he say no go there.'

'I'm just kidding you,' says Luca, grabbing my hand. 'There's no ghosts down there, just fun stuff. Come on.'

He pulls me down the stairs and we tumble into a dark, windowless room. There is a cord hanging by the entrance. Luca pulls it and a weak light, cast by a solitary bulb in the centre of the ceiling, illuminates the room. Stacks of cardboard boxes line the walls and there is a rail on which hang countless fur coats and hats. The air smells musty and damp, like the vaults in the church back home, which were only opened up at Easter time so that the congregation could view the relics of the saints.

'Hey, look at me,' says Luca. 'I'm putting on the Ritz.'

I turn to see him, clad in an oversized brown fur coat and shiny top hat, a jewelled cane in his hands.

'May I escort you for cocktails, my lady,' he says, in a voice that sounds like Ronald and the men who read the news on the wireless.

144

He takes my arm and marches me up and down the room, waving the cane from side to side, the top hat falling over his eyes. He looks so silly I start to laugh.

'Now, what's so funny, young lady,' he says, pushing the hat up with the back of his hand. 'Is that any way to treat a gentleman?'

He throws his hands out and sends a pile of boxes flying to the floor.

'Oops,' he cries, as we scramble to retrieve the scraps of paper that have escaped from the boxes. 'Better clear this up before they find us.'

As we are gathering the papers, something catches my eye. It is a newspaper clipping with a familiar name written across the top: *CONSTANCE MARKI-EVICZ*. After which is written: *TEN YEARS SINCE HER DEATH, WE EXPLORE HER LEGACY*. There is another piece of paper stapled to it, obscuring the rest of the story. This paper is lined with faint gold and has writing scribbled on it. I recognize it as a page from Mary's diary, in her distinctive messy handwriting. I wonder why she ripped it out.

While Luca busies himself with repacking the boxes, I take myself off into the corner of the room so I can look more closely at the paper. Lifting up Mary's diary page, I see a colourized photograph of a woman in a green uniform. She is looking directly at the camera and holding a gun. 'This is Constance,' I whisper to myself, mesmerized by the image, her powerful stare, and the confidence with which she holds the gun. This is the woman who came to Mary's house in Ireland, who helped her find work in London. I stare at the photograph while the long-dead woman stares back at me. There is something about her expression, her determined stance, that reminds me of Katalin. There is a lengthy article below the image that I cannot understand, so I turn to the diary page. There, in Basque, Mary has scribbled: *Ten years and still nothing. Options: Give a child a home? The perfect front? Keep up the façade. Keep them happy. Make them think I am one of them. Mrs Davidson: the quintessential English woman. The perfect mother? Accept Lorea's mission?*

I am about to read on when I hear footsteps on the stairs. Then Mary's voice calling.

'Luca? Teresa? Are you down there?'

'Time to go,' says Luca, grabbing the papers from me and placing them on top of one of the boxes. 'No more ghosts today, my lady.'

Mary is standing in the hallway when we emerge. Her arms are folded across her chest and her face is set in a deep frown.

'What did Ronald tell you about the underbelly?' she says crossly. 'You're not to go there. It is dark and dangerous; you might fall.'

'I'm sorry, Mary,' I say, feeling my cheeks burning with shame. The last thing I want is to upset Mary and Ronald on my very first day.

'There's no need to be sorry,' says Mary, her face softening. 'It's just there are so many delightful parts of the house, it's a shame to waste time in the dark and dusty corners. Now, let's go and find Ronald. It seems he was wrong – the rain has held off and it's still bright blue skies out there.'

Ronald is collecting eggs from the chickens when we return to the garden, his sleeves rolled up to the elbows.

'Would you two like to help me?' he calls, when he spots us. 'I think this might require smaller, steadier hands than my great shovels.'

'I would love to, Mr Davidson, but I had better be getting back,' says Luca. 'Papa will need my help preparing the bread for tomorrow.'

'No rest for the wicked, eh,' says Ronald, his eyes brightening as he brings out a large white egg from the coop. 'Cheerio, Luca.'

'Cheerio, Mr Davidson. Mrs Davidson.'

Then, turning to me, he leans forward and kisses me lightly on the cheek. He is very handsome and, as I smile back at him, I feel a funny sensation in the pit of my stomach, like a bird is flapping its wings in there.

'Cheerio, my lady,' he says, and before I can respond, he leaps over the back wall and disappears into the café.

Later, Mary shows me to my bedroom. It is high in the eaves of the house and has a curious V-shaped window, with a little cushioned seat beneath, that looks out onto the garden. A perfect reading spot. The walls are decorated with red-and-green floral-patterned wallpaper with little gold birds hidden in the leaves. 'Birds to sing you to sleep, dote,' says Mary, her eyes twinkling. My bed is much larger than the one I had at home and that in the convent. Mary said it is a queen-sized bed, so that must make me royalty. It has iron posts with a golden globe at the top of each, and is covered with soft, fluffy pillows and a thick eiderdown that matches the flowers on the walls. I prop the doll that I was given at Southampton Docks so she sits upright on the top of the covers.

As Mary takes a soft cotton nightdress from the drawer and hands it to me, I think about the newspaper cutting and the words Mary scribbled on it. What does it all mean? I am desperate to ask her, but it would mean admitting that I have invaded her privacy. She was cross enough that we had disobeyed her wishes and gone down to the basement. If she finds out I was rifling through her personal belongings she might send me back to the convent – or worse, to an orphanage. So, instead, I keep quiet, slip on the cool nightdress and curl up in bed.

But as Mary tucks me in, I cannot stop thinking about Constance, defiant in her green uniform, her hands clasping the gun.

'Mary,' I say, as she sits on the bed beside me. 'Do you think it is right for women to be soldiers?'

'Whatever makes you say that, dote?'

'I was thinking about my sister,' I say, which is only half a lie, as Katalin is never far from my mind. 'Having to stay behind in Spain and do as the men do. Fight. It doesn't seem fair.'

'Well, not all women choose to fight,' says Mary. 'And your sister's involvement with the Loyalists was her choice.'

'But aren't women supposed to be gentle?' I try to imagine Katalin shooting or killing someone. 'Aren't they supposed to look after people, not harm them?'

'In war, it is about defending yourself and your cause,' says Mary, her face growing serious. 'Rather than setting out to intentionally harm another person. And I think that a woman can be both warrior and nurturer. Don't you?'

'In Spain, women are not seen as soldiers,' I reply. 'At least they weren't until this war. It sounds like things were different in Ireland. There it seems acceptable for women to wear uniforms and fire guns.'

Mary looks at me, her green eyes narrowing. But then, to my relief, her expression softens.

'Have I ever told you the story of Queen Maeve?' she says, her eyes regaining their spark. 'The warrior queen of Connaught?'

I shake my head, eager to hear the story.

'Well,' says Mary, folding her hands on her lap, 'Queen Maeve was a mythical figure, but that doesn't make her story any less inspiring. That's not to say she was perfect. Far from it. According to legend, our Maeve was impulsive and headstrong and so hungry for power she fought a furious battle with her husband, King Ailill, over a prized bull, of all things.'

'A bull?' I say, my eyes feeling heavy with sleep. 'Why would you fight over a bull?'

'Well, as I said, Maeve was impulsive and fiercely competitive,' continues Mary, her bright eyes displaying not a hint of tiredness. 'And because her husband had obtained a white bull, which was highly prized, Maeve made it her mission to have a bull to rival his. She found one at a place called Cooley, and was about to take ownership of it when the seller changed his mind and withdrew his offer. As you can imagine, Maeve exploded with rage and waged war on Cooley. She assembled an army, and they stormed the place and captured the promised bull. When she got back home, not content with having equal wealth with her husband, the pair decided to pitch their bulls against each other. The two beasts ended up dead, and Maeve and Ailill were back to square one.'

'Maeve sounds awful,' I say – feeling, for the first time, discomfited by one of Mary's stories. 'Why would you wage war and kill people and animals just because you want to look powerful?'

'You're right, dote,' says Mary, gently stroking my face. 'War is a terrible thing. And waging it over a bull?

Come on now, why would anyone take up arms and fight for such a futile cause, you may ask. Well, like you, when I first heard the story of Maeve, I thought she was ridiculous – a flighty, arrogant woman who wanted wealth and power at all costs. But now that I am grown up and have lived a little, I see that Maeve was simply trying to be seen as equal to the men around her, which was no mean feat in those days. Your sister Katalin, I imagine, is doing something similar. What I am trying to say, dote, is that whether it is a prize bull, an independent Ireland or a Spain free of fascists, if you believe in something strongly enough then it is worth fighting for.'

'What happened to Maeve?' I ask, trying to dispel any thoughts of my sister and war. 'After the bull died.'

'Well,' says Mary. 'When her time came, she asked to be buried in a standing position, facing her enemies in Ulster. There's a big mound in Sligo, known as Maeve's Cairn, where they say she stands to this day. Like I said, it is a mythical story, but I know that whenever I feel sad or hopeless, I think of Maeve standing there facing her enemies with a smile on her face for all eternity, and it gives me strength.'

My eyes are closed now but I feel Mary kiss my forehead. As I listen to her footsteps disappearing down the wooden staircase, I am filled with a deep sense of contentment. Maybe it is the sunshine or the smell of flowers or the taste of cinnamon buns and morello cherries still lingering in my mouth, or the image of Maeve standing firm in the face of her enemies, or the warm feeling I got when Luca called me his lady, but for the first time since I arrived in England I feel like the sadness stone has fallen away. I feel like I have come home.

16

Mary
APRIL 1926
WESTMINSTER

I was still in shock from that kiss when I brought the children down to breakfast the following morning. I felt rather nervous as I led Daphne by the hand down the grand staircase, Albert hurtling ahead of us. What would I say to Ronald when I saw him? Would he know that I had spent the entire night lying in my narrow bed, running over the kiss in my mind, remembering how his lips had brushed against my cheek, how it had made my insides feel like they were filled with fizzy pop? In the end, my nerves were all in vain, as we were greeted by an empty dining room. Peggy sashayed in with a tray of boiled eggs, toast and tea. As she placed breakfast on the sideboard, Peggy informed me that the Air Marshal and his wife had left early for an engagement in Rutland, while Master Ronald had left even earlier to catch his train back to Oxford.

Even though I had only spent a few hours in his company, the news that Ronald had left made me feel hollow inside. I sat down at the table and, after persuading Albert to eat a couple of mouthfuls of toast and wiping egg yolk from the front of

Daphne's white dress, I found my appetite had evaporated. Silly girl, I said to myself, as I readied the children for their morning's lessons. What were you thinking, letting yourself believe that someone like Ronald would have feelings for someone like you? And look at how I had embarrassed myself by wading after him into the water. What must he have thought? I tried to put all the memories of the previous day to the back of my mind as I got on with the morning's tasks. Once Albert was settled in the nursery with his tutor, and Daphne had occupied herself with her needlework, I returned to my bedroom to do some needlework of my own.

My mind was busy with my list of chores when I pushed my door open and saw a letter lying on the floor. I stooped to pick it up. My name was scribbled on the front of the envelope, but there was no stamp or postmark. When I opened it, my heart leapt in my chest. Inside was a return train ticket from London to Oxford, with a scribbled note that read:

Dear Mary,

I am sorry I did not get the chance to say goodbye. I had to return to Oxford on the early train as I have an exam to prepare for, worse luck. I really enjoyed talking to you last night, though the evening went by far too quickly. I am keen to continue our conversation and was wondering if you would like to visit me in Oxford this Saturday? I heard Father say that was your day off. If so, I could meet you at the

railway station at eleven o'clock. I have enclosed a
return ticket I had spare. Please feel free to use it.

Yours,
Ronald

*I could not believe what I was reading. Ronald wanted me to
visit him in Oxford! The idea was as fanciful as visiting him on
the moon. What would I wear? What would I say to his clever
friends? My nerves returned with gusto, but I knew that I could
not refuse. Constance had told me that I should take advantage
of every opportunity, and this was an invitation into the heart of
English society. If I made a success of this, who knows what it
might lead to? I recalled Fintan's declarations round the dinner
table when he had first joined the Republican cause: 'The trick is
to watch the English carefully, learn their ways, observe their tactics, mimic their gestures. Then, when the time is right . . . bam,
you strike.' My father had grimaced at this overt display of patriotism but, though I was only young, I knew what Fintan was
getting at. I needed to be fully accepted into this world, and to do
that I would have to convince Ronald that I was one of his kind.*

*Two days later I was sitting on a train bound for Oxford. I
was so apprehensive I had not been able to eat a morsel at breakfast. I was wearing my only 'good' dress: an emerald-coloured silk
shirt-waister that Señora Alvariz had given me as a Christmas
gift. For the whole journey, I practised what I would say when I
saw him. 'Good morning, Ronald. Thank you so much for the
kind invitation.' I muttered it over and over, under my breath,*

making sure my English accent was as perfect as could be, all the way to Oxford. However, when I alighted from the train and saw him standing on the platform, impeccably dressed in a three-piece tweed suit and brown felt cap, the sun glowing behind his head, my mind went blank. He seemed to sense my awkwardness as he hurried over, kissed me on the cheek and told me how wonderful it was to see me. As soon as I inhaled him, that unique scent, part woodsmoke, part spice, I began to settle. Then he clasped my hand and swept me out of the station, whispering in my ear that it was time we went on an adventure.

Oh, how to describe the day, though it was only a few short hours. First, Ronald took me to the glorious Bodleian Library, explaining how it housed over one million books. I could not even imagine what that many books looked like, but I was eager to find out. We were stopped at the door by a man in a waistcoat and bow tie, who informed us women who were not students were not permitted into the library. As we skipped away giggling, Ronald gave a little smirk and suggested that he should have told the grim-faced chap that I was a visiting professor. 'A professor of mythology,' I added. 'From the University of Padua,' added Ronald, 'specializing in unicorns and dragons' teeth.'

Any disappointment at being denied entry to the library soon disappeared as we spent the afternoon rowing along the river, or 'punting' as Ronald told me it was called. The boats were narrow and looked rather unstable, but as I settled in and Ronald took up the pole, I found it to be most peaceful. We drifted along the river, Ronald pointing out various landmarks: the Botanic Garden; the towers of his college, Magdalen, peculiarly pronounced 'maudlin'.

Later, after we had returned the boat and were sitting on the riverbank enjoying the pork pies and bottled beer that Ronald had packed, he began telling me more about his studies. About his tutor and the story he was working on. He mentioned the name of his college again and that is when I slipped up. Heady from the ale and fresh air, I commented on how, where I come from in Ireland, Magdalen is pronounced as it is spelled, like Mary Magdalene, the fallen woman of the Bible. It was only when the words had left my lips that I realized what I had said. Ronald looked stunned for a moment and then he burst out laughing. 'You're ... you're Irish?' he said, his eyes widening. 'Yes,' I replied, my shame giving way to pride as I stared into his bright eyes. 'Do you have a problem with that?' 'Not at all,' he said, smiling. 'It actually makes me like you even more. But how on earth did you manage to get a job with my father?'

I explained how it had all happened, told him what London meant to me, how mesmerized I was by it and how dearly I wanted to stay. 'So, you pretended to be English?' said Ronald, laughing again. 'Well, I have to hand it to you, Mary, you are some woman. Not many people could fool my father, but you have somehow managed it. I have nothing but admiration for you.'

Even though it was true, I didn't feel comfortable with Ronald thinking I had tricked Air Marshal Davidson. I did not want to rouse Ronald's suspicions, for him to see me as an Irish woman set on fleecing a grand, English family. He seemed to sense my discomfort, for he placed his hand on mine and stroked my skin tenderly. 'Look, if today is a day for confessions,' he said, his face growing serious, 'then I have one of my own. My father thinks that I am going to join the RAF after graduation, and I have no intention of doing so. Never in a million years.' Then, after he handed me another bottle of beer, we raised a toast. 'Here's to staying true to ourselves,' he said, clinking his bottle against mine. 'And never wasting a single second of our lives.'

While we were apart, Ronald and I exchanged letters, in which I told him more about my life in Ireland, a subject he seemed intrigued by, and he sent me the latest instalment of his story, The Other Lands, *a tale which I was totally enchanted by. Of course, our relationship had to be a strict secret. If his father found out about us, he would have dismissed me immediately. As hard as it was at times, we both knew that it was imperative that we always practise discretion. This was put to the test this weekend, when Ronald came home for Easter.*

It was rather comical, the display we put on at dinner, the two of us sitting there rigid as the statues on a church altar, asking the other to 'Kindly pass the salt' and 'Would you care for some tartare sauce for your fish?' The Davidsons had guests for dinner, a couple of rather dour old RAF officers. Their conversation was dull, but I recognized an opportunity to inveigle myself into another strand of English society. Trying not to meet Ronald's gaze, for fear of dissolving into laughter, I began asking the men about their work, about the planes they flew, the battles they had been involved in, the ranking system of the Air Force. It was intriguing to me, but I could hear Ronald trying to suppress his laughter when I asked one of them if the food was any good in the officers' mess. The man stared at me, his eyes boggling in his red face, like I had lost my senses. I knew that, with Air Marshal Davidson present, I was playing a dangerous game. After all, I had presented myself to him at my job interview as a respectable English girl from Surbiton. Surely such a girl would be familiar with the prowess and achievements of the RAF. Yet Davidson, for once, seemed relaxed, and began offering his own anecdotes about his exploits in the skies. Perhaps the port had loosened his tongue, or perhaps, and I am wary to even dare to articulate this, I had managed to pull it off. Perhaps I had convinced them that I was indeed 'one of them'.

Afterwards, when everyone had retired to bed, Ronald and I scurried back to our spot on the front step and at last let out all the mirth we'd been holding back.

'Would you kindly pass the salt?' Ronald scoffed, nudging me in my side. 'Oh, do tell me more about your work, Group Captain Bleacher. I have always been fascinated by the aeronautical business. Honestly, Mary, you should consider a career on the stage. You're a natural.'

Once the laughter had subsided, we sat for a moment in silence, watching as the smoke we exhaled drifted, mingling, into the black night sky. I felt a deep sense of contentment in the pit of my stomach. I had managed to maintain the façade for an entire evening. They believed in the person I was pretending to be, without question. Constance would be so proud of me.

'I have some news, Mary,' Ronald said, breaking into my thoughts.

He took my hand and told me that he had been offered a job in a publishing house. A friend of his tutor's, the proprietor of the publishing house, had lunched with them the previous week. Impressed by Ronald's passion for literature and his predicted first class honours degree, he had offered him a role as an editorial assistant for a new imprint he was launching, based in Bloomsbury. If Ronald wanted it, the job was his.

I exclaimed with excitement over the wonderful news. It was everything he wanted to do. Ronald went quiet then, and told me how his father had taken him to his RAF club the previous evening and told him he would be expected to turn up for training on 1st July, just three days after graduation. When Ronald had protested, his father was stony-faced.

'You'd be willing to ruin my reputation, to bring shame on this family, just to fulfil some boyhood flight of fancy, would you, Ronald?' his father had asked, an electric current of fury coursing beneath his words.

I was reminded of my father's reaction when Constance had visited the house that day, the shame that my parents perceived Fintan's actions as having brought upon the family, and my head burned at the injustice. Fintan had done what he thought was right, he had stood up for his beliefs. He was a great man. Before I could stop myself, I had blurted all this out to Ronald, fully expecting him to be as open-minded as he ever was. But when I had finished, Ronald looked at me strangely, like he was seeing me for the first time.

He shifted away from me on the step. 'Ronald?' I said, putting my hand on his arm. 'What is it?'

'Listen, Mary,' he said, lowering his voice. 'I completely understand your reasons for lying to my father about your background, and I do not agree with his views on the Irish. He is bigoted and narrow-minded. However, when it comes to . . . Republican activity, well, there are people here who would not take kindly to knowing who your brother was or what he did. In fact, that sort of talk could get you arrested, Mary. Do you understand?' Ronald's intense gaze on me, I nodded my head, feeling well and truly admonished.

When I went up to bed I lay there for hours, wide awake, running over the conversation in my mind. I heard Constance's voice in my head: 'Tread carefully.' How could I have been so stupid? So trusting of Ronald was I, so full of giddy feeling, I had let my mouth run away with me.

This morning, my worst fears were confirmed. I was summoned to Air Marshal Davidson's study and given an instant dismissal. When I asked him why I was being fired, he told me that I had committed fraud. That not only had I lied about being English, but I had also been extolling my brother's involvement in an attempt to overthrow the British government that was tantamount to treason.

'I should call the police and have you arrested,' he said, barely concealing his fury. I suspect the only reason he didn't was because he would be loath to expose that he had been tricked into hiring me in the first place. The Air Marshal was not one to grant mercy to anyone.

Instead, he told me I had twenty-four hours to get out of the house and that he would pay me only what I was owed. 'That will be all, Miss O'Connor,' he snarled, spittle flying from his tight lips as he emphasized the 'O'. My whole body was trembling as I gripped the banister and made my way up to the nursery to pack.

I could not believe it. That after everything we had been through, after all he had said about his father, Ronald had betrayed me so cruelly. Now, here I am, homeless and jobless, and it is all because of him. The man who wooed me with his dazzling eyes and sharp wit is nothing more than a Judas. Constance was right; the English are not to be trusted. I will never make that mistake again, and I will never forgive Ronald for what he has done to me.

17

Corinne
PRESENT DAY

'Rochester Place,' says Jimmy, shaking his head. 'It's been a long time since I heard that name, I can tell you.'

We are sitting in his cosily cluttered living room, sipping strong tea out of cracked china cups. I'm perched on the edge of a sagging, well-worn sofa, while Jimmy reclines opposite me on a brown, padded chair that looks like it was found at an office clearance sale, his laptop open at his feet. There is a gas fire and, above that, a plasterboard mantelpiece crammed with glass ornaments and porcelain figurines. A framed photograph of the Queen and Prince Philip hangs above the mantelpiece, their faded faces illuminated by the glow of the fire. The house and its contents feel borrowed, as though Jimmy is simply existing here, amongst the car boot sale cast-offs and discarded office furniture.

'Nidra said you know the area,' I say, placing my cup on the wooden fruit crate which has been repurposed as Jimmy's coffee table. 'That you grew up on Larkin Road, during the war.'

'Is she still going on about ghosts?' he says, his blue

eyes lighting up and a smile creeping across his weather-worn face. 'I don't know. She's got quite the imagination, has Nidra.'

'This isn't about ghosts, no,' I reply, curious that he immediately jumped from my innocent-seeming question to supernatural activity. 'It's about Rochester Place, and the people who lived there.'

His smiles fades, and a shadow darkens his face momentarily. I pause, recalling the stories Gran used to tell me about the people who lived through the war, how they don't like being reminded of it. I realize I need to tread carefully. Also, I haven't given Jimmy a suitable reason for asking about the house. I can hardly tell him that I think I might have received a call from the woman who lived there, a woman who I know died in 1940. So I decide to use my secret weapon.

'I'm asking on behalf of my Uncle Robin, actually. Robin Cunningham. He's a historian.' I hope that the mention of Mr House Detective will lighten the mood.

'Robin Cunningham? The chap from the telly?' interjects Jimmy, with a grin.

'Er, yes, that's him. He's been investigating the area for . . . for a project.'

'I see,' says Jimmy contemplatively, his eyes fixed on the table.

'I was just wondering if your father ever spoke about the people who lived there,' I say. 'The Davidson family.

They lived there up until 1940 – before your time, I'd imagine.'

I realize then that I have no idea how old Jimmy is. Looking at his thin shoulders poking through the threadbare fleece cardigan, the deep lines on his forehead and round his eyes, he could be anywhere from late sixties to early nineties. Despite his frailty, there is something so youthful about his demeanour.

'She was trapped.'

'I'm sorry?'

'Both of them were,' he says, a frown line deepening between his eyebrows. 'Trapped under rubble. Apparently, the house collapsed like a pile of Lego. My father . . . he . . . he never got over it.'

'Are you talking about Mary and Teresa?' I say, feeling rather unsettled suddenly. 'I read their names on the plaque in the spot where the house used to be. It said they had lost their lives there.'

Jimmy nods his head, his face grave. 'They lived there.'

'Did you know them?' I say, feeling a chill running through me.

'Not really,' says Jimmy. 'I was just a kid back then. I had no interest in the neighbours. I remember Rochester Place backed onto an Italian café. It was on the spot where your missus's gaff is now. Mario's, I think it was called.'

'My goodness,' I gasp. Another coincidence. 'I never realized. Do you know anything about the people who ran the café? It was Italian, you say?'

'I think so,' says Jimmy, glancing up at the carriage clock on the mantelpiece. 'But like I said, I was just a kid.'

'Did the Davidsons frequent Mario's?' I try to imagine what the café must have looked like back then. It feels good that, in some way, Tulsi is helping to keep a small part of the past alive.

'I have no idea,' says Jimmy, brusquely. 'I have very little recollection of those people. We kept ourselves to ourselves, my folks and me. My old man, he was a very private person. He . . . he suffered a lot during the war.'

He pauses and takes a sip of tea. I notice, when he sets it down, that his hands are trembling.

'Jimmy? Are you alright?'

He nods unconvincingly.

'He never spoke a word to me of what happened that night,' he says, fixing me with his pale blue eyes. 'I was sound asleep when it happened. It was Mum who filled me in, years later. It had been a particularly brutal air raid, she said, and Dad had come out of our house with a group of neighbours to see if they could find any survivors along that bit of road. When they got to Rochester Place, it was clear that no one would be left alive. The house was nothing more than rubble. He used to work on the underground like me, my old dad, and he was used to "jumpers" – you know, the poor souls who jump in front of trains? Well, Dad saw a lot of them, and he had to . . . clean up afterwards, you know? He never talked about it much, but when I asked him once how he could deal with it, he said it was best never to dwell on things like that. That the sensible approach was just to focus on what you had to do, and get it done.'

I nod my head. It is the same mantra I apply at work.

'So, it wasn't anything gruesome that affected him that night,' says Jimmy, drumming his fingers on the chair arm. 'It was the fact that, in the midst of all this smoke and rubble and mayhem, he spotted a woman's shoe – bright red it was – lying on the ground, virtually undamaged. After weeks of dead bodies and twisted limbs and air-raid sirens, it was this simple sight that affected him. But it was what happened the next day that really shook him to his core.'

The atmosphere alters suddenly, like the room has constricted. I am aware only of my breathing and the faint ticking of the carriage clock.

'Now, my dad was as solid as they come, a proper no-nonsense South Londoner,' continues Jimmy. 'Ghosts? "You're having a laugh," he'd say. But what he saw the day after the bombing changed him forever.'

'What did he see?'

'A woman,' says Jimmy. 'Standing at the top of Larkin Road, looking towards what had once been Rochester Place. She was dressed all in black, he said, with a green hair clip in her hair and a pair of red shoes. Now, this would all seem very normal, except my dad knew this woman. And he also knew that she had been killed in an air raid the day before. He was sure of this because he had helped remove her body.'

'Mary Davidson?' I say, flinching as a pile of junk mail comes through the letter box and lands with a thud on the mat. 'Your dad thinks he saw . . . her ghost?'

'Listen, I think it might be best to stop there,' says Jimmy, shifting in his seat. 'Tell your uncle to be careful round this story. When it comes to Mary Davidson, some things are best left alone.'

He drains his tea and picks up his laptop from the floor.

'Got a bit of work to do now,' he says, easing himself out of the chair.

I take the hint and follow him to the door.

'Thanks for the tea,' I say, as he lets me out. 'And for taking the time to talk to me about the house. I'm sorry if I touched a raw nerve, mentioning your dad.'

'My dad was a troubled man,' says Jimmy, clutching the laptop to his chest. 'Like many folk who lived through those years. As for me, don't worry about it. I like to talk about the past. Helps me make sense of today's nonsense.'

He nods his head then disappears back into the house. I stand for a moment, trying to take in what I have just heard. Yes, there is a great ghost story there, courtesy of Jimmy's dad, and it was interesting to learn about Tulsi's history, but as for the mystery phone call, I am still none the wiser. With a heavy heart, I make my way back to the flat. I am almost there when my phone beeps with two messages. Relief floods through me when I see the first. It's an email from Gran, sent yesterday but only now coming through:

Hello darling heart. I'm sorry that I haven't been in touch. I've had a bit of unexpected business to attend to here, which I shall tell you about in good time. Typing this on my PC as have mislaid my phone. Tell Robin I've signed his petition, hopefully it's not too late to save that beautiful tree. Sending all my love to you and Nidra. Please don't worry about me. I shall explain everything soon. Gran x

Unexpected business? I think to myself. Gran? The only business she ever has to deal with nowadays is how much seaweed she can gather in one armful on her daily walks on the beach. This sounds awfully intriguing. But why can't she tell me what it is?

I close the email and open the text message. It's from Nidra. *Posted an hour ago*, she has written. Underneath is a link to the Tulsi Twitter page. I feel sick as I read it. Someone with a Twitter handle called 'FREE THE UK' has posted underneath Tulsi's pinned tweet, which shows Rima accepting the award for local business of the year: *AVOID THIS MUCK. EAT LOCAL. EAT ENGLISH FOOD. LEAVE BRITAIN FOR THE BRITISH. FREE UK. DEATH TO FOREIGN SCUM.*

18

Teresa
JULY 1939

'Teresa, dote, will you go and collect some eggs for breakfast?'

I look out of the window. The sun is shining, and I cannot think of anything more perfect than a freshly boiled egg.

'Of course, Mary,' I reply, in my now almost-fluent English. 'It would be my pleasure.'

She smiles at me as I skip out into the garden, while Ronald peers over the top of *The Times*, with its harrowing headline: *JEWS FLEEING NAZI TYRANNY TURNED AWAY AT PORT*. I shudder as I recall Adolf Hitler's vicious-sounding voice on the wireless, and my own journey to safety. What if Katalin hadn't secured my passage on the SS *Habana*? What would have become of me?

I try to sweep such dark thoughts away as I stroll through the dewy grass towards the chicken coop, bees buzzing gently round my head. It is two years since I first arrived at Rochester Place, and in that time I have been filled with more joy than I ever thought possible.

From the moment I got here, Mary and Ronald went out of their way to make me feel welcome. Using the recipes she had learned at Señor Alvariz's house, Mary recreated delicious Basque dishes: pisto, bacalao, celery drenched in vinegar, olive oil and garlic, and roasted asparagus with Idiazabal cheese. Flavours that I never thought I would taste again, let alone in a grand English house. She bought a vinyl record of Spanish folk music which we listen to every evening – the three of us prancing about the drawing room like it's a festival day in the town square at Guernica.

I yearn for my sister every day, but particularly now, when this country stands on the brink of war.

Sometimes, at night, I dream of that moment when life in Guernica changed. In the dream, Katalin and I are standing, as we did that autumn day in 1936, arm in arm with José near the famous Tree of Guernica, the symbol of freedom for the Basque people. It was under the branches of this mighty oak, in past centuries, that each Lord of Biscay made their vow to uphold the liberties of the Biscayan people. We stand and listen, as loud-speakers broadcast across the square the election of José Aguirre as president of the new Basque republic.

I remember how Katalin's eyes shone as she listened to the new president declare, emphatically, that the Basque region would remain loyal to the Republic until the fascist scourge was defeated. 'We must do all we can to support the Republic,' said Katalin, squeezing my hand. 'It is what our parents would have wanted. To fight back against evil.'

I gulped down my fear. Talk of evil made me think of the fairy tales Katalin would read to me from my bumper book of stories, where innocent children were kidnapped by monstrous hags or brave knights had to defeat wicked rulers. To me, such evil stayed locked inside those books. It had no place in Guernica, my safe and magical home.

'We will support him every step of the way,' added José, kissing Katalin lightly on the nose. 'The bakery will be our HQ. After all, every loyal Republican needs his daily bread.'

At the time, I had thought José was simply expressing his desire to feed the members of the resistance. Now I know that Katalin, José and I were part of a complex web of facilitators, delivering tactics and messages to the fighters in the hills via bags of cinnamon buns.

'Say cheese.'

I turn round and see Luca hurtling towards me, holding an imaginary camera.

'Hey, Toto,' he calls, using his nickname for me. He thinks Teresa is a far too grown-up name. 'What are you doing?'

'What does it look like?' I say, pointing to the pile of eggs in my basket. 'Would you like to stay for breakfast?'

'No offence, but I prefer Papa's eggs,' he says, grimacing. 'That's why I came over. To see if you would like to come and have breakfast with *me*.'

'At the café?'

'Where else?'

I am torn. Though I love going to Mario's café and drinking endless cups of his delicious frothy coffee, the thought of Mary's boiled eggs and buttered soldiers makes my mouth water. However, Luca's smile wins me over, and I tell him to wait while I deliver the eggs to Mary.

The café is warm and bustling. As we sit sipping our coffee and nibbling sweet breakfast rolls, Luca shows me his latest wildlife book. Animals are Luca's obsession; he hopes to be a conservationist when he grows up. 'Papa is going to take me to London Zoo for my birthday in October,' he says excitedly, as he flicks the pages. 'Would you like to come too?'

I am just about to answer when there is an almighty crash. Instinctively, I throw myself onto the floor and cover my head with my hands, the noise taking me straight back to the market square. I hear the people at the next table gasp and Luca letting rip with a stream of expletives, but I cannot hear his father. My heart pounds as I raise my head but I am relieved to see Mario standing by the broken window, his feet covered in fragments of glass.

'Papa, we cannot let this go on,' cries Luca, rushing

to the door. 'I will go after whoever it was. I will make them pay.'

'Leave it,' says Mario, his voice barely a whisper.

I get to my feet and put my hand to my forehead, checking for wounds.

'Papa?'

Luca stumbles towards his father and takes the brick that Mario is holding in his hands. Without a word, he brings it over to me. There is a piece of paper wrapped around the brick, held in place with an elastic band. On it are written four words: *DEATH TO FOREIGN SCUM*.

'Who would do this?' I say, shakily. 'Why?'

'People think we are the enemy,' says Mario, walking over to the counter. 'They think we support Hitler, as Mussolini does.'

'But that's ridiculous,' I say, sitting down on the tall metal stool by the counter. 'You're not on Mussolini's side any more than my sister was on Franco's. Why can't people understand that?'

'Because they believe what they hear on the wireless,' says Mario, shrugging. 'And the nonsense Fred Harding spouts in the pub.'

'That old bigot,' says Luca, with a snort. 'I bet it was him that threw that brick.'

'Surely even he wouldn't stoop that low?' I say, recalling Harding's eyes as I walked down the street that first day – the hatred that no number of my smiles or 'good mornings' has been able to dispel.

'It seems that after months of shouting about the vermin that have invaded his country,' says Luca, 'he's now started targeting certain businesses, including ours.'

'Targeting? In what way?'

'Leaflets,' says Luca, almost spitting the word out. 'He's had a load of them properly printed out and all.'

'What do they say, these leaflets?'

'That foreigners such as me and Papa and Mary and you, Toto, are a "threat to national security",' he retorts heatedly, his voice rising in anger. 'That we are not to be trusted. That we are likely plotting against the state and that our businesses should be boycotted.'

'Forget Harding for now,' says Mario, visibly shaken. 'And come and help me clean up this mess.'

He hands us each a dustpan and brush and we set to work.

Later we return to Rochester Place, a sombre pair. Mario has sent a package of fresh mozzarella, tomatoes and olive oil for Mary, who takes them gratefully. 'Olive oil, how wonderful,' she says, turning the bottle over in her hands, like it is a precious jewel. 'Sure, we can only get the stuff at the chemist. Now, are you two hungry? I've got some soda bread warming in the oven. Perfect for mopping up that oil.'

She pauses then, noticing our grim expressions.

'What is it?' she says, placing the bottle on the kitchen table. 'Come now, let's find Ronald.'

She ushers us into the library, where Ronald is sitting,

working on his story. When we explain what happened, Mary's face darkens.

'I knew it,' she whispers, glancing nervously at Ronald. 'I knew we'd be scapegoated. Oh, to have English blood, eh?'

She snorts derisively then goes to the window and draws the heavy silk curtains.

Ronald sits silently, pen in one hand, the other resting on a pile of papers. After a few moments, he looks up at us and smiles, his face a welcome light amid the darkness of today's events.

'It is interesting to hear the methods Fred Harding is using,' he says thoughtfully, placing the pen behind his ear. 'Because they are as old as time. Bigots and tyrants like to think that they are bringing something new, something revolutionary, to the table, when really they are just following a tired old pattern. The good news is that they never win. It's what this story is all about. Here, let me read some of it to you.'

I watch as he flicks through the papers on his desk, his eyes sparkling. Ronald appears to enjoy working as an editor, often regaling us with funny tales: impersonating the poet who suffers sneezing fits if he gets a bad review, or the woman who turns up on the doorstep of the publishing house each morning with the latest instalment of her scandalous romance novel ('a little racy for our readers' tastes,' Ronald will mock-whisper as an aside). But it is clear that his passion lies in storytelling.

'Ah, here it is,' he says, pulling out a thick sheaf of papers. 'Now this little tale was inspired by a man called Clive Lewis, who taught me at Oxford University, and it tells the story of the inhabitants of a fictional place known as the Other Lands.'

'Sounds very interesting, Mr Davidson,' says Luca, sitting down on the bottom rung of the bookshelf ladder. 'I like adventure stories.'

'Now, Luca, this is more than just an adventure story,' says Ronald, looking up from his papers. 'It is a story as old as time.'

Mary is still standing by the window. I have never seen her this quiet before. I go across to her and take her hand. Then we sit side by side on the little window seat, my hand still in hers, but she seems tense and irritable, and she pushes my hand away. I wonder if she is thinking about her brother, how he fought to protect his own land from what he saw as an aggressive invader.

'The inhabitants of these lands,' continues Ronald, 'had lived and thrived there peacefully for centuries until, one misty morning, a fearsome ship docked in the harbour. On board was an army of warriors, formidable giants who said they came from a place called the Superior Land. The Superior Landers dominated the land and seas across much of the globe, and they had set their sights on the Other Land as the next target to conquer. From that moment, the Other Landers had to battle to defend their land, their culture, their language and their freedom from the invaders. Their darkest hour arrived in the form of Urick, a Superior Lander, who gave an impassioned speech one day – a speech that would change the course of the Other Landers' history.'

'Good luck to them,' says Mary drily, as Ronald pauses to turn the page. 'Though I don't hold out much hope. Look what happened to Ireland.'

'Never give up hope, my darling,' says Ronald softly. 'Now, where were we?'

'You had got to the bit where Urick, the Superior Lander, had given a speech,' says Luca, swinging his legs back and forth on the ladder.

'Ah, yes,' says Ronald, returning to the page. 'The delightful Urick. Now, in this speech he declared his manifesto outlining the aims of the Superior Landers, which included the outlawing of freedom of speech, the banning of religion and the enforcement of one language, with all others forbidden. He told the Other Landers they must give up their fight and conform, or else they would be imprisoned. This was his truth, his firm belief, and he was steadfast in this. No other view would be tolerated.'

'Like Fred Harding and his leaflets,' says Luca with a snort.

'He can't do that.' Beside me, Mary's voice drips with anger. 'Surely it's against the law. We should report him.'

She glances at Ronald for affirmation, but he simply shrugs.

'I'm afraid, my darling,' he replies with a sigh, 'in this country, unlike the Superior Lands, there is such a thing as freedom of speech which, unfortunately, applies to all – bigots like Harding included.'

'You see,' exclaims Luca, jumping down from the ladder in frustration. 'This is why I prefer animals.'

Though we have tried to view what happened at Mario's café as an isolated incident, it has turned out to be just the beginning of darker times. I can sense it as I go about my day – a palpable feeling of dread. Where before the house was filled with the sound of Mary's records blasting out of the gramophone, now all we hear is the news on the wireless.

Something bad is brewing, and I know that it is connected to Adolf Hitler, but I'm too scared to listen to the news reports. Memories of Guernica come flooding back when I hear talk of gathering troops and potential invasions.

Lying in bed at night, I remember the look on Katalin's face in the weeks following the bombing.

'We must get you out of here, Teresa,' she declared one day, as we huddled in José's car. 'It is not safe.'

'I am staying with you,' I told her, as José drove us away from the safe house we had been staying at in Bilbao. 'I can help you. I can collect the special buns from the bakery when we go back home.'

'Oh, Teresa,' Katalin yelled from the front passenger

seat. 'There is no home. There is no bakery. There is no anything in Guernica any more. It has been destroyed. Franco pulverized it.'

Katalin had never spoken to me like that before. The shock of her anger combined with the gravity of her words made my lip quiver. Soon fat tears were pouring down my cheeks.

'Shh, little one,' said Katalin, turning in her seat and placing her hand on my face. 'It is all going to be fine. There is a plan in place for the children. The British are organizing a ship to take you to England until the worst of it is over.'

'But I don't want to go to England,' I screamed. 'I want to stay with you.'

'It will only be for three months, Teresa,' said Katalin, her eyes filling with tears. 'I promise you. It will be a little holiday for you while José and I deal with what needs to be done here.'

'Why can't you come with me?' I cried. 'Don't you want to be safe too? Why do you have to keep on fighting, Katalin? You are not a soldier; you are my sister.'

They exchanged looks then – wary expressions that made my legs feel weak with fear. 'Three months will be over in a blink,' said José, as the signs for the station loomed up ahead. 'You'll be home before you know it. And until then you will be in England. It is safe there.'

I believed those words. England was safe. Rochester Place even more so. I felt sure, even when the first news reports from Germany began to trickle in, that we would remain untouched by war here at Rochester Place. Mary and Ronald were immune to all that, I reasoned. They lived in a separate, magical world, a world of stories and flowers and poets who sneeze.

I believed that right up until this morning, when Ronald calls me into his study and tells me that he has enlisted in the RAF.

'You can't do this,' I cry. 'You can't just leave us. And why would you join the RAF? I thought you didn't want to be like your father.'

Ronald raises an eyebrow at me. I realize my mistake straight away, for he has never mentioned his father or his involvement in the RAF. But I can't help exclaiming at his decision. It is not just the fact that he is following his dreadful father. I cannot understand how Ronald, the kind, gentle man who loves books and gardening and dancing to sentimental songs, would want to fly a plane and drop bombs on people. Noticing how distressed I am, he comes over to me and calmly takes my hand.

'Teresa,' he says, his soft eyes glistening, 'you must understand that this decision has not come easily to me. There is nothing I want more than to stay with you and Mary in our lovely home. Yet, if I don't act now, this home, this country, our freedom and everything we hold dear may be taken from us. This is not about wanting to drop bombs; it is about fighting back against evil. The

Nazis want to destroy our way of life. They are like the Superior Landers in our story and, to overcome them, we must be strong like the Other Landers and fight back. Do you understand?'

I nod my head sombrely. Of course I understand. I have seen this all before, in another country, in another war. I understand it so well that when I look up at Ronald, I do not see the kindly man who adopted me, the smartly dressed Englishman with a twinkle in his eye and a flower in his lapel. I see my sister, my Katalin, heading for her doom.

19

Mary
DECEMBER 1926
TOOTING

As I hauled my suitcase down the steps of Pevensey House, I saw a familiar figure standing by the railings. Ronald, his face pale and drawn. 'Mary,' he said, rushing towards me, arms out-stretched. 'I just heard the news. I'm so sorry.' I told him where to stick his 'sorry', then I pushed past him and marched off down the road. I could hear him running after me, so I hurried even faster, but he was soon on my heels.

'Mary, please,' he said, putting his hand on my shoulder. 'It's not what you think. It wasn't me who told my father about you. It was Albert.'

'Albert?'

I could not believe what I was hearing.

'But how?'

'He must have overheard us, on the step,' said Ronald, his face stricken with concern. 'Little brat has a habit of eavesdropping.'

I was so overcome with shock and relief I started to cry. I told him I was sorry that I had doubted him, but that I had no choice but to return to Ireland. It was clear I did not belong in London, or England for that matter.

'You can't do that,' cried Ronald, his voice trembling. 'I can't let you walk away from me, from us. The truth is, I have fallen in love with you, Mary. I think I fell in love with you the moment I saw you wading towards me through that bloody lake. I can't lose you. Not now. It would be . . . it would be like losing a part of myself.'

At those words, I felt a strange sensation wash over me, a mix of elation and terror. Ronald went on. He'd come up with a plan: I could return with him to Oxford. Now that his housemates had finished their studies and gone home, there was room in the cottage for me. We could stay there for a couple of months until the lease ran out, gather our thoughts. I was in such a state that I could not fully grasp what he was saying. Though I had strong feelings for Ronald, I had imagined that our relationship would blossom slowly. Now he was suggesting that I go and live with him, in sin. I thought of my parents and what they would say if they knew just how far I had fallen. All they wanted for me was to have a comfortable life with someone secure and reliable, like Pat McGinty; to be a mother, a homemaker, to be God-fearing and respectable. As though reading my mind, Ronald knelt in front of me, right there on the street, and took my hand. He told me that we would live alongside each other chastely, that he would honour and respect me, and that when the two months were over, we would have a plan. 'Or you can return to Ireland,' he said. 'The choice is yours.'

The decision was not a difficult one to make. In a duel between head and heart, love will always be the victor. I accompanied Ronald back to Oxford, where I found work as a waitress. In the weeks that followed we fell into an easy routine, with me working in Clark's tearoom while Ronald spent the day in the library immersed in The Other Lands.

Despite our closeness, there were still times when I had to stay in the shadows. When he graduated with a first class honours degree in English literature, I could not be there to see him do it. Once his parents had returned to London, Ronald and his house-mates came to find me at the tearoom. We spent a merry evening in the pub, where we toasted their success with pints of ale and mopped it up with a supper of pie and peas. I had never seen Ronald look so happy. It made my heart ache, as I knew what was coming. Soon he would be summoned to RAF Tangmere in Sussex. What would become of us then? Well, if Air Marshal Davidson got his way, then Ronald would embark on the life he had planned out for him, a life that didn't include being with an Irish woman from a family of Fenians. But I had outwitted his father once before and I knew I could do it again. I had not come this far to falter at the first sign of trouble. I had come to this country with a plan, and I intended to see it through.

I soon discovered that I would not need to battle any further, as it turned out that Ronald was stronger than I had given him credit for and had no intention of following convention. One even-ing, he poured us a dram of whisky each, and we sank into the velvet sofa by the roaring fire in the little snug. As the whisky loosened his lips, Ronald began to talk, for the first time, about his mother, Air Marshal Davidson's first wife.

Rosemary Stephenson had been a free spirit, born ahead of her time. She had studied the arts, modelled in a photographic studio

185

and planned to travel the world. By the time she was eighteen years old, her bohemian family, who lived in a rambling pile outside Oxfordshire, were heavily in debt. It was arranged for Rosemary, the eldest daughter, to marry a friend of the family, Oliver Davidson, in return for a small sum of money which would keep them afloat. Davidson, at the time a socially awkward man who had never been able to establish a relationship, in turn would gain a beautiful, intelligent wife to parade around on his arm. Ronald told me how he had found old letters written from his mother to his aunt, describing her unhappiness at the match and how Davidson treated her as dismissively as he would a servant. He barely spoke to her, and tolerated her in his bed for the sole purpose of producing an heir for the illustrious Davidson line. It did not take long for Rosemary to fall pregnant, and her spirits lifted somewhat when Ronald was born, not least because it meant, as a nursing mother, she would be spared the indignity of lying with Oliver in his loveless bed.

Rosemary adored her small boy, and Ronald recalled happy outings to the seaside with her – she had loved the sunsets at Whitstable – as well as trips to the theatre and the glasshouses at Kew, all accompanied by liberal hugs and kisses. It was a halcyon period for both mother and son, but then Oliver insisted on sending Ronald away to boarding school at the tender age of four, and the happy times came to an end. Rosemary was devastated to be so far from Ronald and fell into a deep depression. When Ronald was eleven years old, she couldn't take it any longer.

Pouring another tot of whisky, Ronald took a shuddering breath as he told me that his mother's death had been brought

186

about by despair, and not, as his father had announced in the Times *obituary*, a short illness. 'Did she kill herself?' I asked him, feeling sick to my core that someone could be so unhappy as to think death was the only escape. Ronald didn't answer my question, but his silence said all I needed to know.

We sat up all that night, talking. Ronald told me how he thought he had never been able to bond with his father because he had so much of his mother in him: his looks, his joie de vivre, his desire for adventure. All the things that terrified his father. She was the woman Oliver Davidson couldn't tame, who had refused to bend to his will. He hadn't cared that she didn't love him. It was the fact that she didn't respect him that had rankled most. That, and the fact that she was more intelligent than him. She was forever quoting Shakespeare and Blake and giving her thoughts about art and music and books. To Oliver Davidson, Rosemary was an alien species, a threat to his traditional views. Ronald believes that a large part of his father was relieved when he walked into the bedroom that day and saw what she had done. He was finally free again. Free to remarry a woman like Celia, a young skittish socialite who would hang on his every word, and give him, in Albert and Daphne, a son he could mould in his image and a timid daughter to be bullied into obedience.

And then, as the dawn was breaking and a shaft of pale morning sun trickled into the room, illuminating his tired face, Ronald told me something that made me sit up. His mother had known that Ronald might face difficulties once she was gone. She'd known that he didn't fit into the family, just as she hadn't, so she'd made provisions for Ronald before she died. She bequeathed him

187

a house that had been in her family for generations, and a small trust fund she had spent years investing shrewdly. It was something just for Ronald, something of his own that Oliver could not get his hands on or try to control. It could be, said Ronald, the key to our freedom.

The house, more of a mansion than a mere house really, is everything I thought it would be and so much more. It is located in Tooting, an area of South London that I have so far been unfamiliar with. As we strolled to the house, Ronald told me a little of its history. It was built in 1824, planned as part of a crescent of grand houses, but the developer had run out of money and only one house was completed, Rochester Place. Ronald's great-uncle, Charles Stephenson, a solicitor and amateur naturalist, bought the house at a discounted price and set about turning it into a horticultural haven, a little piece of the countryside in the heart of South London. On his death, Charles bequeathed the house to his niece, Ronald's mother, who with remarkable foresight put it in Ronald's name, to be given to him when he turned twenty-one.

Yet I rather thought Ronald had taken a wrong turning as he led me down Larkin Road. It was just an ordinary urban street. This was no place for the kind of house he had described, the grand Georgian pile bursting with plants and oddities, I thought to myself as we passed a rather rundown strip of terraces. But then Ronald took a left turn and we found ourselves walking down what appeared to be a quiet country lane, with a cobbled path, toffee-coloured stone walls and bramble bushes lining either side.

The sounds of omnibuses and street sellers fell away as we walked. It felt as though we were stepping into a fairy tale.

At the end of the path, I caught a glimpse of chimney and a flash of railing which, as we drew near, transformed into a house.

'Welcome to Rochester Place,' said Ronald, taking my arm and leading me through the wrought-iron gate. 'Now don't let its current state put you off. I'm afraid it's been left to decay in recent years. It was leased to a charity after Uncle Charles's death and then stood empty for decades. If we do decide to live here, we'll have a lot of work to do to restore it to its former glory. And, darling, I fully understand if you'd rather just sell it. After all, it's not in the most desirable part of town.'

But as Ronald chattered beside me about rusty railings, chipped paint and broken windows, I stood there, enchanted. It was the most breathtaking house I had ever seen. Squinting my eyes, I had a vision of how it must have looked when it was first built. I saw past all its flaws and into the true heart of it. The peeling paint on the door had once been a glossy red, the colour of ripe cherries; the overgrown garden had been a haven of plants and flowers, herbs and vegetables; the broken lantern above the door had once glowed with light, beckoning Charles Stephenson home after a long day at the office.

'This is it,' I said, turning to Ronald, with a certainty that I had never felt before. 'This is our home.'

A month later Ronald and I were married at Balham Register Office. It was a small but intimate ceremony, attended by a couple of Ronald's Oxford friends and Peggy the housemaid, who I had remained close to. After a picnic of champagne and lemon sponge cake, nestled on blankets on Tooting Common, we returned to our ramshackle old house as man and wife.

That evening, drunk on love and champagne, we danced to our favourite songs on the gramophone and promised each other the world.

'Vow to me you will write your book,' I said to Ronald, as he spun me around the room.

'I will,' he said, still dressed in his wedding suit. 'And of you, my love, I ask only one thing.'

'What is that?'

His face grew serious. He stopped dancing and took my hand in his.

'That you will never hide your Irishness again. That you will always be proud of who you are and where you come from.'

I thought back to that morning in Pevensey House when, raw from what I thought was his betrayal, I had vowed to take revenge on Ronald. I loved this man, yet I couldn't help but hear Constance's voice in my head, the words she'd left me with when she said goodbye outside Pevensey House that day: 'Tread carefully, Mary.' In this country I will always have to be on my guard, and there may be a time when, to protect myself, I have to cover up my Fenian past.

'I swear that I will always be your Mary,' I said, taking his face in my hands and kissing him deeply. With that, he twirled me round the room until we both got so dizzy we collapsed in a giggling heap onto the sofa. That night, we made love for the first time as man and wife, and I fell asleep in his arms. Surely no two people had ever been happier.

Then there was no time for dancing. We had our work cut out restoring the house, not simply to its former glory but to what we wanted it to be. A warm and welcoming home. At first it was a daunting prospect, but help came in the shape of a long-dead uncle. A few weeks after the wedding we were clearing out the great library, a vast space that takes up almost half of the first floor, when we came across a book. As we leafed through the time-worn pages of The Diary of an Urban Naturalist, *we soon realized it was penned by none other than Charles Stephenson. I took the book to bed with me every night, so captivated was I by the voice of Ronald's long-dead great-uncle – not least his meticulous documentation of how he had transformed the garden. Leaving Ronald to focus on the interior, I set about applying Charles's advice to the tangle of undergrowth that currently constituted the Rochester Place garden.*

'Though we are in the dead of winter' – Charles's entry for this date in 1826, one hundred years ago – 'there is life bubbling and fizzing under the soil, little bulbs and seedlings waiting patiently for their day in the sun.'

Those words give me hope, as I sit here watching my husband drape holly leaves and mistletoe across the fireplace. We have toiled and strained these last few months. Now it is time to rest, and wait for the fruits of our labour to ripen.

And as the buds ripen, I feel something else begin to stir, deep within me, hidden away for the winter months. A baby.

20

Teresa
AUGUST 1939

In the week since Ronald told me he was leaving to join the RAF, I have been plagued by a recurring nightmare. Each time it is the same: Rochester Place is on fire, and I am trapped behind railings calling out for Ronald and Mary. In an attempt to lull my frazzled mind, last night Ronald strapped me into the passenger seat of his shiny black Austin 18 and took me for a drive through the slumbering streets of South London. Within ten minutes, the steady hum of the engine sent me into a deep sleep. I woke just as we were pulling up outside Rochester Place, where Mary was standing in the rain, opening the gates.

She carried me from the car and tucked me into bed. I slept through the night undisturbed by dreams. This morning, for the first time in a while, I feel rested as I walk down the stairs to breakfast, the smell of buttery scrambled eggs in the air making my stomach rumble.

Mary greets me with a kiss as I walk into the kitchen.

'Morning, dote. You look a lot better today.'

As she finishes preparing breakfast, I hear a loud

banging noise coming from outside. I go to the window and see Ronald and Mario, shirtsleeves rolled up, grappling with a huge piece of tarpaulin.

'What are they doing?' I ask, as Mary plates up the eggs.

'They're building an Anderson shelter,' she says. 'Ronald thinks we're going to need one if war is declared. Come on now, eat up your breakfast.'

I have never heard of an Anderson shelter, but Mary explains that it is somewhere safe to run to when the bombs start falling. A little bunker that you half bury in the ground, then heap a load of earth on top. The corrugated material is very strong, and can apparently withstand the force of a bomb.

As I chew my eggs, I can't help but imagine cowering underground in the damp darkness while bombs explode overhead. Still, better that than being above ground.

After breakfast, Mary and I go outside to see how the men are getting on. Ronald is hammering the tarpaulin into place while Mario holds it steady. They look up as we approach, and Ronald asks us what we think.

'It looks good,' says Mary, placing her hand on Ronald's shoulder. 'Well done, lads. I bet you're gasping for a cup of tea. Why don't you take a break and come inside? I've got a tray of shortbread just out of the oven too.'

When the adults have gone, I stand looking at the strange intrusion. It seems so out of place, a harsh, ugly object in our lush garden.

'Hey, Toto.'

I look up and see Luca climbing over the wall.

'What do you think?' I say, pointing to the shelter. 'Apparently this thing is going to protect us if the Nazis start bombing.'

'It reminds me of a badger's sett,' says Luca, peering inside. 'A good idea. This is how most animals protect themselves from predators. They burrow underground.'

'But we're not animals. We're people and we live in houses.'

He sees my desolate face and his eyes light up. 'I have an idea. How about we make it more homely. Decorate it.'

'With what?'

'Anything we like,' he says. 'Let's start with some flowers to brighten it up.'

I watch as he runs over to the hydrangea bush and starts plucking off the blue flowers. Returning to the shelter, he places the blooms across the top.

'See, it looks better already,' he says. 'Now, I have just the thing. Wait here.'

He jumps back over the wall, then returns a few minutes later with an armful of garden gnomes.

'The old man who used to live in our flat left these behind,' he says, with a glint in his eye. 'Papa thinks they're silly, but I think they will look good on here. They will be our watchmen.'

We set to work placing the cheerful gnomes around

the shelter. While we are arranging more foliage, Luca haltingly admits he is scared about the impending war. 'What will happen if we don't get to the shelter in time? I don't want to die, Toto. Not yet anyway.'

'Ronald said there will be a siren,' I say, taking a cluster of hydrangeas and threading them round the gnomes' feet, 'when a bomb is coming. The siren will give us the warning so we will have time to get to the shelter. In Guernica, we were not so lucky.'

'What happened in Guernica?' he says, looking up from his work.

I stare at the blue flowers and the rosy-cheeked gnomes, then, taking in a deep breath, I begin to tell Luca what happened that day at the market square.

Katalin and José had gone up into the hills with a reporter from a French newspaper who they had met in a bar a few days earlier. He was hoping to take some photographs to accompany a piece he was writing on the war, and needed help locating resistance fighters who were hiding out in the hills. They had sent word to their contacts and had arranged to drive out there to set up a shoot. Katalin explained all this to me that morning consolingly, when I protested that I didn't want to stay with our elderly neighbour, Señora Babette. I knew she was doing something exciting and I wanted her to take me with them. Señora Babette was no fun. All she talked about was cooking and cleaning and her painful knees. When I realized that Katalin was not going to budge, I relented and accompanied Señora Babette to the market, trailing behind as the old lady rooted around the boxes of soil-covered vegetables. While she was trying to find an unspoiled pepper, my attention was drawn to the flower stall, where a display of tall pink lilies was filling the air with its sweet scent. The enticing fragrance of those lilies overpowered the usual market smells of raw meat and earthy vegetables and I wanted to get close to it, to fill my nose with its loveliness.

But as I leaned forward to smell the flowers, an almighty roar blasted through the air. It sounded like a thousand engines all starting up at once. I looked up and saw what appeared to be a huge flock of geese, dark shapes moving in formation, their wings splayed out across the afternoon sky. But as the shapes got closer, I saw that they were not birds, they were fighter planes, and they were heading straight for us. I don't recall much more after that, besides the fierce wind whipped up by the planes, which caused the market stalls to topple over. Some hurtled through the air, knocking down shoppers like skittles, while, in the sky above, the might of the Condor Legion prepared to unleash hell. The next few moments are not so much a memory as fragments – broken images that appear then shatter in my mind's eye whenever I try to recall what happened. As I describe it to Luca, the smell of lilies lodges itself in my nose, just as it did when I hit the ground as the first of the bombs exploded, the weight of the kindly stall holder who had smiled at me just moments earlier pressing down on me. I stayed there for what seemed like hours, trapped underneath her body, before getting up and stumbling through the smoke and the broken bodies towards the Iglesia Santa María, where, miraculously, Katalin found me huddled next to the broken remains of the statue of St Barbara. She gasped when she saw me, and asked me if I was hurt. I saw that she was staring at my dress. When I placed my hand on my chest, it was wet and sticky. When I looked down I saw that the dress I was wearing, my favourite pale pink one with embroidered black flowers on the skirt and sleeves, was drenched in blood.

Katalin quickly checked me over for wounds, but I only had some scratches on my knees from where I had thrown myself on the ground. The thick red blood was not mine. And then I remembered the flower stall holder pressed down on me, her eyes lifeless, blood spilling from her open mouth. Katalin tried to get me to change my clothes when we reached Bilbao, but I refused to take the dress off. I doggedly held on to that dress as the scarlet turned dark brown and crusted, until it was eventually cut from me and burned by the medical examiners at Southampton Docks. When I arrived at Stoneham Camp, I had been scrubbed clean, yet I would never forget the horror, never forget that blood.

When I have finished, I look up at Luca. He has tears in his eyes. It is then that I realize he is the only person I have ever spoken to in such detail about that day. Not even Mary knows what happened. Better to show her my smiles than my pain – no one wants a sad child.

'I want you to know, Toto,' he says, taking my hand and kissing me on the cheek, 'that if that happens here, I will be right next to you. We will fight those Nazis together.'

'How can we do that, Luca? We are only ten years old. It is adults who make the law, adults who start wars.'

'I don't have any belief in the laws of men,' says Luca, puffing out his chest. 'I only believe in the laws of the animal kingdom. We must stick together, Toto, like lions in a pride.'

He flinches and puts a hand to the back of his head, where his dark curls meet the nape of his neck.

'Luca, what is it?'

'Someone threw this at me,' he says, picking up the large stone that has now settled at his feet and glancing around.

'Greasy spics! The state of yers.'

I look up and see a boy standing at the edge of the garden. He has cropped mousy hair and piercing blue eyes. He takes a step forward and I freeze. His hands are full of stones.

'Get lost, sfigato,' shouts Luca, getting to his feet. 'And take your stones with you before I punch your lights out.'

The boy sticks his middle finger up then disappears round the side of the house.

'Idiot,' says Luca, shaking his head as he returns to where I am sitting. 'I swear this area is getting worse and worse.'

Just then, Mary comes out with a tray of lemonade. Luca is shaking with anger. I put my hand on his shoulder.

'Let's keep what just happened to ourselves,' I whisper. 'I don't want Mary to worry. She's got enough to think about with Ronald leaving.'

Luca nods his agreement and puts on his best smile as Mary approaches.

'Well done, you two,' she says, when she sees what we have done. 'It looks beautiful. Like an Irish fairy fort.'

Then Ronald and Mario join us, and we all drink a toast to the shelter.

'God bless this shelter,' says Ronald, raising his glass. 'And may it, and its noble gnomey nightwatchmen, protect us all.'

Three days later, Ronald departs for training at RAF Tangmere, but before he leaves he makes sure that Mary and I know what to do in case of an emergency. He instructs us on how to use the shelter and tells us to run to it as soon as an air-raid siren goes off, without any hesitation, and to stay there until we get the All Clear. He also installs a telephone on the sideboard in the hallway. It is a heavy black one, which Ronald says is made of Bakelite. 'It puts my mind at rest to know that if there is an emergency you can telephone for help,' he says, as Mary and I take turns practising how to dial 999 and memorize the exchange code: BAL 672.

After a farewell tea party, where we are joined by Luca and Mario – who bring delicious cream-filled cannoli to share – and Ronald and Mary dance to 'Spread a Little Happiness', their favourite song, one last time, Ronald packs his kitbag and heads to the station. Mary wanted to go all the way to the station to say goodbye as he boarded the train, but he told her he wanted us to see him off here, standing in the doorway of Rochester Place, the warm and happy home he would be returning to. 'I want to keep that image with me as I go,' he says, pulling us towards him. 'My two girls waiting for me in our lovely home.'

We wave goodbye and, as his tall figure disappears down the cobbled pathway, I hear Mary whisper: 'Keep him safe, God. Please keep him safe.' Something seems to leave her in that moment, a lightness of spirit that has brought me through my own darkness. Now she trudges back into the house like her feet are made of lead, collapses on her bed, and sobs so hard I fear she might break.

21

Mary

It happened in the middle of the night. A dull pain in the base of my stomach that swiftly intensified. I went to the bathroom and what I saw left me in no doubt as to what was happening. I began to scream. Within moments Ronald was by my side, and the next thing I knew I was in hospital, lying in a bed listening as a dispassionate young male doctor informed us, in a sterile, blunt fashion, that our baby had died in my womb. I was told I would need to stay in hospital while 'nature takes its course'.

We returned home two days later. The house, which had glowed with life and possibility for the duration of the pregnancy, now seemed nothing more than an impeccably decorated mausoleum. Ronald settled me into bed, made me cups of tea that I left untouched on the bedside table, kissed my head, held me in his arms, and whispered that he loved me and that I was very brave. But I did not feel brave, I felt broken.

Later he brought the wireless into the room and placed it on the table. 'Maybe a little music and chat might soothe you,' he said, his voice artificially bright. When he left the room, the clipped tones of the BBC World Service filled the air, and I lay on my back, staring at the ceiling as news of cricket scores and a house fire in Wales were delivered in a grave monotone. Then I heard a familiar name: Constance Markievicz. Dead at the age of fifty-nine, of complications related to appendicitis. The newsreader handed over to a correspondent, and I sat up and clutched my knees to my chest as the Irishman reported how, in the weeks leading up to her death, Constance had given away what remained of her wealth and had died amongst the poor, 'where she wanted to be'.

I got to my feet shakily and switched off the wireless. Then I collected my hat and coat and slipped out of the house. The church was empty when I arrived, the air full of incense from that morning's Mass. I went across to the side of the altar and lit two candles: one for Constance, my fallen comrade and the true Queen of Ireland, and one for my baby. 'Look after her, Constance,' I whispered, as I genuflected before making my way out of the church. 'And I promise you both, I will not let you down. I will be strong, and I will carry on fighting until I draw my last breath.'

Almost ten years after I lit those candles, I suffered what was to be my last miscarriage. This one, like the others, occurred late into the pregnancy, and when I was examined, the doctor found that the baby had grown in my fallopian tube. An ectopic pregnancy. I had to be operated on, and when I came round I was told by the doctor, with Ronald – my anchor – gripping my hand tightly, that I could no longer bear children. I had thought that such news would cause me to shout and scream and cry, but instead I just felt numb.

We came home to Rochester Place and set about planning a

childless future. Life resumed its daily rhythms. Ronald commuted to Bloomsbury each day, returning home to eat supper then work on The Other Lands until it was time for bed. I felt him slowly disconnect from me, a ball of grief to be avoided lest it taint the entire house. I busied myself by taking on some voluntary work with the WI at the church. The women there were pleasant enough, but all they could talk about was their large broods of children. I had nothing to contribute to their conversations and I found myself, once again, an outsider. So I quietly withdrew my services.

Thank goodness for Mario and Luca, who recently opened a café on Garratt Lane. The café is the one place I can go to where I feel welcome. Luca regales me with his latest animal facts while Mario tells me stories of his family back in Calabria, and we share a common grief – he having lost Luca's mother to cancer nine years ago. I feel safe with Mario and Luca. Perhaps it is because, like me, they are outsiders.

Last night, after weeks of keeping his distance, Ronald tried to make love. Though I have craved his touch, the feeling of him so close only reminded me of what we have lost. I can never give him children. I am damaged, unhealthy. What kind of woman cannot give her husband a family? Sensing my hesitance, Ronald stopped, asking me if I was alright. Looking deep into the eyes of the man I love, the pain and hurt of the last decade came tumbling out of me. Through sobs I told him that I feared he would leave me, that I had not given him what a wife is supposed to give, that he would be better off finding someone else: a young, healthy woman who will give him babies.

'Do you think that is why I love you?' he said, his eyes filling with tears. 'Because I want you to give me babies? Mary, when I first met you, standing by that lake in St James's Park, I saw a kindred spirit. With you, I knew I would have a lifetime of love and conversation and happiness. Remember what you said to me on the doorstep that evening? Follow your dreams? Well, I did that. But the writing and my job and even our home, they are not my dream; you are. Had we been blessed with babies then that would have been a bonus, but the gods have already given me my treasure. You're my love, Mary, my free-spirited fairy queen. You're all I've ever wanted. All I need in this world.'

Then he held me in his arms, and I fell asleep, safe in the knowledge that I have Ronald, and that I am enough.

People talk of serendipity, of being in the right place at the right time, of destiny seeking you out and, throughout my life, people and situations have been placed in front of me just when I needed them most. It happened in Achill when Constance appeared at the door, and again in St James's Park when Ronald waded into the lake to retrieve my hat. Today, the universe saw fit to present me with another opportunity, one that did indeed seem sent from the heavens, and it happened on Richmond High Street of all places.

I had gone to collect a parcel from the menswear shop near the green that Ronald favours for his shirts. As I was making my way back to the station, I was approached by a striking young woman with thick, dark curly hair and a smile that was strangely familiar.

'Mary?' she said, placing her hand on my arm. 'It is you, isn't it? Do you remember me? You used to look after me when I was a child.'

And then I recognized her. Little Lorea: my turnip-carving companion, the girl with the infectious laugh and beautiful hair, now grown into quite the young woman. We embraced and I found myself shedding a tear. Señor Alvariz and his family had given me my first taste of London. They had treated me kindly and taught me their language and culture, while encouraging and showing interest in mine.

She told me that her parents were still in Bilbao and were happy and well, having lived through and survived the civil war. Señor Alvariz, now retired, has taken up watercolour painting, yet he has lost none of his political zeal and is following the rumblings in Europe with interest. It seemed from her demeanour and her chat that Lorea had inherited her father's spirit. It was clear that the little girl I had regaled with stories of fierce warrior-women had grown up to be quite the revolutionary, and my ears pricked up when I heard what she had to say.

'It is so fortuitous that I should bump into you,' said Lorea, her youthful face growing serious for a moment. 'You see, I am working on something at the moment that could really benefit from the input of someone like you, someone with your knowledge and discretion. I could tell you more about it if you are interested. Though this mission is rather a taxing one, and would require quite a lot of your time, should you choose to come on board. We could, perhaps, go somewhere a little quieter to discuss it.'

I thought about my routine at that point: long empty days

spent in the house, avoiding the nursery, distracting myself by sitting for hours in Mario's café. But there are only so many cups of coffee one can consume, only so many hours one can dedicate to grief. Something had to shift and here, in the shape of my one-time charge Lorea, was an opportunity, a sign, just like Constance's arrival had been. Talking to her over a cup of tea a little later, as she outlined the task, I suddenly felt alive again. There was no question. This job was made for me. I had a duty to do it.

I told her that I would be happy to take it on. And then, pulling a notebook from her handbag, she scribbled down a name and address. 'I shall telephone the contact this afternoon to let her know you're on board,' she said, her face beaming. 'Thank you so much, Mary. I can rest easy knowing that this job is in such safe hands.' We bid farewell then. As I watched her walk away – the child I had cared for all those years ago, now a confident, revolutionary woman of nineteen – I felt a surge of energy course through me. It felt like Constance had sent Lorea to remind me who I am and what I have been sent here to do. In a matter of moments, I was brought back to life.

22

Corinne

It is quiet in the café now that the breakfast rush is over. I agreed to cover for a couple of hours while Nidra and Rima go to the bank to discuss taking out a mortgage for this place. I am keeping my fingers crossed for them. After the shock of receiving those racist tweets yesterday, the last thing they need is the threat of losing the café. It is so much a part of who they are, I cannot imagine how they will cope without it.

I am lost in my thoughts when I feel a presence. I look up. Jimmy's steely gaze is fixed on me, and he has his money pouch in hand to pay for the scrambled eggs and tea he has spent the last hour nursing while typing on his laptop.

'All good?' I say, taking his card and tapping the machine. 'I'm no Rima when it comes to scrambled eggs, but by the look of your empty plate they can't have been too bad.'

'They were just the job, love,' he says, doffing his baker-boy hat. 'I'm no snob when it comes to food. Where are the girls today?'

'They've gone to the bank for a meeting,' I say, handing Jimmy his card and receipt. 'To discuss buying this place.'

'Ah, yes, Rima mentioned something about that,' he says. 'These London landlords are an unscrupulous bunch, hiking up the rents whenever they like. It's criminal. I don't know, I remember a time when Tooting was full of family-run businesses. Now it's just a sea of global chains and . . . well, never mind. Pop the change in the tip box. And tell the girls I send my best.'

'I will. Thanks, Jimmy,' I say, watching as he shuffles out of the café, his red hat a beacon against the grey morning gloom.

I slot the two-pound coins into the tip box that is wedged next to Saira's little glass ornament that has always sat, pride of place, on the shelf by the till. 'That's my lucky charm,' Saira used to say, if anyone tried to move it. 'It was given to me the day I signed the lease for Tulsi, and it has brought me good fortune ever since.'

I smile as I recall my late mother-in-law's belief in fate and lucky charms and karma, and how fully Nidra has followed her mother's beliefs. Our flat is littered with keepsakes, charms, white feathers and lucky pennies that Nidra has collected along the way, and though I don't share in her superstitions, the presence of those talismans gives me a strange sense of well-being – a feeling that, somehow, some way, we are being protected.

'Looks like we got the mortgage, Corinne.'

I turn to see Nidra and Rima, their faces beaming.

'Oh, that's wonderful news,' I cry, running out from behind the counter and swallowing them both in a hug. 'I knew you'd do it. I just knew it.'

'You tell Corinne all about it,' says Rima, extricating herself from us. 'I'd better get a start on the lunches. It's after eleven already.'

Nidra and I pull out a couple of stools and sit at the counter.

'So then,' I say to Nidra, excitedly, 'what did they say?'

'Well, the loan's been approved in principle. There's a few more bits of paperwork to deliver and sign, but the mortgage adviser said it should all go through without any problem.'

'That's amazing,' I say. 'We should go out tonight and celebrate. I'm not working until tomorrow evening.'

'I'd like that,' says Nidra. 'Thought let's not say "celebrate" just yet. I don't want to tempt fate until everything has been signed and sealed. But, when it is, we'll have the biggest party.'

'Definitely,' I say. 'Wait till Gran hears. She'll be over the moon.'

'Can you come and give me a hand with these salads, Nidra?'

Rima's voice reverberates through the café.

'I'd better go,' Nidra says, kissing me on the cheek. 'But it's a definite yes to tonight. We haven't been out in ages. How about we go to the Portuguese place in the market? I fancy a bowl of that delicious fish stew. Meet you there around seven?'

'Sounds great,' I say, draining my coffee as Nidra grabs her apron from the hook behind the counter. She is just fastening it when Rima comes running out of the kitchen holding her phone.

'Look at this,' she says, handing the phone to Nidra.

'Oh my God,' my wife says, her face stricken as she looks at the screen.

'What is it, Nidra?'

'Another tweet,' she says, handing me the phone. 'But this time they've posted a video.'

I take the phone. There is an image of a Union Jack, and a play button. I press it, and after a lengthy pause the video begins. It is a pretty amateurish affair. No audio, just a large piece of paper spread out on a carpeted floor. The words *KEEP BRITAIN FOR THE BRITISH. FOREIGN SCUM NOT WANTED HERE* printed across it As I stare at the screen, the reassuring sounds of Sade's greatest hits and the smell of frying onions fade away, and my body freezes. But it is not the message, vile as it is, that has shocked me; it is the background. The ornaments on the mantelpiece, the framed photo of the Queen and Prince Philip on the wall.

'Nidra,' I say, looking up from the phone in disbelief. 'I know who this is, who has been sending these messages. It's Jimmy.'

23

Teresa

In a bid to help with the war effort, and to distract us from worrying about Ronald, Mary suggested we turn the kitchen at Rochester Place into a food bank. Many of the local businesses, including Mario's, have donated tinned food and packets of rice and beans, and some of the local women have even baked cakes. Quite a feat, as well as being a generous gesture in these days of rationing. Mary spends most evenings poring over her *Stork Wartime Cookery Book*, which gives no end of ideas for economizing, planning meals and baking without sugar. Our days are spent packing boxes with tinned fruit, pulses and wedges of cake, then leaving them by the gate for Luca to deliver to those in need on his bicycle, which he has fitted with a handy trailer. Though our industriousness has helped keep Ronald and his possible fate at the back of our minds during the day, in the evening there is no escaping the dreaded wireless, which is turned up to full volume from 6 p.m. until Mary retires to bed at eleven. I try to avoid it by collecting eggs in the garden or reading in my room, but Luca, who has become something of a newshound, is always keen to fill me in on what I have missed.

Tonight, when he returns with the empty boxes, he comes dashing over to the chicken coop, where I am sitting chatting to Betty and Sheila, the little bantams.

'Toto,' he cries breathlessly. 'Have you heard what's happened at Dunkirk?'

I haven't heard, nor do I particularly want to; but, as always when there is a development, my thoughts leap to Ronald.

'Does it involve the RAF?' I say nervously.

'I don't think so,' says Luca. 'But I heard on the wireless that the Germans have got our troops surrounded. They're trapped on the beach there. You know Mrs Nelson from Number 47? Well, her son is one of them. She's distraught.'

'That's terrible,' I say, thinking of Katalin and Ronald, wherever they may be. 'They will have to be rescued.'

'Easier said than done when you've got German tanks and guns surrounding them,' says Luca, shaking his head. 'And here we are delivering food parcels and cooking pasta, safe as houses.'

I nod my head, as images of the market square, the overturned stalls, the bodies lying pressed together, appear before my eyes.

'Yes,' I say as Luca disappears over the wall. 'Safe as houses.'

A few days later, as Mary and I make our way home after collecting a donation from the WI, we see that Heinemeyer's, the German bakery on Garratt Lane, has been vandalized. The windows are smashed, and someone has daubed *NAZI SCUM* on the door. Mary shakes her head as we pass.

'The Heinemeyers are Jewish,' she says, taking my hand as we step carefully to avoid the broken glass. 'They came to this country seven years ago to avoid persecution by the Nazis. Now they have had their business destroyed because people cannot tell the difference between a German and a Nazi.'

As we walk on, I sense someone watching us. Looking up, I see a shadow standing at the window of the flat above the shop. Mrs Heinemeyer, baker of the most delicious rye and pumpernickel bagels, looks back at me and smiles sadly. I wave up at her, but she has already let the curtain fall.

The following day, when I come down to breakfast, I find Mary hunched over the wireless, black circles of sleeplessness framing her eyes, Churchill's distinctive voice echoing round the room.

'Dunkirk has been evacuated,' she says, not looking up at me. 'Churchill says they couldn't have done it without the RAF. I wonder if Ronald . . .'

'If Ronald was there then he is a hero,' I say, putting my hand on her shoulder. 'He has saved his countrymen.'

Mary flinches at my touch, then stands up and turns off the wireless.

'It is good news, isn't it?' I say, feeling confused at her reaction. 'The men have been rescued.'

She looks at me with an expression I have never seen before. Her face hardens and she seems, for just a moment, like a different person.

'Here,' she says, handing me an earthenware bowl. 'Why don't you collect some eggs for breakfast? The girls have been clucking all morning.'

Her face softens then and she is Mary once more, though I feel strangely unsettled as I take the bowl and head into the garden. I thought I knew her inside out, but it feels like I have seen a different side of her, one that she has kept hidden from me all these years.

The hens are screeching furiously when I reach the coop.

'Shh now, girls,' I say, kneeling beside the wire. 'It's only me. No need to get so feisty.'

I spot three large eggs nestled amid a pile of straw and feathers. Reaching my hand inside, careful to avoid the pecks, I remove each one and place them in the bowl, imagining the heavenly plate of creamy scrambled eggs that awaits me. Just then I hear a noise behind me. Turning round, I see Fred Harding standing by the front gate. He moves towards me, and I instinctively jump backwards.

'Why are you still here?' he says, jabbing his finger towards me. 'Your war's over now, or haven't you heard?'

I try to speak but no words will come. I am frozen to the spot, still clutching the bowl of eggs.

'It's a bloody disgrace,' he says, spittle forming at the side of his mouth. 'Our brave lads are out there facing all manner of dangers while fighting a foreign enemy, and our capital city is giving shelter to aliens like you and that Fenian bitch. You have no right to be here, do you hear me? This is England, and our soldiers are fighting to save it. England is for the English, and this war will settle that once and for all.'

He looks like he is about to say something else, but then he stops and puts a hand to his cheek. Then he rushes towards me, his face purple with anger. At first, I think he is going to hit me, but he pushes me aside and runs across the garden to the back wall, where Luca is sitting, catapult in hand.

'You greasy little spic. I'll tan your behind,' cries Harding as he stumbles towards the wall.

The hens, sensing hostile activity, resume their shriek-ing. I know I should go inside and get Mary. After all, this man is trespassing on her property. But she is in such a strange mood, and I do not want to add to her anxiety, so instead I stand and watch as Fred Harding pulls Luca down from the wall by his hair.

It all happens so quickly. One minute Harding has Luca in a headlock, the next there is a flash of black hair and blue-and-white striped apron as Mario leaps across the wall and lands a punch on the man's chin. I watch, open-mouthed, as Harding stumbles backwards into the blackberry bush. He puts his arms out to stop himself from falling, but as he does so Luca launches another pebble from the catapult. It hits Harding in the chest, and he falls to his knees in the prickly thorns.

'My goodness, what is going on?'

I turn to see Mary running out of the house. Something about the chaotic scene seems to snap her out of the reverie she has been in. Her eyes blaze as she runs to confront Fred Harding, who is desperately trying to unhook himself from the bramble bush.

'You had an intruder, Mary,' says Mario, placing one arm protectively round Luca's shoulders. 'He was threatening the children.'

'You bloody spic bastard,' splutters Harding, as he finally gets to his feet and staggers to the gate. 'That's assault, that is. My brother-in-law's a copper. You wait till he hears about this. He'll have you banged up.'

'Mr Harding,' says Mary, calmly, 'I have no idea why or how you came to be on my property, but if you don't leave immediately then it will be me calling the police. Do you understand?'

Harding pauses, his hand on the latch of the gate. Then, leaning his face towards Mary, he starts to laugh.

'Your property?' he says, his mouth just inches from Mary's face. 'This ain't your property. This house belongs to Mr Davidson, a man currently fighting for the country your lot would like to see destroyed. Poor fella. How did he end up saddled with a bog-trotter like you? Marry him for a passport, did you? Or were you just good in the sack?'

My chest tightens as I listen to Harding's vile tirade. Placing the bowl of eggs on the ground, I slowly make my way to where he is standing.

'Mr Harding, I won't tell you again,' says Mary, folding her arms across her chest. 'Get out of this garden, now.'

'Or what?' he sneers. 'You'll set your spic boyfriend on me, you Irish whore?'

At those words, a red mist descends on me, and before I know it I have leapt at Harding, pummelling his round belly with my fists.

'Don't you talk to her like that,' I cry, my eyes filling with tears of rage. 'You horrible man.'

I hear an Italian voice behind me, and a pair of hands grabs me round my waist.

'Come now, Teresa,' says Mario, lifting me into his arms. 'He's not worth it.'

'Bloody foreign lunatics,' yells Harding. 'This is what happens when do-gooding liberals interfere in overseas politics. That kid shouldn't even be here. She should be back in Spain in a concentration camp like the rest of the socialist scum.'

'Don't listen, piccolina,' says Mario, as he carries me into the house. 'He has no idea what he is talking about.'

He puts me down on the chair in the drawing room. My heart is racing, and my knuckles are red from where I punched him.

'Wait here now,' says Mario, wiping beads of sweat from his forehead. 'I must see if Mary is alright.'

I hear voices coming from the garden, then all is quiet. A couple of minutes later, Mary appears at the door, her face drained of colour.

'I wish you hadn't done that,' she says, clasping her hands together. 'I was dealing with him calmly. I've told you before, you must never resort to violence.'

'He was saying terrible things about you, aingeru,' I cry. 'He can't be allowed to talk to you like that.'

She looks at me and shakes her head.

'Oh, dote, if I had a shilling for every time some bigot like Harding has called me names, I'd be a rich woman,' she says. 'But if I had punched every one of them I would be in trouble. Not only that, but I would show myself to be just as bad as them. Do you understand?'

'Mario punched him too,' I say, looking up at her. 'Is he going to be in trouble?'

'I don't think so.' Mary crouches in front of me and takes my hands in hers. 'People like Harding tend to operate in the shadows. He knows that if he went to the police then I could report him for trespassing. He also knows that Ronald could return at any time, and he, being a patriotic Englishman, wouldn't want to upset a man who is fighting for his country.'

'Ronald is nothing like Fred Harding,' I say. 'Ronald is a good person.'

'Yes, he is,' says Mary.

'And I think Ronald would be proud of what I did today. I fought back against an evil person, just like Ronald is doing with the Nazis, just like the Other Landers did with the—'

Then the mood changes, and that dark expression comes over Mary's face again.

'Enough now, Teresa,' she snaps. 'Please. I know you think you did the right thing, and of course we should fight back against evil, but all Harding saw just now was an out-of-control foreign girl with a reckless foreign guardian. By behaving like you did, you played into his hands, you proved his opinions right. Now, I am going upstairs to lie down. I can feel a headache coming on.'

Later, when I am lying in bed, after an evening spent watching Mary frowning over a supper of boiled bacon and cabbage – an Irish dish that I know she only makes when she is feeling sad – I hear a noise outside. I stay there for a moment, my heart racing. What if it is Fred Harding, returning to finish me off? Then I hear it again. It sounds like a stone hitting the window. I jump out of bed and go to look. Opening the curtains, I am relieved to see a familiar face looking up at me.

Luca.

He beckons me to come outside. Pulling on my thick dressing gown, I tiptoe downstairs, across the chessboard hallway and through the orangery. Then, unlatching the door, I make my way out into the garden.

'What are you doing?' I say, as Luca comes towards me. He has a wicker basket in his hand.

'I couldn't sleep after all the drama today, so I thought I'd bring you a midnight feast,' he says, taking a gingham tablecloth out of the basket and laying it on the ground. 'I have leftover marinara sauce and some warm bread. Oh, and a bottle of lemonade, made from lemons Papa found in the street, ha!'

I have never had a midnight feast before and, to be honest, after the bacon and cabbage I am not really that hungry, but it is so good to see Luca's friendly face after an evening of Mary's silence.

We sit down on the grass. Luca pours some lemonade into a metal mug and hands it to me. It is sweet and delicious.

'Thank you for what you did today,' I say, watching as Luca tears a strip from the focaccia and hands me a piece.

'What did I do?'

'You saved me from Fred Harding.' I squeeze the soft bread between my finger and thumb. 'When you appeared with your catapult.'

'I did not save you, Toto,' says Luca, with a chuckle. 'I think we all know that you, more than any of us, are perfectly capable of saving yourself. I couldn't believe my eyes when I saw you going for him. You were like a lioness.'

'Mary said it was wrong of me,' I tell him. 'She says that I let myself down and proved all his prejudices correct.'

Luca is silent for a moment. He nibbles some bread, dips another piece into the marinara sauce, then looks up at me.

'Toto,' he says, his dark eyes glimmering in the moonlight. 'Will you promise me something?'

'Of course,' I say.

'Promise me,' he says, 'that no matter what happens in the next few months and years, you will keep that courage of yours.'

'I don't feel courageous,' I say. 'And most of the time I'm more mouse than lioness.'

'That's not true,' he says, lowering his voice so as not to wake Mary. 'You are one of the strongest and bravest people I know. Look at what you have been through and survived. I can't imagine what it must have been like to leave your home and family behind and sail away to a strange new country. When my parents came here, they were already married, and my mama was pregnant with me. They were a family heading for an exciting new home. It's not fair that you had to make that journey alone.'

'Yes,' I say, recalling the panic that set in when I watched Katalin walking away from the station's barriers, the terror of the storm, the strangeness of the camp. 'It was scary. But then I met Mary and Ronald and I felt like I had been given a new home, a new family.'

'I wish I had your bravery,' says Luca.

His words remind me of something Ronald wrote in *The Other Lands*.

'Wait here,' I say, getting to my feet. 'I have something for you.'

I run inside, across the chessboard floor and up the stairs to the library. Ronald's desk is just as he left it: the Anglepoise lamp tilted over a pile of papers held in place with the green butterfly paperweight Mary gave him for Christmas a couple of years ago, his beloved Parker fountain pen wedged in its stand. I open the top drawer and see the pile of crudely bound paperbacks that Ronald had printed a few months before he left. Slipping one into my pocket, I close the drawer and make my way downstairs.

When I return to the garden, Luca is lying on his back looking up at the starlit sky. When he hears me approach, he sits up and smiles at me and my stomach flutters. He has such a beautiful face. Sitting down beside him, I take the book out of my pocket and hand it to him.

'This is for you,' I say.

He holds the book up to the light.

'*The Other Lands*,' he reads. 'By Ronald Davidson. He's made it into an actual book.'

'Not quite bookshop quality,' I say, laughing. 'More a first draft, but I know Ronald would love you to have it.'

'Thank you, Toto,' he says, kissing me on the cheek. 'I will treasure it.'

I bid him goodnight and head inside to bed, thankful that, despite all that is bad in the world, I still have my friend Luca.

Yet, the following morning, as Mary and I set out on an errand, we see a sight that turns my world upside down all over again.

Two police cars are parked outside Mario's café, their sirens flashing. As we draw closer, we see four burly policemen bundling Mario and Luca out of the café.

Mary shrieks and runs towards them.

'What are you doing? These are innocent people.'

'Step away please, madam.' The policeman puts out his hand to hold her back.

'What is happening?' cries Mary. 'Why are they being arrested?'

'We are being interned,' shouts Mario, his face red and sweating. 'On Churchill's orders. And, more than likely, it has something to do with those two.'

He points his finger towards the street, where Fred Harding is standing with the boy who threw the stones at us a while ago.

'That's right,' yells Mario. 'Start them young. Fill your poor son's head with your racist nonsense.'

His son? I did not know Fred Harding had a son. As his father waves his fist at Mario, the boy stands silently, his head down, his hands clasped tightly together.

'That's enough now,' barks the policeman, struggling to get Mario into the car.

'Mary,' says Mario. 'Look after yourself and Teresa. Be careful, please. These are dangerous times and—'

Before he can finish, the policeman shoves him and he falls into the back of the car. I run round to the other side and see Luca in the back seat. He looks out of the window at me, his beautiful eyes expressionless.

'We will help you,' I cry, pressing my hand against the glass. 'I will come and rescue you. I promise.'

He shakes his head and, as the policeman starts the engine, he holds something up to the window. His crumpled copy of *The Other Lands*.

In that moment I feel my scarred heart break into pieces, along its newly healed fault lines.

'Goodbye, Luca,' I whisper, as the car pulls away. 'Have courage.'

24

Corinne

'Are you having a laugh?' says Jimmy, when Nidra and I confront him a few minutes later at his house.

He is standing on the doorstep, arms folded across his chest, his pale face reddening.

'I wish we were,' says Nidra, tears welling in her eyes. 'How could you, Jimmy? We have only ever been kind to you.'

'As I have to you,' he says, his voice trembling with anger. 'I'm your most loyal customer. And I don't deserve being accused of something I haven't done.'

'Jimmy, it's all here,' I say, handing him my phone, the video paused on the screen. 'Your living room is not hard to identify. That royal wedding photo is pretty distinctive.'

He glares at the screen as the video plays, then he looks up, his eyes blazing.

'The little sod,' he cries. 'I'll bloody kill him.'

'Who are you talking about, Jimmy?' says Nidra, glancing nervously at me as we follow him into the house.

We stand by the door as Jimmy strides towards the staircase.

'Jaden,' he yells up the stairs. 'Get yourself down here now!' Returning to us, he says, 'I can't believe it. It's his handwriting. I'd recognize it anywhere.'

We stand in silence for a moment, then we hear footsteps on the landing.

'What do you want?'

The voice is young and strangely familiar.

'I said get down here now,' yells Jimmy.

A few moments later, a small figure emerges from the stairs. As it steps into the light of the living room, I gasp. It is the boy from the café, the one Rima shouted at. He looks at me and Nidra, then back at Jimmy, who thrusts the phone in front of his face.

'It was just a joke,' says Jaden when the video finishes. 'I wanted to get back at that stuck-up cow who runs the café. She took the piss out of me in front of all my mates.'

'You mind your language in front of these ladies,' says Jimmy, grabbing his arm. 'Now get your coat. You're going to go and apologize to Rima.'

'You're actually going to let him work here?'

Nidra shakes her head as Rima explains how Jaden turned up at the café full of contrition. He confessed to everything, and offered to work for free every weekend.

'It will be good for him,' says Rima, as she carefully

writes up the day's specials on the board. 'Show the little fool just what it was he was trying to destroy. Remember how Mum used to say that everyone should be given the chance to redeem themselves. Well, if we can set Jaden on a better path, then that's our good deed done.'

'Hmm, I feel uneasy about it all,' says Nidra. 'The stuff he sent was hardcore. I mean, where did he even learn all that? Jimmy seems like such a good person.'

'That's right, I am.'

We look up to see Jimmy standing at the door, a bunch of carnations in his hand.

'I've come here to say sorry,' he says, walking over to the counter, where Nidra and I are standing. 'Listen, I'm not going to make excuses for him because there aren't any. All I'll say is, after talking to him last night, it seems he's been frequenting these online chat rooms where they spout racist crap. A load of spineless keyboard warriors blaming everyone else for their own inadequacies. You know the kind. Anyway, Jaden wasn't having a good time of it at school. He was getting bullied. He's always been a loner, but this year, when his folks split up and he came to stay with me, it just got harder for him. Then he finally found a group who wanted to hang round with him, the ones who used to come in here, causing trouble, and . . . well, you know what happened next. I totally understand you chucking them out that day, Rima, but he was shown up in front of his mates. It felt, to him, like the final straw.'

'I'm sorry, but that's no excuse for what he went on to do,' says Nidra. 'You don't just become a racist because someone tells you off.'

'No, Nidra,' says Rima, coming round to the front of the counter. 'I was wrong to do what I did. Throwing them out was one thing, but what I said was cruel and unnecessary.'

'It's not your fault, love,' says Jimmy, handing her the flowers. 'I blame the lowlifes in that chat room. Jaden stumbled across it when he was angry and confused, and they filled his head with poison. Those sites need bringing down. Anyway, he's promised me it will never happen again.'

Rima nods her head.

'Thanks, Jimmy,' she says, taking the flowers. 'I hope I'm right to give him a chance like this. After all, the language he used in those messages was deeply disturbing and offensive. As I told him last night, one strike and he is not only out but he'll be reported to the police . . . Right, I'll go put these in water. Oh, Nidra, by the way, Jaden told me something else last night. It wasn't just the messages. Apparently, he was behind the ghost sighting too.'

'What?'

'Yep,' says Rima. 'I asked if he had anything else to confess to, and he said he'd overheard you talking about ghosts and he wanted to scare you, so he and his mates dressed an old shop dummy in black clothes and placed it at the window. That was what you saw that time.'

'The little shit,' cries Nidra, glaring at Jimmy. 'And there I was telling you I thought I was being haunted.'

'Listen, love – as I said, I had no idea about any of this,' says Jimmy. 'All I can say is that he wasn't brought up to behave like this. I feel terrible about the whole thing.'

Nidra nods, then goes to join Rima in the kitchen.

'They don't blame you,' I say, as Jimmy sits down next to me at the counter. 'It's just been a big shock for them. A lot to take in.'

'I love those girls,' says Jimmy, his voice cracking. 'This café has been a haven for me this past year. I've always felt like an outsider, wherever I've been. I've always found it hard to quieten my old man's voice in my head, telling me not to trust anyone. But coming back to Tooting and finding this café . . . well, I've felt part of a community for the first time in years. Those girls truly welcomed me. I feel sick to my stomach that someone from my family has brought this to their door. It's like history repeating itself.'

'What do you mean?' I say, watching as he takes a handkerchief from his coat pocket and wipes his eyes.

'Oh, nothing,' he says, regaining his composure. 'Just my old man, that's all. I suppose I didn't have the best role model when I was a kid. I made some mistakes, did things I'm not proud of. The truth is, love, when you asked me the other day about Rochester Place, about Mary and Teresa . . . well, I wasn't all that honest with you. I did know them. In fact, truth be told, I had a little crush on Teresa back in the day. But she only had eyes for the Italian kid from this place – Luca, his name was. I'm afraid I got rather jealous. I called them names, horrible names. Then, when Italy entered the war, they rounded up all the Italian nationals, and poor Luca and his old man were arrested and sent away to an internment camp. I tried to make amends after that but it was no use. I'm ever so ashamed of it now, but, like I said, I was a kid with an ignorant old man. I had to learn the hard way that what he'd taught me was a load of cobblers.'

'Oh, Jimmy. Why didn't you tell me?'

'I was embarrassed, love,' he says, his eyes filling up again. 'Embarrassed and very sad. It broke my heart, what happened to her. My old man tried to atone for it. Before we left Tooting, he had a plaque made up and placed on the bench in what had been the Davidsons' garden. It wasn't much, but it was his way of saying sorry for all that he'd put them through. Anyway, I've got something for you. I don't know how useful it'll be to you and your uncle, but I feel I need to give it away. This thing has weighed on me like a curse all these years. It's time to let it go.'

He reaches into his rucksack, takes out a small leather notebook, and hands it to me.

'What's this?' I ask, turning it over in my hands. The leather is sun-bleached and the spine is ripped.

'Have a look inside,' he says, leaning towards me.

I open the book. The pages are yellow and wafer thin. There is handwriting inside, but the ink has been smudged, as though the book was left out in the rain. A lot of the words have been obliterated, but those that I can read appear to be in a foreign language, one I am unfamiliar with.

'Whose notebook is this?' I say, looking up at Jimmy.

'Have a look at the first page again,' he says. 'It's easy to miss as it's so weather-worn.'

I turn the pages and hold it up to the light. There, in the left-hand corner in faded ink, is a name. *Mary Davidson.*

'My goodness, Jimmy,' I cry. 'This is her diary?'

'Yes,' he says.

'How did you come by it?' I ask, opening it up again and gazing at the childish writing.

'I found it in the rubble,' says Jimmy. 'The day after the bombing.'

'And you kept it?'

'I just felt it needed saving,' he says, his voice trembling with emotion. 'So much had been destroyed. And I felt so guilty for how I'd treated them. I reckoned the diary would be a reminder for me. A warning, if you like, to never succumb to my old man's hatred again.'

'I understand,' I say. 'Now I know what you meant by Jaden's behaviour bringing it all back.'

Jimmy nods.

'Anyway,' he says, looking up at me, his eyes red with tears. 'I tried to read it, but it seems Mary wrote using some sort of code. It's certainly not a language I've ever come across before. But as I went to close it, I saw something poking out of the back pages. A photo.' He reaches into his pocket and pulls out a tiny plastic wallet. 'Here, meet Mary, Teresa and Ronald.'

He hands me the photo and a shiver slices through my body.

The photograph, taken in the garden of Rochester Place, is faded and worn, but I can still make out the three subjects. Ronald, broad-shouldered and handsome, stands in the centre, his arms around Mary and Teresa. Mary's dark shoulder-length hair is pinned back at the sides in the 1930s fashion. She has a beautiful face with bright eyes, and a dazzling smile. Teresa, a thin, wiry girl with curly black hair, looks nervously at the camera.

'They seem so happy,' I say, handing the photo back to Jimmy. 'To think what happened to them, to the house . . .'

'That's why I want you to keep this,' says Jimmy, pressing the photo into my hands. 'And the diary. If they can be of some use to your uncle as a record of social history, then I've at least done something right. I've been haunted by their story nearly all my life. It's time to lay it to rest.'

He smiles sadly, then, with an apologetic nod to Rima and Nidra, makes his way out of the café.

I sit quietly for a moment, the diary and photo in front of me. My eyes rest on Mary. I try to equate the dazzling woman in the picture with the terrified voice on the phone pleading with me to save her child. Just then my phone rings, and I see Uncle Robin's name flashing on the screen.

'Uncle Robin, you're never going to believe what's happened.'

'Can I tell you my news first?' he says, sounding rather giddy. 'I think you're going to want to hear it. It regards our Mary.'

'Of course,' I say, running my hands across the plastic cover, Mary's eyes boring into me. 'Go on.'

'Well, it seems Mary was not who we thought she was,' he says. 'She stood accused of working against the British government, and was about to be arrested for what was, at the time, one of the most treacherous of crimes – a crime that carried the death penalty. Corinne, Mary Davidson was a spy.'

25

Teresa
OCTOBER 1940

The skies are exploding above London on a nightly basis now, and though at first we thought that the Luftwaffe would continue to target the East End docks, in the last few days bombs have been dropped on Clapham, Croydon and as close as Tooting Bec. When the siren sounds, Mary and I drop whatever we are doing and hurry out to the Anderson shelter, where we sit huddled together on the wooden cots Ronald built, sipping cocoa and trying to distract ourselves from the explosions by retelling stories of Grace O'Malley, Queen Maeve of Connacht and Mari the mountain goddess. I can see Mary wince each time the German bombs are met with anti-aircraft fire, wondering if it is Ronald up there, trying to protect England the way he protected us.

Yet, though I worry for Ronald and pray, each night, that the shrill whistle flying overhead is not a bomb with his or our names on it, I am learning to live with the air raids, to read them, to work with them. I have learned to identify the level of threat of a bomb by the sound it makes. If the sound is shrill and high-pitched, then it's more than likely it is heading our way, but if it's a deeper, low growl, then it's probably someone else's problem. I tell myself that, if I am vigilant, if I continue to watch and listen, then I will not be caught off guard as I was in the market square. That innocent moment of stopping to smell a bunch of lilies feels like a lifetime ago.

The bombings in South London have meant more work for the Rochester Place food bank, and we spend most of our days packing up emergency parcels for those who have lost their homes. Mary and I started work at seven o'clock this morning, and by lunchtime we are still only halfway through the packing. We are just debating whether or not to have a break or work through lunch when there is a knock at the door. Mary's face grows pale, her thoughts immediately turning to Ronald. These days an unexpected knock at the door can mean a visit from the dreaded telegram man.

'You get it, dote,' she says, knocking over a tin of condensed milk in her agitation. 'I've got to finish this packing, or we'll be in trouble.'

I do as she asks, but as I take the latch off the front door my chest tightens. What if it *is* bad news? What then? But when I open it, I see a young man walking away down the path who is clearly not the telegram man. I recognize him instantly. It is Fred Harding's son.

'Hey,' I call after him. 'What do you think you're

doing, knocking on our door and running off? Don't you think you've caused enough trouble?'

He turns on his heel and comes back up the path, his face surprisingly contrite.

'I'm sorry,' he says, looking down at his scuffed shoes. 'You took ages to answer, and I thought you were out.'

'What do you want?' I say, barely able to suppress my anger, the memory of Luca in the back of that police car still fresh in my mind.

'I came to say I'm sorry,' he says. 'I never meant for it to go this far. It was just a bit of a laugh to begin with, the brick through the window, the stones, but I never meant for them to get taken away. I swear I didn't.'

'It was you,' I say, my heart lurching inside my chest. 'You threw that brick? And the horrible message attached to it? What was it again? Oh yes, "death to foreign scum". How could you? I don't want your apologies. I don't want you anywhere near me. And besides, it's too late. Luca and Mario have been taken away. He was my best friend and now I'll never see him again. Get away from me, do you hear me?'

I go to shut the door, but he puts out his hand.

'Wait,' he says, his face reddening. 'Hear me out. I understand that you hate me, and you don't accept my apology. There's nothing I can do about that, but I can do something to try to atone for what I did.'

'I don't want anything from you,' I cry.

'I know where he is,' he says, staring at me with those

236

strange blue eyes. 'Luca. I know where they took him. And it's closer than you think.'

'What?' I say, my stomach flipping over. 'Where is he?'

'I'll explain everything on the way,' he says, his voice brightening. 'You grab your coat and I'll take you. Be quick. The next bus leaves in five minutes.'

As we sit on the bus, the boy, who introduces himself as Jimmy, tells me how one of Fred Harding's drinking buddies from the pub works as a guard at a newly built internment camp on Wimbledon Common. Jimmy overheard his father talking to this man, who confirmed that Mario and Luca had been taken there, along with a couple of hundred other Italian nationals.

'Churchill wanted the lot of 'em rounded up,' says Jimmy, as we alight from the bus. 'Said they were enemies of the state.'

His words sear through me as we make our way across the common.

'There it is,' he says.

He points towards a cluster of makeshift tents up ahead. As we draw closer, I see a camp, not unlike the one I was taken to at Stoneham when I first arrived in England. Yet, instead of jolly bell tents and smiling volunteers, music and laughter, here there are barbed wire, snarling guard dogs with bared teeth, and soldiers holding loaded rifles. I try to imagine Luca in there, trapped and cold and afraid. The thought is unbearable.

'Oi, you two.'

We look up and see a khaki-clad guard, a rat-faced man with pock-marked skin.

'What are you doing, poking round here? Go on, hop it.'

'It's no use,' I say, disconsolately. 'Why did we even come? Of course we're not going to be able to see him. It's a prison camp.'

I feel even worse than I did when they took him away, knowing that he is so close. But Jimmy, seemingly ignoring the man, is marching off to the other side of the camp.

'Ignore that old goat,' he says, when I catch up with him. 'Kenneth, the chap from the pub, has agreed to let us have a couple of minutes with Luca.'

'What?' I exclaim, my heart lifting. 'But why didn't you tell me?'

'I didn't want you to get overexcited,' he says. 'In case Kenneth don't turn up. Mind, he should do. I gave him some whisky my old man had stashed away. He'll kill me when he finds out but . . . I just wanted to make things better. Look, there he is.'

He gestures to a heavy-set, middle-aged man who is standing by the wire fence up ahead. The man nods his head as we approach.

'Two minutes,' he says, sternly. 'And I'll be straight back. No mucking around, you hear me?'

'You have my word, Ken,' says Jimmy, with a wink. 'Enjoy your Scotch, eh?'

The man glares at him. 'Wait here. And keep your voices down.'

He disappears round the corner while we wait at the wire. A couple of moments later a figure appears on the other side of the fence.

'Luca,' I cry, as he shuffles towards me.

He puts his finger to his lips.

'Shh, Toto,' he says. 'We don't want to summon the other guards.'

He has lost weight, and his usually well-groomed hair is lank and unwashed. There are dark circles under his eyes and his lips are dry and cracked. I put my finger through the wire and wrap it round his.

'Darling Luca,' I whisper. 'What can I do to get you out of there?'

'Just keep being brave, Toto,' he says, squeezing my finger. 'I will find a way back to you, I promise.'

'How is Mario?' I say, trying to hold back my tears.

'As well as can be expected. He is very angry. They all are. The adults. There is talk of some of us being deported.'

'No! They can't do that. I can't lose you.'

'Whatever happens,' he says, as Kenneth the guard appears behind him and gestures to his watch, 'I will find a way back to you. I promise.'

And then the words spill out of me, unbidden.

'I love you, Luca.'

'I love you, Toto.'

Then he lets go of my finger and follows the guard back into the camp.

My eyes are so raw from crying when I arrive back at Rochester Place half an hour later that, at first, I do not notice the uniformed boy on the bicycle making his way down the path. But as I draw level, he takes off his cap and nods solemnly, and I know, with sickening dread, what this means.

'No,' I shout as I run up the path and pull open the door. 'Please, don't let it be him.'

But when I get inside, my worst fears are realized. Mary is slumped on the chequered floor, her shoulders hunched, her knees pulled up to her chest. She does not look up as I approach, just sits there, like a broken queen on a chessboard. Then I see it, a flash of white on the black tile. The telegram. I bend down to pick it up, and with shaking hands read the message:

ON BEHALF OF THE ROYAL AIR FORCE IT IS MY SAD DUTY TO INFORM YOU . . .

26

Corinne

PRESENT DAY

'A spy?' says Nidra. 'Blimey, this is turning into the best episode of *House Detective* ever.'

We are sitting round Uncle Robin's cluttered table, drinking coffee and nibbling on smoked salmon and cream cheese bagels from Robin's favourite bakery on Brick Lane.

'An enemy of the state, no less,' says Robin, brushing crumbs from his sweater. 'Likely working with the Germans . . . Oh, that is just what the doctor ordered. You know, I've always said there is something about a Brick Lane bagel that can cure all ills.'

'I thought that was chicken soup?' I say, taking another bite of the soft but chewy bagel.

'Ah, yes, Jewish penicillin. That too,' says Robin, dabbing his mouth with his hand and then taking a large bite of the roll. 'But for me, the bagel is king.'

'So then,' asks Nidra, 'how did you find out she was a spy?'

'Well, I'd begun looking into the background of Mary's husband, Ronald Davidson,' he says, pausing to

241

take a glug of coffee. 'And, from there, managed to find their marriage certificate, which featured Mary's maiden name, O'Connor.'

'An Irish name,' says Nidra. 'Oh, Corinne, that gives me goosebumps. You said the woman on the phone had an Irish accent.'

'Yes, she did,' I say, willing myself not to be drawn down the rabbit hole of ghost theories. 'But I'm still convinced that the person on the phone was real, and that she was in trouble. This story, as fascinating as it is, may have nothing at all to do with the call.'

'What? An Irish woman called Mary rings you and says she's trapped under rubble in a house that no longer exists, a house that was bombed in the Blitz, and you say it isn't linked? It's beyond spooky, Corinne. Anyway, sorry, Robin. I interrupted you.'

'Ah, where was I? Oh, yes, as I was delving into Ronald's background I managed to trace his father,' he says. 'A rather decorated figure by the name of Oliver Davidson. An air marshal, no less. Anyway, to cut a long story short, as he was the only person in our search with a relatively high profile, I decided to go along to the British Library to see if I could find any record of him in the newspaper archives. Lo and behold, I found an obituary, and a few bits and pieces related to his military career, but then I decided to type in Mary's name next to his and that's when things got really interesting.'

'What did you find?' I ask, fearing that any moment

now he is going to cut to a commercial break, after which 'all will be revealed'.

'Well, it was extraordinary,' he says. 'I found an interview with Davidson's son, Albert, published in *The Times* in February 1960. He had followed his father into the RAF and was, at that point, rather high up in the ranks. Towards the end of the interview he was asked what he had learned from his father. He spoke a bit about values and honour and courage, and then he said, almost as an aside, that his father had taught him to always be on guard. His father had been stung by an employee, he said, back in the 1920s – a young Irish woman by the name of Mary O'Connor, who had inveigled her way into the family's employment and run off with Davidson's elder son, and who had then been killed in an air raid. Albert said that, just before she died, a warrant had been issued for Mary's arrest.'

'For spying?' says Nidra, helping herself to another bagel.

'It seems so,' says Uncle Robin. 'Albert Davidson was quite adamant. He and his father firmly believed that Mary had rather questionable reasons for being in England, and for being married to Ronald for that matter. It appears her death saved her from a more public reckoning. Corinne, can you pass me that blue folder from the sideboard?'

I get up and walk over to the large iron display cabinet that sits in the recess between the kitchen and the hallway. It contains all Uncle Robin's curios, objects I remember from childhood visits – such as a Victorian doll's head, an Edwardian automaton birdcage which I used to spend hours winding up to let the birds move their beaks and tails and sing, the first edition of *Punch* magazine, the print stamp from Virginia Woolf's Hogarth Press, a pair of tiny Victorian lady's shoes and a chipped bust of Mozart. I see that he has added to the collection since I was last here, as there is a large glass sand-timer. I pick it up and turn it on its head. Then, as the grains of sand trickle down, I grab the folder and return to the table.

'When I was in the library, I discovered something else.' Uncle Robin's voice is solemn as he takes the folder from me.

'What?' I say, a chill running through me. 'What did you find?'

'Well,' says Uncle Robin, peering at me over the top of his spectacles, 'I remembered what you said about the plaque you found in the garden, on the bench.'

'*In loving memory of Mary Davidson and Teresa Garro, who lost their lives here . . .*' I begin.

'On the fifteenth of October 1940,' says Uncle Robin, finishing my sentence. 'I simply put those names into a tracker I have that brings up the names of those who were killed on any given date during the Blitz, and there she was.'

He pauses to clear his throat, then continues.

'On the night in question, it seems they didn't make it to the Anderson shelter in time. I'm guessing that a house of that size and status would have had one in the garden. The house was hit on that date, and they didn't make it out. Teresa Garro was just eleven years old. A child.'

As I sit here, I feel my chest tighten, like all the air has been sucked out of the room. I think of the phone call, Mary's stricken voice. *She's just a little girl. Eleven years old.* My hands start to tremble, and I sit on them to try to steady myself.

Opposite me, Uncle Robin and Nidra seem oblivious to my distress.

'The house was irreparably damaged, reduced to rubble,' says Uncle Robin, shaking his head. 'The shell of it survived for a few more years but then it was finally cleared in 1946, after the war. The name, Rochester Place, went with it, and that area now is seen as an adjunct to Larkin Road, the place where residents leave out their bins to be collected. In fact, there's an application pending from the council to clear the garden and build some lucrative garages there. What a terrible waste, eh? A beautiful Georgian house, gone. Just like that.'

He clicks his fingers, and the noise makes me flinch.

'I realize it's a lot of information to take in, my dear,' he says, getting up from his chair. 'Let me get you a glass of water.'

He takes a tumbler from the shelf and fills it from the tap.

'Here you are,' he says, handing it to me.

'It must be just a strange coincidence.' I take a drink of water, my hands still trembling. 'It has to be. None of it makes sense otherwise.'

'I think we have to keep an open mind,' says Nidra, in between bites of bagel. 'Some things just defy logic.'

'Well,' says Uncle Robin, returning to his seat, 'I've not much time for ghost stories, as you know. There must be a logical explanation. I wonder whether your caller has some morbid fascination with wartime London. It does happen. I've met my fair share of them over the years. The steampunk ones stick in my mind, obsessed with Victoriana, then there's the Charles Dickens aficionados and the Jack the Ripper ghouls. They turn up on the doorstep from time to time, asking questions and getting their London geography confused. It's most tiresome.'

Robin carries on talking, suggesting other possible explanations, but none of them make sense. I know that Mary was real, that her fear and terror were real. But if it wasn't a prank or, as Robin thinks, a ghoulish Blitz obsessive, then . . . what?

'Well, whatever it is, my curiosity has been piqued,' says Uncle Robin, gathering up his papers. 'We must get to the bottom of this mystery. I suggest I put a notice out on my various house-history pages, all the social media doo-dahs too, asking if anyone has any information about Rochester Place, the Davidsons and Teresa Garro.

Who knows, my dear, someone out there might be able to solve this puzzle for us and put your mind at rest. I can see it's troubling you.'

'I'm fine, really, Uncle Robin,' I say, getting up from the table and slipping my coat on. 'It's these night shifts. They can be a killer.'

'I can only imagine,' he says, leaning back in his chair. 'All those poor souls in peril on the other end of the line. I don't know how you do it. I really don't. Still, you've always had a calm head, even when you were a child. Anyway, back to our spy story. It seems the Davidsons had proof of Mary's transgression. There was an incident at the dinner table one evening where she doggedly quizzed a pair of Air Marshal Davidson's high-ranking RAF colleagues on their work. And, according to Albert, his mother witnessed her meeting with Constance Markievicz, the famed Irish freedom fighter, right outside the house. Apparently she was handed suspicious-looking papers, and the pair of them – according to Mrs Davidson – appeared to be acting shiftily, though it wasn't until years later, when Constance Markievicz died and her photograph was splashed across the newspapers, that Mrs Davidson realized who it was that Mary had been meeting. When the Davidsons learned of Ronald's death they knew they would have to act on their suspicions. They had physical proof too. A pile of papers they found in Mary's room, written in code.'

It is then I remember the diary. I stuffed it into my bag when Robin called. Taking it out, I hand it over to him.

'I'd almost forgotten about this,' I say. 'Jimmy from the café gave it to me. It's a long story, but he grew up near Rochester Place and found the diary among the rubble after the bombing. What you just said about Mary writing in code – well, this diary seems to back it up.'

'How extraordinary,' says Robin, running his hands across the leather-bound cover. 'May I?'

'Of course.' I watch as he opens it carefully. 'Jimmy wanted you to have it. Said it might hold some clues.'

'Corinne, is that your phone ringing?' says Nidra, gesturing to my bag. I was so engrossed in the diary I hadn't noticed. I lean across and take the phone out. It's Annie, Gran's neighbour, calling.

'Annie,' I say, my stomach lurching. 'Is everything okay?'

'Oh. Corinne,' she says, choking back tears. 'Thank goodness I got hold of you. I went to your gran's to drop off the phone this morning. I was supposed to pop it back yesterday, but I lost track of time. Anyway, there was no answer at your gran's front door, so I went round the back and . . . and that's when I saw her. She was just lying there on the living-room floor, not moving. I'm so sorry, love. It's not good news.'

27

Teresa

It has been a week since we received the telegram. This morning, when I come down for breakfast, I find Mary lying on the sofa in her nightgown and slippers, while the gramophone plays 'Spread a Little Happiness'. She has played that song so many times it is now lodged in my head, and I have grown to hate it.

I ask Mary if she would like something to eat, but she just shakes her head dolefully and carries on staring at the ceiling. I leave her to it and go out into the garden to collect some eggs. While I am out there, I hear a knock on the front door. Peering over the side gate I see a young woman standing on the step. She is very elegant, tall with light blonde hair, and is smartly dressed in a grey coat and matching hat. I am about to call out to her to ask if I can help her, when I hear the door open and Mary cry, 'I've been waiting for you.' She comes towards the young woman and makes to embrace her, but the woman steps back as though recoiling from Mary's touch. Then she hands Mary something, and says in a voice as sharp as glass, 'I can't be seen to be here, Mary. Just read this and take it as a warning. Do what you need to do. But don't leave it too late. They're already closing in.'

With that, she turns and walks away, her smart brogues clicking down the path like a ticking clock.

Taking my basket of eggs, I run inside and find Mary sitting at the kitchen table, her eyes red and puffy.

'Aingeru,' I cry, running towards her. 'What is it? What is the matter?'

Then she does something she has never done before. She brushes me off.

'Leave me, dote,' she says, getting up from the table, her shoulders hunched. 'You need to stay well away from me now, if you are to be saved.'

She is not making any sense, and it is scaring me. I follow her into the drawing room and watch as she pours a large measure of Ronald's special whisky into a tumbler and drinks it in one gulp.

'Is this because of the woman who came to the door?' I ask, as she pours another measure. 'What did she want? She said something about a warning.'

Mary puts the glass down and comes towards me, her eyes blazing.

'You did not see anything, and you did not hear anything, is that clear?' she says, her face pressed so close to mine I can smell the whisky on her breath.

I have never seen Mary like this before.

'Please, dote,' she says, her voice softening. 'You have to listen to me. I have never let you down, have I?'

I shake my head. No, she has never let me down.

'But in this case, for your own safety, you have to pretend that what you saw just now on the doorstep never happened. Can you do that?'

I try to reason with her, try to get her to tell me what is going on, but she just puts her hands up as if to silence me.

'Teresa,' she says firmly, 'can you do that?'

'Yes,' I whisper, hoping in my heart that I am doing the right thing. 'I can do that.'

'Good,' she says. 'Now go up to your room. We must stay in the house for the next few days. We must hide away until . . . until the danger passes. You can entertain yourself with your books, can't you?'

'You mean we can't go out at all?' I say, panic rising up my body. 'We're imprisoned.'

'Oh, Teresa, don't be so dramatic,' Mary sighs. 'It's just for a few days. You have a beautiful house and a well-stocked library. It is hardly prison. Now run along. I need to clear my head.'

I do as she says and go upstairs to the library. A shaft of light pours down onto the shelves, exposing the cobwebs and dust motes that have built up since Ronald left. I go to his desk, hoping to find solace in a chapter or two of *The Other Lands*, but as I sit down, I notice the telegram wedged underneath Ronald's inkpot. I slide it out and read it again:

> ON BEHALF OF THE ROYAL AIR FORCE IT IS MY SAD DUTY TO INFORM YOU THAT YOUR HUSBAND, GROUP CAPTAIN RON-ALD ARTHUR DAVIDSON, IS PRESUMED TO HAVE BEEN KILLED IN ACTION . . .

Though the message is horrifying, the hopeful part of me can't help focusing on one particular word: 'presumed'. Not confirmed, then. Whoever sent this telegram was not imparting solid facts, but presumptions. My heart lifts a little as I fold up the telegram and slide it back under the inkpot. There is hope. The presence of Ronald's clutter on the desk gives me further confidence that he is still alive. If Ronald were dead, I would feel it, deep in my bones, and as I sit reading through the scribbled last chapters of *The Other Lands*, I can hear his voice as clearly as if he were sitting next to me. He cannot be dead, I tell myself, because he promised us he would return, and Ronald never breaks his promises.

Yet the following morning, when I come down to breakfast and share my thoughts with Mary, she just shakes her head and says that hope deserted her a long time ago.

After breakfast, as we sit in the drawing room listening to the wireless, there is another knock at the door.

Mary leaps from the armchair, clutching her chest, the colour draining from her face. I offer to go and see who it is, but she tells me to stay in the room and not make a sound. When I hear the front door close, I creep out into the hallway. Mary is standing in the middle of the floor, holding a telegram in her hands. 'Ronald,' I cry, running towards her. 'Is it news from Ronald? Is he safe?' She looks at me, and the expression on her face is so alarming that I stagger backwards. Her eyes, always her best feature, so full of life and light, have clouded. It is as though there is nothing left inside her – whatever it is that makes her Mary, Ronald's sweetheart and my aingeru, has gone.

'Mary,' I say, my voice trembling. 'What is it? Tell me what has happened.'

But she does not reply. Instead, she folds the telegram, puts it in her pocket, then walks back into the drawing room and closes the door.

Later, as I am sitting on my bed trying to read, I hear the telephone ring. I creep out of the bedroom and peer over the banister. I can hear Mary talking but I cannot work out what she is saying. Finally, I hear: 'Yes, I understand. I will wait for you to arrive. I will be ready.'

What can it be? I think of the young woman on the doorstep, Mary making me swear I had not seen her, then hiding ourselves in the house like two hermits. I need to know what is going on. I need to confront Mary. After all, she promised me, back at the convent, that she would always tell me the truth. Now the truth is what I am going to get.

However, when I walk into the kitchen, I am greeted with the most extraordinary sight. There is Mary, her hair and make-up done, dressed in the red dress that Ronald loved so much, the emerald clip she has not worn since the news of his death now glittering in her black hair. She has tied an apron round her middle and is standing by the stove, the smell of tomatoes and garlic wafting through the air. When she sees me in the doorway, she puts down the wooden spoon she is holding and comes towards me, arms outstretched.

'Oh, my dote, there you are,' she says, kissing me on the forehead. 'I have a little surprise for you. Come and see.'

I go to the table and see boxes of tinned sardines, eggs from the chickens, wild garlic, fresh tomatoes and beans from the garden.

'I had these put away in the larder,' says Mary, returning to the stove to stir the pot. 'For when Ronald next came back. But I thought, instead, you and I would make a special dinner tonight. You said you'd like us to go to Guernica together one day. Well, I thought I would bring Guernica to you. What do you think?'

I do not know what to say. I am confused. One minute Mary is dead-eyed and silent, telling us we are not allowed to leave the house, the next she is dressed to the nines and cooking up a feast. I want to tell her how

I feel, to ask about the phone call, but it is so good to see the old Mary back, to bask in her glow, that I decide to keep my thoughts to myself. There is always tomorrow, I tell myself, as Mary puts the Spanish folk music record on the gramophone and swings me round the room, so for now let us just enjoy this moment.

Later, after a meal of salty sardines, spiced eggs, beans roasted in olive oil and garlic, and hunks of homemade bread, Mary and I sit in front of the fire in the drawing room, watching the flames bouncing off the black grate.

'That was a feast, aingeru,' I say, as Mary wraps a thick blanket around my shoulders. 'We'll be eating the leftovers all week.'

Mary looks at me then, and her eyes fill with tears.

'What is it?' I ask. Then I remember the telegram. 'Is it Ronald? Please, Mary, tell me what has happened.'

'You know how much I love you, dote?' she says, pulling me closer.

'More than there are stars in the sky, more than there are people on the earth, more than anything,' I say, repeating the line she has spoken each night as she tucks me into bed.

'More than anything,' she says, a tear falling onto her cheek. 'And that will never change.'

She kisses me on my forehead, then tells me that we are going to go on a little trip. She wanted it to be a surprise, she says. A fun adventure for the two of us. She tells me to get my hat and coat and then we will head off.

But as I get to my feet, two things happen simultaneously: there is a loud pounding at the door and the air-raid siren goes off.

'I have to get that,' cries Mary. 'Come now, dote. Quickly.'

She goes to grab me, but I am already darting towards the kitchen. I remember what Ronald taught us. We have to get to the shelter.

'Teresa, come back,' she cries.

There is the pounding on the door again, this time more insistent, and I hear Mary running down the hallway to answer it.

It takes me thirty seconds to get to the shelter. Once inside, I light the oil lamp, sit on the edge of the bed and wait for Mary to come.

28

Corinne

I am just stepping out of the taxi at the hospital when my phone rings. With shaking hands, I pull it out, praying that it is not bad news. But when I see the name on the screen, my panic subsides.

'Hi, Uncle Robin,' I say, balancing the phone in the crook of my shoulder as I wheel my suitcase behind me. 'I've just arrived at the hospital. Have you heard anything?'

'No, dear,' he says, though he sounds dazed. 'I haven't heard anything from the hospital.'

'Robin, can I call you back later?' I ask, as I reach the entrance. 'I really want to get inside and see Gran.'

'The photograph,' he says, his voice a dull monotone. 'The one in Mary's diary. I just found it.'

I can't believe that he is still talking about Rochester Place, after everything with Gran.

'Look, Uncle Robin, I'm sorry,' I say, as an ambulance pulls up beside me in the loading bay. 'But this really isn't a priority right now. I have to get to Gran.

The Rochester Place stuff will have to be put aside for now. It's not important.'

'Corinne, I think you'll find it is,' he says. 'Please hear me out.'

'Robin, what is this?'

'The little girl in the photograph,' he says, his voice almost drowned out by the ambulance engine. 'The Spanish refugee.'

'Yes,' I say, wishing Robin would not choose this of all times to do one of his cliffhanger TV reveals. 'What about her?'

'I recognized her instantly,' he says. 'The unruly hair, the shy expression, those eyes. Corinne, the girl in the photograph is not Teresa Garro. It's your grandmother.'

Five minutes later, I am still standing with my phone gripped in my hand outside Castlebar Hospital. Gran was brought here as it is the nearest hospital to Achill, the remote island off the west coast of Ireland that she has called home for the last five years. An odd choice, we thought at the time, seeing as Gran had no connection to Ireland beyond a love of its folklore and a taste for strong Irish tea.

Yet now that decision, if nothing else, seems to make sense.

It is just getting light. A pale morning sun shines onto the glass building, bathing it in a pinkish glow. As

I walk into the hospital, I replay Uncle Robin's phone call in my head, but no matter how hard I try, I just cannot fathom it.

How can the girl in the photo be Gran? Gran is as English as fish and chips. You only have to listen to her Surrey-honed accent to know that. She grew up in Sutton, the only daughter of Derek and Freda Cunningham, a dentist and his wife, and has never, for as long as I have known her, spoken of Spain. Uncle Robin, though twelve years younger than Gran, grew up on the same street as his cousin. Surely he would have detected something? If Gran had been adopted then it would have been known amongst the family, wouldn't it? None of it makes sense.

Yet Uncle Robin was adamant that the girl in the photo is Gran. 'It's her, Corinne,' he said, as I stood half-dazed, the phone pressed to my ear. 'I don't know how or why, but it is Joyce. There is no doubt about it.'

Robin grew up with Gran. He knew her when she was young and would have seen photos of her from when she was in her teens, and though Uncle Robin can turn on the dramatic tension for the TV cameras, he is not someone who jumps to wild conclusions. If he says it's Gran, then I have to believe him.

But then Jimmy said the girl, Teresa, had been killed alongside Mary at Rochester Place that night, and the plaque on the bench that a guilt-ridden Fred Harding had erected confirmed it. Yet how to explain how a seemingly dead Spanish orphan came to take on the identity of a suburban, Surrey schoolgirl called Joyce? And, even more curious, how did her long-dead foster mother come to call me on my mobile begging for help?

My head feels like it is about to explode as I make my way along the strip-lit corridor. Annie said that Gran was in the ICU, so following the overhead signs I make my way to the elevator. When I step inside, I catch a glimpse of myself in the mirror. It may be the fluorescent lighting inside the elevator, but my skin has taken on a greenish tinge. I look . . . ghostly.

I explain who I am to the duty nurse, a large woman with rosy cheeks and a kind smile who introduces herself as Michelle, and she leads me down the corridor to the private room where Gran has been placed.

'She was talking about you earlier,' says Michelle, turning to me and smiling. 'I asked her if she had any other family, and she said she had two lovely girls in London. Is that your sister she was referring to?'

'My wife,' I say, wishing with all my heart that Nidra were with me now.

'Ah, I see,' says Michelle, nodding. 'To be honest, your gran hasn't been making much sense, though we think that's because she suffered a mini-stroke either before or after she fell. Though she's lucky her neighbour found her when she did. She's a little confused still, so you'll have to be patient with her. Though Annie tells me you're a first responder, so you'll be used to keeping calm in a crisis, eh?'

We stop outside a glass-panelled room. There is a piece of card wedged on the door with *JOYCE SIMP-SON* printed on it. I look at the name and a peculiar feeling comes over me. It is like I am about to meet a stranger.

'Here we are,' says Michelle, pushing the door open. 'Hello, Joyce. Look who's come to see you.'

Gran looks up at me from the bed, where she is lying with her head propped up. She has a cannula inserted into a vein on one hand and an ET tube in her mouth. Beside the bed, a machine monitors her heart rate. I stare at the numbers, reluctant to look Gran in the eye. The room smells of detergent and bodily fluids.

'Here,' says Michelle, taking a plastic chair from the corner of the room and placing it by the bed. 'Sit yourself down, Corinne.'

I swallow the unease that is rising like bile in my throat and sit down on the hard chair. Clasping my hands on my lap, I keep my eyes lowered while Michelle takes a reading from the machine then walks across to the door.

'I'll leave you to have some time with your gran,' she says. 'If you need me, I'm just outside the door, at the nurses' station.'

'Thank you, Michelle,' I say, as she closes the door.

Then, with a pounding heart, I turn my head towards

the bed. Relief floods my body. It is still Gran. Her familiar soft brown eyes look up at me and, as she puts her hand on mine, the tears that I have been holding in since I first got the call come pouring forth.

'There now, dote,' she says, croakily. 'Don't be upsetting yourself now.'

I take Gran's hand in mine, forgetting for a few moments about Teresa Garro and the photograph. All that matters is that Gran is here – that she is safe.

'They said you had a stroke,' I say, rubbing her soft skin. 'Do you have any memory of what happened before Annie found you? How you fell?'

Gran goes to answer, then her eyes dart to the door. I turn round and see an elderly man standing there, dressed in a dark overcoat and a bright red wool scarf. He is rather short, with crinkled olive skin and cropped white hair. As he removes his coat he looks up and meets my eye. His face is familiar.

'Look who's here, darling,' says Gran, gesturing to me. 'It's our beautiful granddaughter.'

My stomach knots. Did I hear her correctly?

'You mean?' I say, staggering to my feet. 'You're . . .'

The man comes over to me and puts both hands on my shoulders. His eyes fill with tears, and he shakes his head. I look back at him, remembering the photos in Gran's old album. This man, holding my infant mother in the garden of our house, tanned arms and black hair, aviator sunglasses; one of him and Gran at Mum's First

Holy Communion, Gran demure in her favourite burgundy twin set, he smartly dressed in a three-piece suit, my mother in the middle, her face obscured by a white veil. My grandfather. The man who Gran swept all trace of from the house, the only memory of him a few Polaroids in a dusty old album. Here he is.

'It's uncanny,' he says, his voice trembling. 'The resemblance. It's like looking at . . .'

'She's her mother's daughter, alright,' says Gran, raspily. 'With those eyebrows. Though she has my temperament, thank goodness.'

He guides me back to the chair, then sits on the other side of the bed and places his hand on Gran's.

'You're . . . you're my grandfather?' I say, my face flushing. 'Grandad Len?'

'I am, yes,' he says, sorrowfully. 'Though I suppose that title ought to be earned. I haven't been around for you, Corinne, though hopefully when you hear our story, you'll understand.'

He looks at Gran. She gives him a little nod, then they both turn to me.

'For now, it's probably best you call me by my first name,' he says, his mouth trembling with emotion. 'The name I was born with. Luca.'

29

Teresa

Mary still has not come. It must be at least fifteen minutes since the sirens sounded. Now, with explosions pounding the air above, there is little chance of her making it out here.

Please, Mari. Please keep her safe.

I have never been in the shelter alone before. Though I have a torch, it is casting strange shadowy shapes on the walls, like sea monsters or wolves with sharp teeth. I am writing this in the back of Mary's diary, which, unbeknownst to her, I hid underneath my bed down here. Though I know almost everything that is contained in the diary, it gives me comfort to look at it from time to time. Now, though, reading is not enough. I have to do something to stop my hands from shaking, and writing helps keep the fear at bay. This pen is my sword, and I shall strike back at every bomb with a word or a sentence, just as Ronald would tell me to.

But what would Mary do? What would she say if she were here? Well, she would hold me in her arms, her dark head propped up on the pillow, and she would tell me stories about Grace O'Malley. 'Do you think a few explosions would have scared our pirate queen?' she would say, stroking my arm to stop me trembling, the

264

scent of her rosewater perfume filling the air. 'The girl who cut off her hair and pretended to be a boy so that she could join her father's naval fleet? The girl who marched into the court of Elizabeth I, refusing to bow, and demanded the release of her imprisoned son as well as the right to claim her ancestral lands? Goodness, no.'

Mary's soothing voice would calm my nerves as it did the first day I met her, back in the convent, when I heard the news that Bilbao had fallen and called out for Mari, the goddess of the mountains, but was sent an Irish storyteller with cherry-red shoes instead.

'And what about Constance Markievicz?' she would continue, while I closed my eyes and pictured the woman who had fought alongside Mary's brother in the Easter Rising and had saved Mary from a miserable life with the fat old farmer. Constance, with her deep-set green eyes, her tall, formidable frame, and her kind heart, which she gave freely to those who needed her help. 'I don't think she would have been cowed by a few bombs.'

Thoughts of Mary and Grace and Constance, the holy trinity of fearless women, flit through my head as I sit here in the half-light, trying my best to keep my nerve. But I am only eleven years old. I am just a child, and I am scared.

There was a lull in the bombing just now, and I thought the All Clear might sound, but a faint rumble in the distance makes me think that I will be here for most of the night. I think back to earlier, when the siren sounded at the exact moment there was a knock at the door. Why did Mary answer it when she knows to run for cover immediately when the siren sounds? Did she think it might be Ronald? Or perhaps that woman who came yesterday, the one who made Mary behave strangely. Whoever it was, Mary has surely risked her life by answering that door.

Yet I am here, alive, and I need her. I need her so much my heart burns. Up above, the rumbles grow louder. Soon the explosions will return with a vengeance, and I will be back in the market square, terrified and alone but this time there will be no Katalin to save me. I feel the solidity of the prism in my pocket, try to recall Katalin's words about life after death, but I am not ready for death, not now. I am just a girl. Then I remember something the nuns used to do at the convent. On Sundays, they would ask us girls how we were feeling and what we wished to pray for that day. Then they would write down the names of the saints they felt could help us with our problems, and we would read the names out loud and ask them to help. Maybe if I do the same with the names of everyone I have known and loved then they will hear me and help me.

Here goes . . .

Katalin! José! Mary! Ronald! Luca! Help me!

Padre Armando! Ana!

Mario! Rosaria! Eider! Veronica!

Sister Bernadette!

Jimmy!

Grace O'Malley! Queen Maeve! Mari, oh Mari!

Please, someone, help me.

Then, my head fills with the image of Ronald and Mary that last day, dancing to their favourite song. I can hear Ronald's crisp clear voice singing along: 'Even when the darkest clouds are in the sky . . .'

266

'Write, Teresa,' Ronald's voice whispers in my ear. 'Keep writing until the All Clear sounds.'

I am doing as he asks but, as this pen strokes the page, I hear other voices. All the people I love are singing the song.

'Spread a little happiness as you go by.'

The bombs intensify, but they are now just a backdrop to the rousing rendition, a timpani drum keeping time.

'Write, Teresa,' cries Ronald. 'Write what you are wishing for.'

I wish for the voices to be real. I wish that all the people I love and care for could be in this room, sitting with me, joining hands and singing along.

'Write it as though it is real, Teresa,' says Ronald, his voice rising above the singing.

There is Katalin sitting by the wall, her black hair swept back in a ponytail, the sleeves of her linen shirt rolled up. José is beside her, holding a bag of cinnamon buns. They tap their feet in time to the music as they eat their treats, faces beaming, as though they haven't a care in the world. Next to them, Mary and Ronald nuzzle together, lost in each other, as they sing along to their favourite tune. Luca winks at me from beside Ronald. He has never liked singing but, God love him, he is mouthing the words as best he can, his hands joined with Mario, who sits beside him, his face now free of worry.

'Keep writing,' Ronald implores me. 'Not long now until we get the All Clear.'

I do as he says and see Padre Armando link arms with Sister Bernadette as they belt out the song with as much passion as if they were singing a hymn. Veronica, Ana, Rosaria and Eider giggle, their faces flushed as they swing their hands and tap their feet. They are all here to keep me company.

And then, at long last, I hear it. The All Clear. The singing stops and they dissolve into the shadows. Ronald, Mary, Katalin, José, Luca and Mario, Padre Armando and Sister Bernadette, Jimmy and the girls, the friends and family I have brought to my side with a stroke of my pen.

'You can stop now, Teresa,' says Ronald. 'No more writing tonight.'

30

Teresa

It was still dark when I emerged from the shelter. The air was eerily silent; the Luftwaffe, having wreaked their havoc, had moved on elsewhere. My legs were numb from sitting on the bed, and as I got to the top of the shelter steps, I lost my footing and fell onto the grass. The gnomes that Luca had lovingly placed at the entrance of the shelter were lying on the ground beside me, their cheery faces cracked and broken. I scrambled to my feet, my eyes slowly adjusting to the dark, and then I saw something so horrifying I could barely breathe.

The back of the house had disappeared, exposed like a giant doll's house. Where the kitchen door had been was now a heap of glass and rubble, with black smoke rising from it. In the coop, the chickens were screeching and frantically flapping their wings. In a daze I staggered onwards. Then I saw something glinting in the moonlight, on the ground by the coop. As I drew closer, I saw that it was Mary's handbag, the silver clasp undone.

She wasn't in the kitchen, I told myself, as I stumbled out of the side gate, which was hanging from its hinges, and made my way to the front of the house. She was going to answer the door.

The front door, on the other side of the building. She will be safe.

Yet, when I reached the front garden, any hope I may have been clinging on to evaporated. It was not just the kitchen that had been hit. Rochester Place, my home for the last three years, was nothing more than a smouldering ruin. Smoke rose like evil spirits from the bricks. I saw a flash of red: the exquisite front door laid like a stretcher across the surface of what had once been the path. The timber frame of the house wobbled precariously, as if it were about to crumble.

And then, as the smoke cleared, I saw the outline of a body. A woman was lying amid the rubble, her arms spread out like Christ on the cross. I saw the distinctive dark hair, the black coat she had thrown on to answer the door, the red shoes . . . Oh, Mary. Oh, my heart.

Then I heard a loud whining noise. At first, I feared another attack, and was about to throw myself onto the ground when I recognized it was a siren. Help was coming.

There were other sounds too. Screams coming from nearby Larkin Road and beyond. I stood frozen to the spot, unable to move, unable to speak, to cry, to scream. I heard the sirens drawing closer. Soon they would arrive. They would put out the flames. The wardens would then take out a stretcher from the back of the ambulance and they would scramble around the rubble. They would find Mary and they would bring her out.

I could not see them do that. I could not see my Mary hauled out of there like the shoppers in the market square, broken and crushed. I had to leave before they arrived. I had to get so far

270

away that I would not be able to hear them say that she was dead.

So, I ran back down to the shelter, where I sit now, trying to block out the horror by writing through it.

Mary's voice punctures the air. The words of courage she spoke to me at the convent, and again when war was declared, mean more to me now than when she first said them. Back then Ronald was safe and well, the house was intact and as warm and secure as ever, Mary was not grief-stricken, Mario was serving frothy coffee and fretting over whether he could get fresh garlic if rationing came in, and Luca's only concern was the fate of the Asian elephants at London Zoo.

And Katalin? Katalin was in a prison camp. Will I ever see her again?

I want to scream but no sound will come from my lungs. I feel like all the air has been sucked from me, from the room, from the world.

I will stop writing now and leave this diary where it belongs, at Rochester Place. Whoever finds it will learn about the people who once lived in this little corner of South London and, hopefully, be able to piece together our story. I have no need of it any more. To keep it with me, to read about Mary and Ronald and Katalin, of Mario and Luca, the people I love and who have loved me in return, would be too much to bear. So, I will let it go. I have committed its contents to memory, and it will live on in my heart for the rest of my days.

31

Corinne

Sitting on the sofa in Gran's cottage, cradling a cup of strong Irish tea in my hands, I go over the events of the previous day, still stunned by the revelations. By the fact that the person I thought I knew more than anyone in this world, the person who raised me, who told me bed-time stories and rocked me to sleep, who queued up outside HMV on Oxford Street with me when I was seven years old so that I could meet the Spice Girls – the woman who has been a constant when everything else in my life has fallen apart – was to all intents and purposes a stranger.

As I sat by her hospital bed, with Luca holding her hand, I told Gran about the phone call, about Mary, about Robin's investigations into Rochester Place and the discovery of the diary.

'It was Robin who recognized you,' I told her. 'He said he'd know that unruly hair anywhere.'

'Darling Robin,' whispered Gran. 'Oh, what must he think of me? What must he think of both of us? Lying to him for all these years.'

'We didn't lie, Toto,' said Luca. 'We did what we had to do to survive.'

'Tell me what happened, Gran,' I said. 'Tell me who you are.'

Gran turned to me then, and between rasping breaths, she told me the story of her early life. She told me of Guernica, the lovely market town where she had been born and raised. As she spoke of the apartment where she had grown up, with its terracotta tiled floor, its balcony that overlooked the town square, and the ginger cat that came to the stairwell each day to be fed, her face changed. She was no longer Joyce Simpson, the jolly lady from suburban South London who entertained children with her stories at Tooting Library. She was Teresa Garro, a survivor.

Now, sitting in her cottage – the place I have visited countless times – with only the sound of the sea for company, I notice things that I hadn't before. The Basque cookbook wedged on the shelf by the Aga, the black lace mantilla draped across the back of the armchair, the framed print of Picasso's *Guernica* hanging above the fireplace. Gran has displayed her Basque identity in plain sight, as she never did, or maybe never felt she could, back in London.

I recall how her eyes misted over in the hospital when she spoke about Guernica, how she stopped and let out a noise that was half sob, half shout. Worried that talk of her past would raise her blood pressure, I told her that we could resume the conversation later, but she insisted we continue.

'I have kept this secret for eighty years,' she said, composing herself. 'If I don't tell you now, my dote, I may not get another chance.'

So she continued, painting a vivid picture of a life and a family I had been completely unaware of. My great-grandparents, who died in a rail accident when Gran was a baby; my brave, fiercely independent great-aunt Katalin, who became guardian to Gran when she was just sixteen, and the songs she sang in the town square, the delicious pepper stew she would cook in the tiny kitchen, the love and security she bestowed on her little sister.

'She was my first love,' Gran said, her eyes fixed on that spot in the middle of the room that she had addressed the whole story to, as though talking to a ghost. 'My protector.'

Her shoulders tensed as she spoke about the first stirrings of war, the talk in the cafés and bars of men and women having to do their bit to fight fascism. 'But to me, that's all it was,' she said, shaking her head. 'Just talk. As far as I was concerned, the war and Franco and fascism were happening elsewhere, in big cities like Bilbao. It was absurd that it could come to a small backwater town like Guernica.'

Then, as she described what happened next, how her childish hope had been ripped apart on an ordinary

Monday afternoon in April 1937, I was suddenly living through it with her. I could smell the scent of the lilies that she had stopped to look at, just moments before the German Condor Legion unleashed hell from the skies above the market square. I could taste the fear Gran had felt as she cowered underneath the flower stall, tucked into the chest of the stall holder, the smell of smoke and death filling the air.

Outside the cottage window, the Atlantic Ocean whips and sprays, while here in the warmth I recall how Luca sobbed as Gran told her story. She had emerged from the shelter and stumbled across the ruins of Rochester Place.

'That's when . . .' she said, squeezing Luca's hand. 'That's when . . . oh, my heart, it was torn in two. But I thought it was her . . . I had no idea it was my . . . it was my . . . Oh, it's too much, I can't . . .'

'Shh, now, Toto,' Luca whispered, pressing his head to hers. 'You heard what the nurse said. You must try to keep calm.'

'I'm fine,' said Gran, though her voice was trembling. 'I have to get all this out before . . . before it's too late. Corinne needs to hear it. There's been too much hiding, more than I even realized, but she has to know the truth. This is her family.'

But before she could continue, Nurse Phelan came in and told us that visiting time was almost over. A camp bed had been arranged for Luca to sleep on. He had promised Gran that, this time, he would not leave her side. I wanted to ask them what had happened, how it could be that you could lose the love of your life not just once but twice, but I could see that Gran was tiring and, with Nurse Phelan lingering by the door, I realized that those questions would have to wait.

'I'd better get going, Gran,' I said, squeezing her hand. 'Though I'll just be at the cottage, and I'll have my phone with me throughout the night if you need me. I'll come back again tomorrow. Try to get some rest now, won't you?'

She looked up at me then, and met my eyes for the first time since I had arrived.

'They say that your life doesn't necessarily begin the day you are born,' she said, smiling her gentle smile. 'It begins the day you choose life over death. When I heard the ambulances arrive, I climbed out of the shelter and started to run. I ran and I ran until I no longer knew where I was. On a busy high street I was found by a young woman with cropped red hair. Seeing that I was in distress, she took me to the nearest Salvation Army shelter, where she sat with me all through the day. Her name was Corinne, and I never saw her again. Though when you were born, I suggested your mother call you that, after the calm, kind girl who sat with me when my heart was breaking. You know, my darling, seeing how you have turned out and the work you do, staying on the phone and calming people when they are at their most vulnerable, I always think how it was just the right name for you.'

I smiled, accepting the blessing granted to me – the name of a stranger who had appeared in Gran's hour of need.

'I never forgot Rochester Place,' Gran said, her voice weakening. 'I even went back there a few times over the years, though all that's left is an overgrown garden.'

As she spoke, the memory of that rainy night returned to me.

'Did you ever take me with you?' I asked. 'In the car?'

'Just once,' said Gran, her expression softening. 'You weren't sleeping. Your grandfather had left, and I was at my wits' end. I didn't know what to do, how to help you. I had no one to turn to. I drove round and round. Then, once you had fallen asleep, I drove to Rochester Place, parked outside the gate, and went to sit in the garden where I had spent that long night huddled in the Anderson shelter. I closed my eyes and asked Mary to help me, asked her if everything was going to be alright. Then the heavens opened, and I got soaked running back to the car, but I knew the rain was a sign from Mary. She had those little Irish superstitions involving the weather. The rain, apparently, was a good sign. I knew it was her telling me not to worry.'

Draining my tea, I get up and walk over to the window, where I stand looking out at a wild, rugged stretch of ocean. The sky, which was the colour of pewter earlier, has lightened and the water is calm and still. Gran told me that Mary had been baptized in the shallows on that very stretch of water, and that Gran, after being placed in a foster home, had given herself her very own baptism of sorts by telling her carers that her name was Joyce and she had been born in Tooting. Teresa had died alongside Mary, she said. From that day onwards, she never spoke of Mary or Ronald or Rochester Place or Guernica again – though, she assured me, she had kept them hidden in her heart.

Stepping back from the window, I pause by Gran's bookshelves, which line the whole of one wall. I spot Uncle Robin's *House Detective* series, his grinning face beaming out from the spine; then there are the classics Gran devoured when I was little – *Rebecca*, *Wuthering Heights*, *The Collected Dickens*. They stir up memories of curling on the sofa with Gran on Christmas Eve, drinking hot chocolate while she read to me from *A Christmas Carol*. She would always pause when the Ghost of Christmas Past led Scrooge back to his childhood home, and though at the time I just thought she was overcome by the emotion of the story, now it all makes sense. I spot a few Hemingways on the shelf too – *For Whom the Bell Tolls* now taking on an extra resonance with the knowledge that Gran actually lived through the civil war that Hemingway wrote about.

Then, I notice something: a thick, hardback book lying on its side on the bottom shelf.

The Other Lands: A Tale of Courage Against the Odds
by
Ronald O'Connor

Opening the book, I see a simple paragraph that makes my heart hurt.

The following story was inspired by the lives of two brave and brilliant young women, Mary O'Connor and Teresa Garro. It is dedicated to them.

I flick back a couple of pages and see that it was published in 1960, twenty years after Ronald was supposedly killed in action.

Closing the book, I trace my fingers over the raised letters of the author's name. Ronald O'Connor. Not only had Ronald seemingly survived, but he took the name of the woman he loved, the woman who had deceived him, and immortalized her in print.

I am about to return the book to the shelf when something slips out. It is a receipt from the Ballina branch of Oxfam. The name of Ronald's book is printed on it, along with the price – five euros – and the date: 5 June 2016.

Gran bought the cottage and moved to Achill the following year, though I remember her going on holiday to Ireland in 2016, just after Saira died. She had returned invigorated and told us that she planned to buy a place in Achill and move there permanently. We were all surprised by this – though Gran had always had a soft spot for Irish culture, particularly the folk tales, she had never expressed a desire to live there. She had always seemed so settled in South London. Now, though, it all begins to fall into place. Gran went to Ireland to see the place where Mary had grown up, and while there she stumbled upon Ronald's book in a branch of Oxfam. I picture her wandering through the shop, idly browsing, then seeing that name, reading that dedication. How shocked she must have been.

My thoughts are interrupted by the sound of a key in the lock. I look up and see Luca striding into the living room.

'Your gran's okay – just resting. She sent me home. I know it's early, but I could do with a stiff drink,' he says. 'Will you join me?'

I should be angry with this man. After all, he abandoned Gran in her darkest hour. But, somehow, in the wake of all that has happened, anger seems redundant now.

'Yes, please,' I say, watching as he goes to the drinks cabinet and takes out a bottle of Jameson and two crystal tumblers.

'Saluti,' he says, handing me a glass. 'Or should I say, sláinte.'

'You're forgetting "salud",' I say. 'Though that's Spanish. I wonder what the Basque word is.'

'It's "topa". Your grandmother used to whisper it whenever we made a toast. It was one of the few Basque expressions she still used. Don't you remember?'

I shake my head.

'She probably packed it away along with my old shirts,' he says, flopping onto the sofa with a sigh. 'Too many painful memories.'

'What happened, Luca?' I say, sitting down next to him. 'When they took you away?'

He takes a long slug of whisky then, with his eyes fixed on his glass, tells me how, after being interned in a camp on Wimbledon Common, he and his father were separated. Mario was deported and sent to Canada, while Luca was sent to an orphanage on the south coast. It was a brutal place, and he quickly learned that if he were to survive, he would need to shake off his Italian identity. So, Luca De Santis became Len Simpson. His background, his mannerisms, his whole life history was erased, and it was a different, quieter, broken young man who emerged from that institution in 1947.

'Everything had been taken from me,' he says, choked with emotion. 'But there was one thing I was determined not to lose, and that was my Toto. I bought a one-way ticket to Waterloo station and headed for Tooting. It took me eighteen months, but I found her.'

He pauses to take a sip of whisky before continuing.

'One of the chaps in the insurance office I was

working in told me about this lovely young librarian who had enchanted his young son and daughter with her stories at Tooting Library. He said she told an adventure story called *The Other Lands* that had kept the kids enraptured all afternoon. As soon as he said that, I knew that I'd found her.'

He leans back on the sofa, his eyes on the ceiling.

Then he turns to me. 'I thought we were cursed. That's why I left her the second time. We had been so happy as children, then our lives fell apart. When we reunited, we had a few blissful years but the darkness crept in again, and I thought I had brought it with me, that I was a bad omen.'

'I don't believe in that kind of thing,' I say, watching as the fire fizzes in the grate. 'I think life is hard, that it throws terrible experiences your way, but those aren't brought about by bad luck or curses.'

'Nothing more terrible than having to bury your own child, Corinne,' he says, cradling the tumbler in trembling hands. 'I thought losing my father had been tough, thought being sent to an orphanage was the worst life would throw at me, but seeing my precious only child struggle with addiction, then having to . . . having to . . . pick out a coffin . . . it's . . .'

He lets the sentence hang, takes another sip of whisky, then, putting the tumbler down, stands up and walks to the window.

'I told your grandmother I was leaving a few months

later,' he says, clasping his gnarled hands behind his back. 'It was the hardest thing I have ever had to do, but I told her it was the only way – that when we were together terrible things kept happening. I looked at you, this innocent little toddler, and I knew I couldn't risk history repeating itself. We had to break the chain.'

A heavy silence falls between us. He steps away from the window and picks up the book I left on the window-sill when he arrived home.

'Ah, I see you found *The Other Lands*,' he says, turning the book over in his hands. 'You know, your gran gave me a draft of this when I was taken away. I used to read it in secret when I was in the camp.'

'That dedication was a surprise,' I say. 'Especially after reading about his death in Mary's diary. Gran must have got such a shock to see that he had survived.'

'Yes, she did,' says Luca, placing the book back on the shelf. 'But that's not the half of it. You know what put your Gran in the hospital? She found out something else. It wasn't just Ronald who survived the war and lived to a grand old age. Mary did too.'

32

Corinne

'Your grandmother had been in touch with a woman called Stella Jones,' says Luca, pouring himself another whisky. 'She was Ronald's niece, the daughter of his sister, Daphne. Apparently, when she found that book and realized that Ronald had survived, she started digging around. God knows how she tracked down the niece but I suppose in this age of the internet, anything is possible. Can I top you up?'

He gestures to my glass, which is still half-full. I shake my head.

'Probably best,' he says, pouring himself a small measure. 'I'll just have a tot to warm me. This Irish weather chills my bones.'

He brings the drink back to the sofa, takes a long sip then places the tumbler on the coffee table. I notice his hands are trembling. I think of my mother, lying in bed surrounded by empty bottles.

'Anyway, where was I?' he says, interrupting my thoughts. 'Oh, yes, Stella Jones. Her mother had recently died, and when the family were going through her stuff, they came across a box full of Ronald's possessions. Apparently, he'd left the contents of his house to his sister, and they were sent to her when he died. When your grandmother told Stella Jones who she was, Stella told her about the box and said that your grandmother should have it. I think your gran thought it would just be keepsakes, old photos, that sort of thing. But when it arrived, she found much more than she bargained for. That's when I got the phone call.'

'Gran called you? But I thought the two of you were no longer in contact.'

'She always knew where I was,' he says, his eyes clouding over. 'I've been living in Italy for the last twenty-seven years. It was the only place I could think to go when I left your Gran. I tracked down some of my father's relatives, found some work, started to build a quiet life for myself, tried to deal with my grief. But I always made sure your grandmother had a contact number for me, just in case . . . well, in case anything terrible happened, I suppose. I knew we couldn't be together, but I have always loved her, Corinne.'

I nod my head, trying to imagine Luca getting on with his life, knowing that Gran and I were in London. Could there be another family, a new wife? I want to ask him, but I don't know how to even begin. He is still a relative stranger to me. I stay silent and wait while he composes himself.

'She was making no sense at all on the phone,' he

says, reaching forward to take his glass. 'She was calling from the landline as she'd mislaid her mobile. The connection was terrible, and I had to strain to hear what she was saying through the crackles. What I could hear though left me shaken. I hadn't heard her this upset since your mother died. I knew she needed my help, so I took the next flight over here. When I arrived, she was in such a state. She was pacing round the room, all agitated, and she looked like she hadn't brushed her hair in days. I managed to calm her down, ran her a warm bath, then we had some dinner. When we'd finished eating, I washed up then went to join her in the living room. She was sitting in front of the television, watching what I thought was an old documentary. There was a woman on the screen, sitting in a big old armchair, in front of a window looking out to sea. Your grandmother told me to sit down, asked if I recognized the woman. Now, my eyesight is not what it used to be, and all I could see was a very thin old lady with white hair tied up in a bun. I told your grandmother I had no idea who it was, and she got agitated again, started jabbing her finger at the screen. "Can't you see?" she yelled. "Surely you can see." I still didn't recognize her, but then I heard her speak. When I heard that woman talking, the years fell away, and I was back in the garden of Rochester Place.'

He pauses, then looks up at me.

'There was no mistaking that voice,' he said. 'And

that's when I knew why your grandmother was so distraught. The woman on the videotape was Mary.'

'But how could it have been?' I say, my eyes drawn to Luca's trembling hands. 'Everyone I've spoken to said she died that night.'

'I think that's what she wanted them to believe,' says Luca.

There is a knock at the door, and we both jump.

'That will be Annie,' I say, checking my watch. 'She said she'd drive us to the hospital.'

'Saved by the bell, eh?' Luca staggers to his feet. 'Come on, let's go find our Toto.'

When we get to the ward, Luca stops by the nurses' station to get an update on Gran's condition while I hurry towards her room. When I open the door, I see a familiar figure sitting by Gran's bed, his back to me, his hair as messy as ever.

'Uncle Robin,' I say, rushing to him, suddenly overcome with emotion. 'I'm so glad you're here. I didn't know you were coming.'

'I got an early flight this morning and came straight here,' he says, shuffling his chair along to make room for me. 'I had to see her.'

Gran's eyes are closed. Her cheeks are sunken and her collarbone is sticking out from the hospital-issue nightgown. She looks like a fragile ornament, like the slightest touch could break her into pieces. Beside her, the heart monitor displays a steady rate.

'She was awake when I arrived,' says Robin, visibly emotional. 'We managed to have a little chat. Oh, Corinne, I still can't believe it. When I saw that photo I . . .'

His voice cracks. I put my hand on his shoulder as he composes himself.

'All these years and she never said anything, not a word,' he says. 'I've spent the last two days re-evaluating every detail of my childhood. Did her parents – well, her adoptive parents – know her background? Did my parents? Good grief, I never even knew she was adopted. We used to remark on how much she resembled her mother, my aunt Freda. They had the same olive complexion, the same dark eyes. I feel like I've woken up in a different universe.'

'Did Gran clarify any of that for you when you spoke to her today?' I ask, glancing at Gran as she lies in the bed, her eyelids fluttering.

'She said that when she was put into foster care, she told them her name was Joyce and that she had been born in Tooting,' he says, shaking his head, still wrestling with the news.

'Yes, she told me that too.'

'I understand that after everything she went through, she might have wanted to block it all out and start again,' says Robin. 'But there must have been moments when she wanted to talk about it. I could understand it when we were children, but as adults . . . well, I feel sad that she felt she couldn't confide in me.'

'I don't think it was personal, Uncle Robin,' I say, placing my hand on his shoulder. 'She kept it from all of us.'

'Corinne, is that you?'

We look up at the sound of Gran's voice. She is awake.

'Hello, Gran,' I say, sitting down at the end of the bed. 'How are you feeling this morning?'

'Like I've been hit by a truck,' she says, smiling weakly. 'A big monster truck.'

'Ah, Toto, you're awake.'

At the sound of my grandfather's voice, Uncle Robin gets to his feet.

'Len,' he cries, shaking his head in disbelief. 'What are you doing here?'

'Hello, Robin,' says Luca sheepishly. 'Listen, how about we go and get some coffee and I'll fill you in on everything. Come on, I'll treat you to one of the vending machine's finest.'

Robin glances at me, then at Gran, as though waiting for permission.

'Go on, you two,' croaks Gran. 'You've got a lot of catching up to do.'

Uncle Robin nods and, grabbing his coat from the back of the chair, follows Luca out of the room.

'Luca told me about Mary,' I say, pulling my chair closer. 'That must have been a terrible shock for you.'

'I don't know, dote,' says Gran, sighing. 'I think part of me always knew, deep down, that she had got out of there. Mary was a survivor. The biggest shock was finding out what happened that night, knowing that she came, knowing it was her that I had lost and not Mary.'

'Who are you talking about?'

Gran starts to weep quietly. I take a tissue from the box by the bed and gently dab her eyes.

'It's okay, Gran,' I say. 'You don't have to talk about it yet if it's too painful.'

'It was all there on that video,' she says, a hint of bitterness in her voice. 'All the missing pieces. That evening, just as the air-raid siren went off, there was a knock on the door.'

I nod my head, remembering the diary.

'Mary told me to wait,' Gran continues. 'Said she had to get the door. She was in such a state, all jumpy, like she was walking on glass. But I was a good girl, and I did as Ronald told me. I ran to the shelter. Oh, my darling sister, if only I had known . . .'

She squeezes my hand. Her skin feels hot and clammy.

'My Katalin would have loved you. You have her strong nature, and her . . . kind eyes.'

She pauses, then whispers something under her breath.

'She had come to find me,' she says, regaining her

composure. 'That's what Mary said on the video. She had been working for the Associated Press as a newspaper photographer, and had managed to get a pass to come to London to document the Blitz. The Basque Children's Committee had given her Mary and Ronald's address, and she chose that night to come for me. Mary had told her I was in the shelter and to go and find me, that she herself had to run. She left Katalin standing in the hallway. She was moments from me. My Katalin, she had come. After all this time, she had come. If only she had arrived just a few minutes earlier, she would have found me.'

She starts to cry then, uncontrollable sobs of pain and anguish that she has spent the last eight decades holding in. I put my arms around her and hold her close.

'I . . . saw her,' she says. 'I saw her. When I came out of the shelter for the first time. With all the smoke, it was difficult to see clearly, and I thought it was her, thought it was Mary, but now, when I think about it, I should have recognized the coat. After all those years, she still had that big old tweed coat.'

'Gran, I don't know what to say. I can't believe you've had to live with this grief all these years. I just wish I could have made it better.'

She pulls away and takes my face in her hands.

'My girl,' she says, her eyes brightening. 'My darling girl. You made everything better.'

'I hope I did,' I say. 'Still, it just seems so unfair that you and Luca had to face so much heartache.'

'I realized early on that my life would be full of contrasts,' she says. 'The highest of highs and the lowest of lows. But there was one constant amid all of it, one shining light, and that was you, my darling. If anyone could be said to be the one true love of my life, it is you. My Corinne.'

'Gran,' I say. 'I . . . I . . .'

I want to tell her how much I love her, how much she means to me too, but emotion gets the better of me.

'As for your grandfather,' says Gran, stroking my arm gently. 'We were never truly apart, despite our geographical separation. We could feel each other's souls. I knew he would always be there for me, and he knew I would be there for him. That's what happens when two people meet as children. Those people understand us on a deeper level, they know our true selves, the child we bury when we grow up. That's why I was so glad you found Nidra again after all those years. She's your soulmate.'

The door opens and Luca strides in. Uncle Robin follows behind in a daze.

'I take it he's told you, then,' I say.

Robin looks at me and nods.

'He certainly has,' he says. 'And I think I may need something a little stronger than coffee. Anyway, look who's arrived.'

I look up and see Nidra at the door, hair scraped back in a messy ponytail, her hot-pink rucksack on her shoulder and her arms laden with Tupperware boxes. My heart lifts. I have never been happier to see someone in my life.

'Right,' she says, placing the rucksack on the floor. 'Who fancies a dosa?'

33

Corinne
PRESENT DAY

'Luca is your grandfather,' says Nidra, shaking her head.
'I can't get my head round it.'

'That makes two of us,' I say.

'Make that three,' says Uncle Robin, with a chuckle.
'Thank God for wine, that's all I can say.'

After leaving Gran to get some rest, with Luca by her
side, Robin, Nidra and I returned to the cottage. Now, as
we sit on the veranda, blankets over our knees, sipping
red wine and watching the ocean, it still feels unreal. It is
just getting dark, though the embers of a golden sun
dance across the waves like a thousand sparks.

'A peaceful place, this,' says Robin, with a sigh. 'No
wonder your gran was so charmed by it. A little too
peaceful for me, though. I don't think I could live without my dear East End bustle. I find the noises of the
city strangely comforting. Always have.'

I nod my head, recalling the evening drives through
South London with Gran, the burr of the traffic lulling
me to sleep, and as I do, Mary's voice returns to me with
a jolt.

Please, you have to help me . . . She's trapped.

'You know, we've discovered so many secrets these last few days,' I say, taking a sip of wine. 'And yet we still haven't solved the mystery that started it all.'

'The phone call?' says Robin, turning to me, his face flushed with wine and the bracing sea air.

'I just don't understand it. How a person from my grandmother's long-buried past could have . . . connected with me like that.'

'I suppose some things can't be explained, no matter how hard we try,' says Robin. 'Some mysteries are meant to remain unsolved. I know a little of what you're feeling from the years I've spent digging around in the past. Once you start to peel back the layers of a house's history, you find all sorts of voices, long-dead voices, coming through, clamouring to be heard.'

'I understand that,' I say. 'But your job means you set out to uncover those things. You initiate the research from which the voices rise. With me, I was simply tidying away my lunch box at work. My mind was on my job. And now we know that Mary didn't die that night, so what? It was the ghost of her later self that called me?'

'Your gran used to say you were an empath,' says Robin, smiling gently. 'And I could see that too, when you were little. You could always spot a person in distress, someone who needed help. You've spent your life feeling people's emotions, their happiness, their pain. And you've spent your working life listening to voices

295

in peril on the other end of the line, a lot of whom won't make it. Think about all those people who died in the Blitz. Their voices fill the air around London. I've felt it myself.'

'Finally, someone comes around to my way of thinking,' says Nidra, laughing. 'Either that or you've had too much wine, Robin.'

'I'm just saying that Corinne might have tapped into something that night,' he says. 'And, in doing so, solved all these mysteries and brought the family together again.'

'I guess so,' I say, taking another sip of wine. 'Yet that call will always baffle me.'

Just then there is a knock at the door. I go to get up, but Nidra stops me.

'I'll get it,' she says, putting her hand on my shoulder. 'You stay and relax. You need it.'

She disappears into the cottage, leaving Robin and me sitting in silence, mesmerized by the waves. I can hear voices coming from inside, and a couple of minutes later Nidra returns.

'That was Annie,' she says, returning to her chair. 'She brought two casseroles and a lasagne for us to freeze.'

'Oh, that was kind of her,' says Robin. 'You don't get neighbours like that in London.'

'She also left this,' she says, handing me a piece of paper. 'The paramedics found it in your gran's hand when she had the fall. They gave it to Annie for safe-keeping.'

I take the piece of paper. There, written in Gran's distinctive handwriting, is my name and my mobile number. Underneath it is Luca's name and what must be his number.

'It was in her hands?' I look up at Nidra.

'That's what Annie said.'

'She must have been trying to call for help but she'd lost her phone. Annie hadn't returned it yet. Luca said he'd gone for a walk at the other end of the island when it happened. Poor Gran. She must have been so scared.'

'Don't beat yourself up, baby,' says Nidra. 'Annie found her, and Luca came back. All was well.'

She's right, but something is still bothering me, something I can't put my finger on.

'What the dickens is that?' says Robin, suddenly. 'Out there on the waves.'

Nidra stands up and looks out to sea.

'I can't see anything,' she says. 'Just mist.'

'Look closer,' he says, beckoning me to his side. 'There's something moving.'

He points his finger and I see a dark shape emerging from the water. Then it bursts forth and leaps into the air.

'A dolphin,' I cry.

'Oh, that is amazing.' Nidra beams. 'Look how graceful she is.'

As we stand watching, the dolphin splashes back into the water then disappears under the waves.

'Well, what a treat.' Robin turns to me, his eyes twinkling in the moonlight. 'Your gran used to tell me about them, but I never thought I'd get to see one for myself. What a blessing, eh?'

'Right, who would like some lasagne?' asks Nidra, heading back inside. 'Annie's made enough to feed an army.'

'Well, maybe just a little portion,' says Robin, following her in. 'I'm afraid I rather gorged on those dosas earlier. I always overeat in times of crisis.'

I stay where I am, glad of the silence, and watch as the sky turns from purple to black. As I stand here, I think of what Gran told me in the hospital – that I am the great love of her life. I think of Luca hiding out in Italy, trying to drown out his grief, running from a curse that neither he nor Gran truly believed in, then coming to her aid when she needed him, just as he had promised. That house I stumbled across on the back of a phone call has brought the story of my family full circle. And yet, despite all the revelations and resolutions, I still can't shake the feeling that there is something else I am not seeing, some final piece that will solve the puzzle once and for all.

'Corinne!'

Uncle Robin's voice cuts through my thoughts.

'Corinne, your phone's ringing.'

'Just coming,' I call, heading into the kitchen. Robin and Nidra are preparing a salad to go with the lasagne, and a local radio station is playing in the background. I hear the opening bars of Elton John's 'Tiny Dancer' as I reach across the counter and grab my phone.

'Hello,' I say, taking it into the quiet of the living room.

'Is that Corinne?' says a soft Irish voice, chillingly familiar.

'Yes, who is this?'

'It's Nurse Phelan. Michelle.'

'Oh,' I say, my heart lurching. 'Is everything okay?'

There's a pause on the other end that seems to last an eternity.

'I'm ever so sorry, Corinne . . .'

34

Corinne
TEN DAYS LATER

A cool evening breeze ripples across the water as we stand at the mouth of Achill Sound, in the shadow of an ancient tower, waiting for the moment when we will release Gran into her final resting place.

I hold the rectangular oak box in my hands, still unable to fully fathom that she is gone and not quite ready to let her go.

Gran stipulated to her solicitor that she was to be cremated in a fuss-free ceremony at the nearest crematorium to her cottage in Achill. When that was done, she wanted her family to take her ashes to a place called Kildavnet, in the south-east corner of Achill Island. There, she said, you will find a tower house, built in the fifteenth century by the O'Malley clan, and known locally as Grace O'Malley's Tower. *All I ask*, she wrote in her will, *is that you do not weep, but rather celebrate my life. Wear red for the goddess Mari, who came to me when I called all those years ago, and do me the honour of singing my favourite song as I go.*

According to Nurse Phelan, Gran fell asleep just after we left and never woke up. Luca, who stayed by her side to the end, said that in those final moments she looked like the young girl he had once known. 'All the pain had left her,' he told us. 'Her soul had flown free.'

We asked Luca to join us for the ceremony, but he declined. He had already said his goodbyes to Gran. In the days they spent at the cottage, they had made their peace. A couple of days after her death he disappeared, leaving a note to say that he had gone to explore the countryside of Ireland for a few days and would be back when the ceremony was over. I began to realize just how alike my grandparents were – two gentle but independent souls who had been rocked by trauma and heartbreak but had never been defeated.

'Are you ready, Corinne?'

I turn to Nidra, who is standing to my left. The wind is blowing her black hair across her face. The long red coat she bought in Westport, 'specially for Gran', complements my cherry-coloured sweater. On my other side stands Uncle Robin in a bright red blazer and scarf, and beside him Annie, Gran's neighbour, huddled in a plum-coloured puffer jacket. 'Not what I'd normally wear to a funeral,' she said, when we collected her this morning. 'But it's the only reddish garment I had to hand.'

The four of us stand in a row, glowing like beacons against the muted grey sky.

'It's time, my dear,' says Robin, gently.

I take a step towards the edge of the water, the box

suddenly heavy in my hands. I can feel the comforting presence of Robin, Nidra and Annie behind me as I open the lid and let Gran's ashes out into the sea air.

As the mortal remains of my beloved grandmother swirl and dance on the cool Irish breeze, and slowly make their way into the ocean, I hear Robin clear his throat as we prepare to honour the last of Gran's wishes.

'One, two, three, four,' he counts. 'And . . .'

As we deliver our very own, rather out-of-key, rendition of 'Spread a Little Happiness', the grey clouds burst, a mist descends, and it starts to rain – light at first, then a heavy, pelting downpour. Beside me, Uncle Robin chuckles.

'Gran's last little joke, eh? Four sopping-wet eejits singing songs in the rain.'

Back at the cottage, after an hour's drive in Uncle Robin's hire car, we sit and dry off by the fire. The box of Ronald's personal items that Stella Jones sent to Gran sits like an unexploded grenade on the table beside us.

'We should watch that video before we return to London,' says Nidra, coming into the living room with a tray of hot chocolate, as direct as ever. 'Where else are we going to find a working VHS machine?'

The thought of watching the video and dredging up all the Rochester Place business does not appeal. I am still feeling raw, like I've woken up in a new and unfamiliar world. Though it's been more than a week since she died and we have just bid farewell to her at Kildavnet, I still don't feel that Gran has gone.

'We said we'd come back in a month's time to sort out the cottage,' I say, taking a sip of hot chocolate. 'Maybe we can watch it then.'

In her will, Gran left the cottage to me, and though Annie has agreed to keep an eye on it in the short term, we need to decide what we want to do. Nidra thinks we could rent it out as an Airbnb, while Uncle Robin has suggested we use it as a retreat – a place to escape to when city living gets too much. Annie, sagely, commented that we could do both. Though they mean well, I still don't have the space in my head to make such decisions, particularly after the revelations and shock of the last few weeks, and I'm hoping that returning to London will give me some much-needed clarity.

'I just think it might be good to get it over with,' says Nidra, tentatively, aware of my oscillating emotions. 'Then, when we come back to sort the cottage, it won't be hanging over us.'

'Okay,' I say, hauling myself up from the sofa and pulling the box towards me. 'Let's see what Mary had to say.'

I peel open the tape sealing the top of the box and peek inside.

'Goodness, look at this,' I say, pulling out a slim, leather book. 'This is the one Mary mentions in her diary. Ronald's great-uncle's nature journal.'

'So it is,' says Robin, placing his hot chocolate on the mantelpiece and coming to join me. '*The Diary of an Urban Naturalist* by Charles Stephenson. How wonderful. And to think this has been lying in a box all these years.'

I continue to dig around in the box and quickly locate the video, which is in a white cardboard sleeve with *MARY INTERVIEW: 7 FEBRUARY 1998* written on it in black ink. I take it out and hand it to Robin.

'Will you play it for me,' I say, my stomach twisting. 'You're more familiar with VHS machines than I am.'

'Of course,' says Robin, getting up. 'They're actually remarkably simple. Much more so than a lot of modern technology . . . Right, I think that's it.'

He presses play, then comes to sit with Nidra and me on the sofa. For the next few moments, none of us speak. The only voice we can hear is the one I heard on the other end of the phone just a few weeks ago.

'I shouldn't actually be here,' says Mary, pushing a strand of white hair away from her face. 'Because, as far as most people are concerned, I died in an air raid in London on the fifteenth of October 1940. In many ways, that would be true. The Mary Davidson who lived at Rochester Place who had welcomed a child she loved with all her heart, who she protected and nurtured and cherished. That Mary is lost in the ruins of Rochester Place.'

A cool breeze seems to swirl through the room, though the fire is blazing.

'It's her,' I say, my eyes still fixed on the screen, where Mary sits by the window, dressed in a brown polo-neck sweater and tweed skirt, the blue Atlantic Ocean just visible behind her head. 'There is no doubt about it. That was the voice I heard that night.'

Nidra shuffles closer to me, rubbing my arm to warm me up.

On the screen, Mary clasps her hands together and looks down at her lap. Off screen, a man's voice begins to speak.

'We're recording this because you wanted to go public,' he says, the Oxford-educated, RAF officer's clipped tones still there in Ronald's voice. 'You wanted to clear your name. Is that right?'

Mary looks up. Her eyes, though wrinkled and rheumy with age, are still bright. She smiles sadly at her husband.

'Yes,' she says. 'That is right.'

'Tell me about Air Marshal Oliver Davidson,' says Ronald.

'Your father?' replies Mary, raising her eyebrow disdainfully. 'Where shall I begin?'

'Tell me what he did when he thought that I had been killed in action.'

'Well,' she says, sighing, 'he did what any loving

father-in-law would have done and tried to get me hanged for espionage.'

'Bloody hell,' says Nidra, beside me. 'I didn't know they were going to hang her.'

'Why do you think he did that?' asks Ronald.

'Because I had stood up to him,' replies Mary. 'And I had committed the grievous crime of falling in love with his son and encouraging him to follow his dreams. To someone like Oliver Davidson, that kind of defiance required punishment. I just didn't realize how far he would go.'

'You found out what he had done before the police had been sent.'

'Yes,' says Mary, looking up at the camera. 'Your sister Daphne came to see me. She said that she had come to warn me, that she had overheard her father talking about me on the telephone. She didn't know who he was talking to, but she understood that he planned to report me to the authorities and that he had evidence to prove that I was an Irish dissident and a spy.'

'Did she tell you what evidence he had?'

'Apparently, they had found some scraps of paper in my chest of drawers when I left his employ all those years ago,' says Mary, shaking her head. 'They were pages I'd ripped out from my diary, just scribblings, written in Basque. Davidson claimed that the notes looked like some sort of code. He also said he had witnesses, his RAF cronies, who were willing to testify that

I had quizzed them about their work over dinner. Sure, I was being polite and inquisitive, but they were twisting it to make it look like I was trying to infiltrate British military intelligence.'

She pauses then, the weight of the accusations still heavy on her shoulders all those decades later.

'That was serious enough,' she continues. 'But David-son had two aces up his sleeve. According to Daphne, while in her father's employ I had been spotted talking to, and receiving papers from, a known Irish freedom fighter. Well that was my friend, Constance. She had fought alongside my brother in the Rising and been such a support to me over the years. She was always reminding me of how unhappy I was when we first met in Ireland, how I was strong enough to push through, because anything was better than going back to the life I had before, and how I deserved a better life – that underneath we are all the same, just people. But that was all. I had no involvement politically. I just wanted to fit in here. To make a success of my life. That day, Constance had come to give me a pile of poetry Fintan had written that had been passed on to her. She thought I might like it, and I did; I treasured it because I loved my brother. That wasn't a crime, but in the eyes of Oliver Davidson, with me having a friend like Con-stance, a brother who fought in the Easter Rising and having lied about my true nationality, he had no doubt as to who he thought I really was. Davidson's claim was that I was a dangerous Fenian who had deliberately targeted a prominent British military family with the aim of passing on highly sensitive information. I was, he said, a danger to the country at this critical hour of war, an enemy of the state and, very likely, collaborating with the Germans. It was vital that I be arrested and made to pay for my crimes.'

'How shocking it must have been for you to receive this news.'

'Well, "shocking" is an understatement,' says Mary, raising her eyebrow. 'The truth is I was terrified, though not for myself. I had little Teresa to think about. What would happen to her if I was arrested? Where would she go? I spent days walking round in a fog of confusion. I even started drinking your whisky.'

She smiles ruefully, then continues.

'But then, a few days later, Daphne returned. She said she had found a way to help me. She knew someone, an old beau from her debutante days, who was now in charge of the Port Authority at Southampton Docks. This young man was so smitten with Daphne, it seems he would do anything for her. Anyway, she told him that I was a dear friend of hers, a widow with a young daughter who had lost all my possessions, including my documentation, in an air raid. I needed to get home to Ireland urgently to tend to my sick mother and there was no time to wait for new documentation to be processed.'

Her voice catches then, and she wipes a tear from her eye.

'Though it was wonderful of her to help,' she says. 'I remember thinking to myself, after the bombing, that Daphne's lie had cursed us, that the fictional air raid had become a reality and I had lost everything.'

'Can you tell me what happened next?'

'Well, Daphne's old beau agreed to help. He told her that he had arranged passage for us on a hospital ship bound for the US, which would be making a stop at Cork. The ship was due to sail at eight o'clock on the evening of the sixteenth of October. The plan was that we would get the train to Southampton on the evening of the fifteenth, where Daphne had booked a hotel for us.'

At this point, Mary breaks down and starts to sob.

'Darling, if it's getting too much, we can take a break.'

'No,' she says, looking up at him with stricken eyes. 'I want this story to be told. I want everyone to know what that man did to us, what he took away from me.'

She takes a deep breath, wipes her eyes, then starts to speak.

'It was a disaster,' she says. 'Daphne had said she would send a car for us at seven o'clock to take us to the station. We'd had a lovely afternoon. I'd used up all the food in the house to make Teresa a Basque feast. After all, we wouldn't be returning for a while, and I didn't want it to go to waste. Everything was going to plan.

The bags were packed. I had decided to tell Teresa where we were going when we got on the train. That way there would be no danger of her telling her friends. I couldn't risk anyone finding out where we were going. But then, just as the clock was creeping towards seven, there was a knock at the door and the siren went off. Right at the same time. Before I knew it, Teresa had darted down to the shelter. I went to follow her to tell her to come back but then there was a knock at the door again, harder this time. I couldn't risk the driver leaving so I ran to get it, but it wasn't the driver, it was a woman saying she was Teresa's sister, Katalin. I recognized her from the photo Teresa had shown me, and there was no mistaking the family resemblance. She had the same soft brown eyes as Teresa, the same measured voice, though she was bigger-boned, and very tall. She was wearing red heels and she towered above me as she stood there, asking if she could see her sister. Looking at her, I felt the ground shift under my feet. I couldn't believe this was happening. I knew I would have to leave, that if I didn't then I would be arrested and executed, but the thought of leaving Teresa made me feel sick.'

'Tell me what you did,' says Ronald, softly.

'I made a decision,' says Mary. 'In that moment. I looked at this strong, capable, woman, a woman who had lived and fought through a bloody civil war and found the strength to come and find her sister, and I told myself that fate had sent her. Teresa was not my child. Katalin had only sent her to England to escape the war. Now that war was over and another one was raging here. Teresa needed her sister. She needed to be safe. What right did I have to drag her on another ship across another ocean to yet another alien country? She deserved better than that. So, I told Katalin where Teresa was, told her to go and find her, and then . . . then I ran.'

'The air raid had begun at this point?'

Mary nods her head.

'There was no sign of the driver,' she says. 'The sky was on fire. I knew I needed to get to a shelter, so I ran along Garratt Lane to Tooting station and made my way to the platform. I huddled there all night, listening to the explosions going off overhead. I spent the night praying for Teresa, praying that she would be safe.'

Her shoulders tremble as she continues.

'The following morning I stepped out of the station and into a Tooting I hope never to see again,' she says, a tear escaping down her cheek. 'The air was thick with choking smoke. There were people standing on the pavements, dressed in their nightclothes, shock making masks of their faces. I saw a woman whose hair had been burned off, and a young lad dressed in torn trousers was pushing an old pram filled with tins of food and a bird in a cage along the road. Then I heard it – the screaming. I staggered towards the noise. I saw Fred Harding, our neighbour, up ahead. He was wearing a thick coat over his pyjamas and he was holding a shovel in his hands. I heard a woman crying, "The whole of Larkin Road . . . it's all gone." I had never felt terror like it before in my life. All the breath went from my body as I ran forwards. I needed to get to Rochester Place. I needed to find Teresa. But the end of Larkin Road was completely sealed off. All I could see was rubble and smoke, so thick it made your eyes sting. And the smell in the air: a mix of gas, smouldering damp wood and charred flesh, like cooked spoilt meat. I never want to smell anything like that again. The next thing I knew, the stretcher-bearers appeared from amid the rubble. They hurtled past me so fast I could just about make out the body they were transporting. It was the red shoes I noticed first, then the mop of dark hair and that big tweed coat. It was Katalin.'

She starts to cry, her whole body jerking with each sob.

'No wonder Gran was in pieces when she saw this,' I say, pausing the video. 'If only I had been here with her. I can't bear to think of her so upset and all alone.'

'Luca came for her,' says Nidra gently, placing her hand on mine. 'She wasn't alone in the end.'

'But what a shocking discovery,' says Robin. 'Poor Joyce . . . er, Teresa. The two sisters had been moments away from reuniting. Such a waste of a young life too. Shall we see what else Mary has to say?'

The truth is I have had my fill of Mary and her revelations. I want to rip the video out of the machine and toss it into the sea. Yet I know we need to hear her out before her voice falls silent forever.

'Okay, let's get this over with,' I say, pointing the dusty old remote control at the television. The film resumes and Ronald's voice echoes through the room.

'Darling, let's have a break,' he says. 'We can get back to it later. This is too much for you right now.'

'No,' Mary cries. 'Please, I have to finish. Then I will never speak of it again.'

'If you're sure.'

'I am sure,' she says, looking up defiantly.

When she continues, her voice is louder, like she is shouting out the story to the world, hoping someone will hear.

'I grabbed the arm of a stretcher-bearer,' she says. 'He was a young man, his eyes glazed from the smoke and fumes. I asked if he had found a child. He shook his head and told me that this was the only body they had found in the wreckage. "If there was a child in there, they wouldn't have stood a chance, love," he said, sweat pouring from his forehead. "It was a direct hit." I felt like my legs were going to give way, but I knew I had to have hope. Teresa was such a sensible girl. She had been on her way to the shelter when I answered the door and she knew that she had to stay there until the All Clear was given. She was alive, she had to be. I spotted a woman then, on the corner of the road. A fire warden. She looked nice. She looked like the kind of person Teresa would trust. I knew that I couldn't stay, knew that if I did, I would be arrested, so I went over to the woman and I asked if she would check on Teresa for me, make sure she was alright.'

She starts to wail then, a low, guttural sound, like a lioness mourning its dead cub.

'"Please",' she yells, her eyes blazing. '"Please, you have to help me. You have to find my little girl. She's trapped. It's the big old Georgian house, Rochester Place it's called, you can't miss it. It's hidden away, behind Larkin Road, down the little pathway. It has a bright red door and a magnolia tree in the garden. Telephone number: BAL 672. Please hurry. I think the house might have been hit. There's so much smoke. You have to help her. Do you promise me you will? She's just a little girl. Eleven years old. Just make sure she's okay, will you do that? My name is Mary. Did you get that? Mary."'

'Stop the video, Uncle Robin.'

I sit on the sofa, staring at the screen, my whole body frozen with shock.

'What is it, Corinne?' says Robin. 'You've gone really pale.'

'That was what I heard that night,' I say. 'Word for word. I can't believe it.'

Mary's face fills the screen in front of me. Her green eyes seem to bore right through me, into my soul.

'I don't understand,' I say shakily.

'Corinne,' says Nidra, getting up from the sofa. 'Didn't Luca say that your gran was watching the video over and over, that she wouldn't turn it off?'

I nod my head, still too shocked to speak.

'I think I know what happened,' says Nidra. 'Where's that piece of paper they found in your gran's hand? The one with your phone number on it?'

'It's in the kitchen,' says Robin. 'I put it in the box they sent from the hospital.'

'Right,' says Nidra.

She heads to the kitchen, then reappears, a few moments later, with the piece of paper.

'Didn't Luca say your gran had been using the landline because she'd lost her mobile?' says Nidra, handing me the paper. 'Well, maybe she was trying to call you when she fell. She would have needed to enter your number manually on the landline, hence the paper.'

'Annie said she was found just by the television,' adds Robin. 'The landline is on the shelf right behind it. Perhaps she was making her way to the phone.'

'I wonder . . .' says Nidra, walking across to the shelf and lifting the landline receiver. Robin and I watch as she puts the receiver to her ear and taps out a number. 'Pass me that piece of paper, Corinne. And a pen.'

I hand them to her. She scribbles something down, then looks up at me and smiles.

'Just as I thought,' she says, triumphantly. 'Last number redial. They still have it on some of these old phones. According to this, your gran *did* call you, but not on the day she fell. It seems we were right; she didn't make it to the phone on time that day. Yet look at when she did connect to you?'

With shaking hands, I read what Nidra has scribbled on the paper. My number and, next to it, the date and time.

'My God,' I say, handing the paper to Robin. 'Look at this.'

Uncle Robin takes his glasses from his top pocket then looks at the phone. When he looks up, I see that the colour has drained from his face.

'She called your number at 1.30 on the morning of the fifteenth of October,' he says.

'The landline number is ex-directory,' adds Nidra. 'Which is why that call came up on your phone as an unknown number.'

'And you heard Mary's voice so clearly because your gran was standing right by the television,' says Robin, handing the piece of paper back to me.

'But why didn't she say anything?' I look down at the paper, trace Gran's neat handwriting with my finger.

'She must have been so distressed at finding out about Mary,' says Uncle Robin, shaking his head. 'Shock can render one speechless. I've seen it happen countless times on *House Detective* when we deliver unexpected news to people.'

'Perhaps she just wanted to hear your voice,' adds Nidra. 'She always used to say what a calming effect you had on her in times of stress.'

I nod my head. Uncle Robin comes over and takes my hand.

'You know what this means, don't you, dear?' he says gently.

'It means that we've solved the mystery of Mary,' I say, a feeling of sadness and relief washing over me. 'At last.'

35

Three Months Later
TOOTING

'Jaden! Will you bring out another tray of those bondas? They can't get enough of them out here.'

Rima smiles, mischievously, as her protégé, impeccably dressed in a crisp white shirt, black trousers and polished shoes, weaves through the partygoers and makes his way to the kitchen.

'Bring two trays if you can,' she shouts after him, her voice competing with the sound of Sade's 'Smooth Operator', her mother's favourite.

Tonight's party is to celebrate Rima and Nidra's successful bid to buy the freehold of Tulsi. After weeks of negotiation, during which the landlord tried to get the sisters to raise their offer by inventing a cash buyer who was prepared to pay three times more than them, they stood their ground and, with no other concrete offers on the table, he was forced to capitulate. Tulsi was finally theirs.

'I wouldn't tell him, but these bondas are almost as good as the ones my mum used to make,' says Nidra, taking a bite out of the crisp potato croquette. 'He's got a real flair for cooking. Who would have thought it?'

'It means the world to see him so engaged,' says Jimmy, balancing a flute of champagne and a plate of food in his hands. 'After what he did, you girls had every right to go to the police. Instead, you took a chance on him, and . . . well, the result speaks for itself.'

'That was all down to Rima,' says Nidra, waving at Uncle Robin, who has got himself trapped by a group of giddy, elderly *House Detective* fans on the other side of the room. 'I'm afraid I didn't share her magnanimity at the time. But Jaden has proved me wrong. It seems some people can change for the better after all.'

'I've always believed that people can be redeemed, that they can see the light,' says Luca, looking rather warily at Jimmy. 'This place is a testament to the power of forgiveness. I know that, if things had worked out differently and he had still been here after the war, my father would have forgiven Fred Harding. He always saw the best in people. I used to think that was a weakness, but now I know it was what helped him to survive.'

Beside him, Jimmy's cheeks flush.

'Luca, I . . . I can't begin to express how sorry I am,' he says, his voice trembling. 'I . . . I never meant for it to get that far. I . . .'

He pauses, emotion getting the better of him.

'Water under the bridge,' says Luca, placing a comforting hand on Jimmy's arm. 'Now, Corinne, my dear. How about a top-up?'

I take his glass and make my way over to the buffet table. As I take another bottle of champagne out of the ice bucket, Uncle Robin appears at my side.

'Dear Lord, I thought I would never get away,' he says, waving politely as the *House Detective* fans make their way out. 'I must say, you've certainly scrubbed up well tonight. I don't think I've seen you in a dress since you were a little girl.'

'Well, I thought I should make the effort,' I say, catching a glimpse of myself in the window. 'As it's such a special night.'

The red dress was a Christmas present from Nidra. At first, I thought it was too much, but then I remembered Gran's story of Mari, always clothed in vibrant red, and I thought it would be a nice touch.

'It's good to see you smiling again,' says Robin. 'These last few months must have been terribly hard for you.'

'They have,' I say. 'But they have also brought a lot of clarity. Solving the mystery of Mary brought everything full circle. I just wish Gran was here to see it.'

'Me too,' says Robin. 'Corinne, there's something I wanted to ask you. I've been thinking about that video and what Mary and Ronald were planning to do with it.'

I nod my head, recalling the afternoon that we sat, in

shock, watching the end of the video. Mary had gone on to describe how, once back in Achill, she had lain low. When Ronald was found in a prisoner-of-war camp in 1945, he returned to London, where his father informed him with barely concealed satisfaction of the bombing of Rochester Place and the deaths of Mary and Teresa. His sister, Daphne, found Ronald living in a boarding house in Pimlico, a broken man. Haltingly, he told his sister he had bought a pistol and intended to use it on himself. Daphne then broke the news about his father's treachery and that Mary was alive and waiting for him in Achill. When he asked about Teresa, Daphne simply shook her head. After that, Ronald cut all ties with his family, except for Daphne, and changed his name to O'Connor.

'Mary wanted to clear her name,' says Robin. 'She wanted to set the record straight, but the book that she and Ronald had planned never came to pass.'

I think back to the letter we found in Gran's cottage from Stella Jones, Daphne's daughter. In it, she wrote of how her mother had kept in touch with Ronald and Mary right up until their deaths: Mary, from a heart attack, in 1998, just a few weeks after recording the video; and Ronald from pneumonia, three years later. Devastated by his wife's death, he had tried to complete the book but passed away before it could be finished. Their ashes, Daphne said, were scattered across the ocean at Achill.

'With all the information we acquired,' continues Robin, 'I think it would be good to feature Mary's story in a special edition of *House Detective*. I would need your permission, of course, but I just think that, as I have the platform, it would be the right thing to finally clear Mary's name.'

'That's a wonderful idea,' I say, looking up to see Rima clambering onto the counter. 'I also think it's important for people to see the other side of the Blitz. Mario's story, for instance.'

'Absolutely,' says Robin. 'And I promise you, Corinne, we'll do them all proud – all your family.'

'I don't doubt that for a second,' I say. 'Now, I think Rima's about to make a speech. I'd better go and top up my grandfather's glass.'

When the last of the guests have gone, I leave Nidra, Rima and Jaden boxing up leftovers in the kitchen and step outside for some much-needed fresh air.

Garratt Lane is alive with the sounds of merriment. Buses and taxis hurtle past; a group of drinkers, leaving the Castle pub, burst into song; the air ripples with good cheer. However, as I stand looking up at the café awning, Mario's faded name now repainted alongside Tulsi's, I feel as lost and alone as I did that night in Gran's car.

'I never thought I'd see this place again, yet alone that name.'

I turn to see Luca standing behind me, his eyes fixed on the shiny new red-and-white sign.

'It must be strange for you,' I say. 'Knowing what happened last time you were here.'

He starts to shiver and puts his hands into the pockets of his overcoat.

'These English winters,' he says. 'I'd forgotten how brutal they are.'

'What happened to him?' I say, finally finding the courage to ask the question that has plagued me all these months. 'To Mario?'

'The truth is, after he was deported to Canada, I don't know what became of him,' says Luca, turning to me, his eyes glistening in the light of the window. 'I asked the people in the foster home I was sent to, but they were as clueless as me. I dug around a little as I got older, even went as far as contacting the Italian embassy, but all searches drew a blank. In the end, I decided to write a new story for my father, one where he left Canada and headed home. I have him living in the mountains of Calabria, a plump, happy old man, with a vineyard and an olive grove and a great big stove. I can see him now, sitting on his veranda, his eyes closed, a smile on his face. I think of that image, and it gives me comfort because I know that, one day, when my time comes, I will join him there.'

'I'm sorry, Luca,' I say, taking his arm. 'You had so much heartbreak in your life. I never really knew my mother – I was so young when she died – but if the grief you felt when you lost her and your father is anything like what I am feeling for Gran then . . . well, I don't know how you survived it.'

'I'll tell you how,' says Luca. 'People like to talk of grief as a temporary state, like a broken arm or a dose of the flu. They assume it to have a beginning and an end. But what I felt after losing my father and then my child, I can only describe as an altered state. Nothing was ever the same again. Everything around me changed – changed utterly. Yet what kept me going was an overwhelming sense that they hadn't truly gone, and the feeling that one day I would see them again.'

'I don't feel like Gran has gone either. I can still feel her all around me.'

'And she is, my darling,' says Luca, kissing my forehead just as Gran used to do. 'She is. Now, I had better be going. I have a flight to catch.'

'But I thought that wasn't until morning,' I say, not wanting to say goodbye. 'I thought you were going to stay at the flat tonight.'

'Being here this evening has made me think of the past,' he says, with a smile. 'The good bits, not the painful parts. And though I would love to spend more time with you, I must embark on this part of my journey alone. I hope that makes sense.'

I nod my head sadly.

'Now, give your grandfather a hug, won't you.'

He wraps his arms around me, and I sink into the warmth of his coat. He smells of almonds and orange blossom and the spice from Jaden's bandos.

'Right,' he says, extricating himself from me. 'I shall go and find a cab to take me to the airport. Until we meet again, my darling.'

He rubs the top of my head, and as I watch him walk away, though I have only just reconnected with him, I feel like an abandoned child.

Turning from the café, I start to walk towards Larkin Road, my feet moving almost independently of my body.

At the corner of what was once Rochester Place, I pause, trying to imagine little Teresa huddled in that Anderson shelter while bombs exploded above her, but all I can see is another scared child, huddled in her Spice Girls pyjamas while her doting grandmother held her in her arms and told her stories of brave pirate queens until she fell asleep.

'Gran, I can't do this,' I cry out into the clear night sky, my eyes raw with tears. 'I don't know how to live without you.'

Just then, I feel someone touch my shoulder. I turn and see Nidra, her face illuminated by the yellow street-light. Without saying a word, she takes my hand and guides me back to Garratt Lane, then we walk home in silence.

*

That night I dream I am on a ship. I am curled up on the deck, a fierce storm raging above me. As the waves crash over the sides, I stumble to my feet. The deck is empty, no sign of life, except for a pile of suitcases stacked in the corner at the stern. Though the wind is fierce, I press against it and make my way towards a row of wooden benches. I see a solitary figure sitting on one of the benches and I know I must get to it before the storm consumes the ship fully.

Rain batters at my face, a thick mist descends, and I can barely see. I hold out my arms and, after a few moments, I feel the solidity of wood against my hands. The mist clears and I find I am sitting on the bench. A little girl sits opposite me, her head bowed. I know instinctively who she is. Reaching out my hand, I touch her shoulder, and when she looks up her face is etched with fear.

'Hello,' I say, not quite able to believe that I am here with her. 'What are you doing back on this ship?'

She puts her hand to the hexagonal sign that is pinned to her coat. On it are the words *Expedición a Inglaterra*.

'You've already made this journey, Teresa,' I say, softly. 'It's time to go home.'

She looks at me and shakes her head.

'I'm scared,' she says, her brow furrowed.

'Don't be scared,' I say, realizing that I am speaking to myself as well as her. 'You're about to see all your loved ones again. Katalin and Mary and Ronald, your little girl too. They're all waiting.'

The sky clears. She looks at something, beyond my shoulder.

'They've arrived,' she says pensively. 'It's too soon. I can't leave you yet. You need me.'

A tear falls down her cheek. I lean forward and kiss it away.

'I'm safe now, Gran,' I say, my heart aching. 'You did a good job. You were the best grandmother anyone could have wished for, but you need to rest now. Your job is done.'

'You won't forget me, will you?' she says, taking my hands in hers.

'How can I forget you?' I say, rubbing her cold skin. 'You're part of me.'

She gets to her feet, her eyes on the horizon, and then she smiles and says something that makes my heart warm: 'Luca, you came.'

'I love you, Gran and Grandad,' I call out as I watch them walk across the deck, arm in arm.

We love you, we love you, we love you.

Their voices flutter through the air like smoke as they slowly fade into the night.

I wake with a start. It is still dark outside. Beside me, Nidra stirs, then curls her arms around my shoulders. The dream still clings to my skin, yet something has departed. Gran wanted to say a final goodbye to me, and now she has gone. I feel something inside me shift.

With the warmth of my wife's body beside me, I close my eyes and, for the first time in years, fall into an untroubled sleep.

Peace has come at last.

Epilogue

Joyce
1996
TOOTING

While the eager young estate agent guides Saira inside the building, I stand for a moment and look up at the name, faded but still visible, displayed on the hoarding, and recall the first time I saw it. Back then, the sign had been freshly painted a vivid red to match the gingham awning and tablecloths. It looked so friendly and inviting, a beacon amidst a sea of grey houses, as I walked down this street with Mary all those years ago. I remember the smell of garlic that wafted through the air as we approached, a comforting smell that reminded me of early evening in Guernica, when supper would be prepared with the kitchen windows flung open and families would gather to eat and talk and reminisce. I used to think that talk of the old days was dull when I was a child. After all, who wanted to dwell on the past when the future held so much excitement, so much promise.

Now, the past clings to me like a second skin. It is everywhere, and yet nowhere.

Mario. Mary. Katalin. Ronald. Names as dusty and

faded as the sign, yet so real to me, so vital. How odd that these major players were written out of my story, just when I needed them most. Yet I feel them around me now as I stand outside the café – a sense that they have played a part in my being here, have somehow orchestrated my return.

Though I only met Saira at the beginning of the year, I recognized something of myself in the timid young mother trying to establish a life in a new country, her family and friends left behind on another continent, and we have struck up a firm friendship. Little Corinne enjoys playing with Saira's two girls. They have become enthusiastic members of the 'Storytime with Joyce' crew, particularly little Nidra, who can't get enough of those real-life ghost-story books we've recently been stocking. What is it about ghosts that appeals to children so much? I suppose it's the thrill of it all, the fear. Once you get to my age you stop fearing ghosts and start to welcome them – will them to come back and haunt you.

It was ghosts that brought me here.

'Joyce, come and see inside.'

Saira's voice snaps me out of my reverie, and I follow her into the rundown building.

'Now, don't let its current state put you off,' says the young man, his eyes twinkling at the thought of his commission. 'There's bags of potential here. Did I tell you, it used to be a café?'

While the young man tells Saira his version of the café's past, I wander around the space and recall my own. Though it is now an empty shell, if I half close my eyes I can see the blue-and-yellow Formica tiled floor, the glass counter laden with bell jars of cannoli and doughnuts; the old silver cash register that pinged with each sale; the framed painting of Mario's hometown in Calabria that hung above the door; the tables covered in red-and-white gingham, pots of salt and black pepper on top. I can smell the spaghetti sauce bubbling in a vat on the hob, the rich scent of tomatoes, red wine, basil and salty anchovies drifting out from the kitchen. I hear Mario's husky voice calling out the orders, hear the soft Italian music coming from the wireless, and the loveliest sound of all, Luca's laugh.

'What do you think?' says Saira, taking my arm and leading me across to the window, where we look out at the traffic on Garratt Lane. 'He's right, it does need a lot of work, which is why the rent is so low, and the girls and I will have to live on bread and water for the next few months to pay for that deposit, but . . . oh, Joyce, I think I can do this. I think I can make it work.'

There was no question that she could. She may be timid, but when it comes to her girls and her tremendous cooking, Saira has the strength of a lion. She has already escaped a turbulent marriage, which even in these enlightened times takes guts. If anyone should have the honour of bringing this café back to life, it is her.

There was also no question of her and the girls starving in order to do this either. I made my mind up as we left the viewing that I would step in and lend her the deposit myself. *You can pay me back when you break even*, I wrote when I sent her the cheque, a few days later. *Now, go and follow your dream.*

Six months later, the café, which Saira has christened Tulsi, after the Hindu sacred herb, has opened its doors to the people of Tooting. As I watch my friend busily cooking and serving and laughing with the customers, I see Mario and Luca, Mary and Ronald. My friends, my family, my ghosts.

'This is for you, my dear,' I tell Saira, leaving little Corinne sitting on the floor with Nidra, the two of them huddled together conspiratorially, and making my way to the counter.

'Oh, my,' she cries, when I hand her the gift. 'A prism. My grandmother used to have one of these on her dressing table when I was a girl. She used to say it brought her luck.'

'Which is why I want you to have it,' I say, trying to keep my emotions in check. 'It was given to me by a very special person, a courageous young woman who believed in family and love and speaking out against injustice. You would have liked her very much.'

'Yes,' says Saira, kissing me on the cheek. 'It sounds

like I would. Thank you, Joyce. I shall put it here, on the shelf, pride of place.'

She smiles at me, then takes a piece of chalk and begins to write up today's menu on the blackboard behind the counter, while I take a seat at the table by the window.

As I sip my coffee, a shaft of sunshine pours in from the window, striking the prism and bathing the café in a dazzling rainbow light, and I am suddenly back in Guernica, safe in Katalin's arms, listening to her gentle voice as she tells me of other worlds, other lands, and of how the beautiful strands of light symbolize life after death and the hope that one day all those we love will come together again. I close my eyes and wonder what became of my sister. Did she escape the prison camp? Did she have a good life? I hope so. Then, as my sister's face fades from my mind, I see Mary standing in the doorway of Rochester Place. I feel her soft hand in mine, smell her intoxicating rosewater scent; I hear Ronald's laughter as he swings me round on the library ladder, shouting out the names of books like a station guard announcing the next destination; and I feel the gentle kiss of the boy who once lived here, the boy who loved animals. The boy whose smile made my knees weak. The boy who told me I had the courage of a lioness.

My first love.

My guardians.

One day, God willing, I will find you all again.

'Are you alright there, Joyce?' Saira's voice cuts into my thoughts. 'Can I get you a top-up?'

'That would be lovely,' I say, handing her my cup. She smiles, then returns to the kitchen while I sit and regard the four empty chairs around the table. 'Thank you, aingerou.'

Acknowledgements

I would like to thank the following people for their help and encouragement as I wrote *The Secrets of Rochester Place*:

My editor, Vikki Moynes, for championing this novel so passionately and believing in it – and its author – every step of the way. It is such a pleasure to work with you.

Harriet Bourton, for your insightful editorial guidance and excellent advice.

Liv Maidment, Madeleine Milburn, and all at the Madeleine Milburn Literary, TV & Film Agency. The best support team an author could wish for.

The incredible team at Viking Penguin. Thanks especially to Ellie Hudson, Leah Boulton and Lydia Fried.

Gemma Wain, for your copyediting brilliance.

Katy Loftus, an exceptional editor and human being who took a chance on my writing and believed I could do it.

Julia Lee, Teresa Sutton and Sharon Hardy, whose father, Fermin Magdalena, was one of the young people who sailed on the SS *Habana* in 1937. Thank you for sharing your father's memories of Bilbao and his journey to England. Thanks also to Victoria Dale for helping to put all this together and for sharing, along with Catherine Connor and Alexandra Winter, some lovely anecdotes about your grandad.

My father, Luke Casey, who set sail for England from the west of Ireland in 1956, aged fourteen. The stories you told me of Granuaile (Grace O'Malley), Queen Maeve, Constance Markievicz, and the Easter Rising, as well as the Great Famine and our family's experiences of it, informed so much of my life. You always said I would write about it one day, and now, my darling dad, I have. Words cannot express how much your love and wisdom inspired me.

My son, Luke, who shares my love of all things historical. Thank you for bringing so much joy and laughter into my life. You have the wisest head and the biggest heart, and I am so proud to be your mum.

I found the following books, pages, blogs and documentaries invaluable as I researched the period detail behind *The Secrets of Rochester Place*:

1916: The Easter Rising by Tim Pat Coogan
Boy in the Blitz: The 1940 Diary of Colin Perry
The Destruction of Guernica by Paul Preston
Forgotten Voices of the Blitz and the Battle of Britain by Joshua Levine
Granuaile: Grace O'Malley – Ireland's Pirate Queen by Anne Chambers

The Great Hunger: Ireland 1845–1849 by Cecil Woodham Smith

Historic Streets and Squares: The Secrets on Your Doorstep by Melanie Backe-Hansen

House Histories: The Secrets Behind Your Front Door by Melanie Backe-Hansen

Only for Three Months: The Basque Children in Exile by Adrian Bell

Renegades: Irish Republican Women 1900–1922 by Ann Matthews

The Truth Behind the Irish Famine 1845–1852 by Jerry Mulvihill

Blitz Spirit with Lucy Worsley: a BBC One documentary exploring the dark side of the 'Blitz Spirit'.

Gernika Lives: a documentary looking at the history and culture of the Basque people, written, produced, and directed by Begonya Plaza.

BasqueChildren.org

HavensEast.org

#HouseHistoryHour: where I was to be found every Thursday evening while writing this novel. A fascinating Twitter thread, run by @HouseHistoryHr and featuring a host of leading house historians. A must for anyone interested in the stories and mysteries attached to period properties.

He just wanted a decent book to read ...

Not too much to ask, is it? It was in 1935 when Allen Lane, Managing
Director of Bodley Head Publishers, stood on a platform at Exeter railway
station looking for something good to read on his journey back to London.
His choice was limited to popular magazines and poor-quality paperbacks –
the same choice faced every day by the vast majority of readers, few of
whom could afford hardbacks. Lane's disappointment and subsequent anger
at the range of books generally available led him to found a company – and
change the world.

*'We believed in the existence in this country of a vast reading public for intelligent
books at a low price, and staked everything on it'*
Sir Allen Lane, 1902–1970, founder of Penguin Books

The quality paperback had arrived – and not just in bookshops. Lane was
adamant that his Penguins should appear in chain stores and tobacconists,
and should cost no more than a packet of cigarettes.

Reading habits (and cigarette prices) have changed since 1935, but
Penguin still believes in publishing the best books for everybody to
enjoy. We still believe that good design costs no more than bad design,
and we still believe that quality books published passionately and responsibly
make the world a better place.

So wherever you see the little bird – whether it's on a piece of
prize-winning literary fiction or a celebrity autobiography, political tour
de force or historical masterpiece, a serial-killer thriller, reference book,
world classic or a piece of pure escapism – you can bet that it represents
the very best that the genre has to offer.

Whatever you like to read – trust Penguin.